I0685016

ENCHANTED
RED CABRIO

LM SELBY

www.hugnfugbooks.com

ENCHANTED
RED CABRIO

FROM HUG & FUG BOOKS

www.hugnfugbooks.com

ALL CHARACTERS AND EVENTS, OTHER THAN THOSE IN THE PUBLIC DOMAIN, ARE FICTITIOUS. ANY RESEMBLANCE TO REAL PERSONS, LIVING OR DECEASED, IS PURELY COINCIDENTAL.

ALL RIGHTS RESERVED.

MORAL RIGHTS OF THE AUTHOR HAVING BEEN ASSERTED.

NO PART OF THIS PUBLICATION MAY BE REPRODUCED, STORED OR TRANSMITTED, WITHOUT PRIOR WRITTEN PERMISSION OF THE PUBLISHER – HUG & FUG BOOKS.

ISBN: 978-0-9924334-4-4

COPYRIGHT © LM SELBY 2016

TO LEARN MORE ABOUT THE AUTHOR, GO TO

http://lmselby.webs.com

• CHAPTER ONE •

'COME VISIT MY ISLAND when you're next in Holland,' concluded Sen. He was known to have a bit of a 'thing' for blondes but how could he be having deeply erotic thoughts of Wanda, after such a brief encounter?

Did he really only meet her an hour ago?

She totally intrigued him and he just had to see her again.

Tingling with arousal, flashes of her teasing him with a stunning naked body, shot around his head like bolts of lightning.

Imagination central had gone into overdrive!

This slim, good looking Australian, from that far off land down under, exuded optimism and overwhelmed him with her energy.

He guessed she must be around his age, which made a big change for him. Not normally attracted to women in their prime but this one was fit and so incredibly sexy.

Mischievous big blue eyes and lightly tanned skin.

Refreshingly witty and clearly very smart, she ran advertising agencies in London and Sydney it seemed and had two adult children, coincidentally working in TV and Radio, just like him.

She was an amazing woman of the world, with stories that captured his interest from the word go.

The scent of her perfume!

The way she swayed confidently, as she walked.

It was all there and he fancied her big time!

Signs were telling him the feeling was mutual but he knew she was leaving the country so he had to make his move and fast. She was about to walk off into the busy streets of Hillywood and he might never see her again.

That said, he was positively stunned by her cheeky but very simple response.

'I would love to!'

As the words came out of her mouth, she jumped up to kiss him goodbye, amazing even herself.

Her lips felt the warmth of his face and he instinctively grabbed her around the waste and held her longingly – leaving them both reeling at the high voltage connection that was made.

If you included the emails and phone calls, she might be able to claim knowing him for a whole day but, in reality, it was just an hour earlier when they first set eyes on each other. Rendezvousing in a busy supermarket, to do business at their post office counter. People rushing all around them, simply fading into oblivion. They'd talked and smiled excitedly, not relinquishing their gaze for even a moment.

Clearly Fug was once again in play with Wanda. She hadn't felt her fiery inner voice take control so totally for a very long time. It was great to have him back.

Images of Medwin sparked through her head, like electric shocks.

Recollections of the long recovery, post him leaving her in Holland seven years earlier and returning to his wife and child in Austria.

It was Medwin's cute broken English that had led to the creation of Hug & Fug, as he and Wanda laughed and shared deep feelings about the different things they liked with hugging and fucking.

The large white feather was suddenly in her mind's eye.

Fug was having a field day!

Wanda melted as she thought back to the way Medwin would gently caress her with it, on waking in their silky soft sheets.

Fug raised her senses so high, she could even feel and smell the special bath and massage oils, they indulged their fantasies with.

Aromas of Ylang-ylang and Patchouli drove her crazy!

Medwin might have gone but Hug & Fug would forever be the characters that drove her deepest thoughts.

The soft and lovable Hug was ever present. Always on hand to lead Wanda with helping anyone feel good, that just needed a hug.

Fug being quite the opposite end of the stick and potentially somewhat wicked. He had not had much play over these past years, although there had been a few occasions, when he managed to entice her into heated expressions of passion.

One very sexy and athletic black man called Earl came to mind briefly.

Yes. It was indeed true what they said!

Now Fug was making up for lost time and Wanda's senses were going wild.

In an instant, Wanda became acutely aware of her Medwin images, being replaced by even raunchier ones of Sen.

Wow! This had never happened before!

And she hadn't even seen Sen naked. Just because he was tall and fit looking, didn't mean he had all the equipment to go with it and yet her inner artist was crafting some incredibly luscious sights.

Her sexual fire had returned!

She'd dated several guys since Medwin but not one had ever started her thinking such hot thoughts so quickly.

Some interesting men but just not 'special' and soon things would sour. Although she could think of nothing more wonderful, than to share her life with an amazing man, she had begun to think there was no such beast out there still to be had.

Maybe she was wrong!

'As fate would have it, I'll be back in Holland at the end of this month for a few days.'

Wanda was out of her brief trance and continuing.

'Can't think of anything I would rather do, than spend some time with you on your island!'

She could play this game. Fug was in full swing and taking control.

Sen was totally gorgeous and she wanted him with outrageous desire.

And yet, could he really be sincere with this sudden invitation?

Wanda desperately hoped so.

Could the simple act of selling her car, had led her to this incredible specimen of a man?

She had always known her enchanted red cabrio had magical qualities.

Now they were kicking in beyond belief!

Sen had an air about him that struck Wanda to the core, at very first sight, and she felt like a spell had been cast, that would change her life forever.

'His smile could melt icebergs and handsome couldn't begin to describe the face it's glowing from,' she thought to herself when they met.

As he towered over her and she gazed up into eyes that spoke of passion and creativity, she was completely drawn to him.

What a great line ....come visit my island!

Maybe he was joking. Time would tell.

In a couple of days, Wanda would greet her son Jay at Heathrow airport, to kick off their two-week long special 'Diamond' celebrations together.

It would be like coming home for Jay.

He and his sister Lou were both born in London, within earshot and sight of Big Ben. Having a Scottish dad, they had been privileged to get dual citizenship at birth.

After their parents divorced, Wanda's career opportunities saw them moving back and forth between Sydney, London and Amsterdam.

The trio had become the epitome of a truly international family.

It was 2008 when Jay and Lou completed their University studies in the UK and decided Australia offered the most opportunities for employment. As they moved into adult life, Sydney became their base.

Here it was 2012 already and Jay had missed the big May events in London for Wanda's special birthday. September was the earliest he could get away from work in Sydney.

Lou, on the other hand, had managed a couple of months in Europe and joined in for all the partying. The TV show she was working on in Sydney, ended in the April and she had happily headed over to share some very special moments with her mum. They were incredibly close and treasured any time they could spend together.

Jay's turn now and the forecast, for September weather, could not have been more perfect for the great trip he and Wanda had planned.

Excited to be visiting London, Jay looked forward to catching up with lifelong friends and University mates. Then he'd be off with his mum to Lisbon, Stockholm and lastly Amsterdam – before flying back to Sydney together, via Malaysia. Finally he'd get to meet his Portuguese and Swedish cohorts, for the gaming cult podcast he created. All the work they did together was online. Great to meet face to face at last.

Lou would fly up to Kuala Lumpur and join Wanda and Jay, for a few days of family fun, before they all made their way home to Australia.

Now it seemed Wanda's last three days in Amsterdam, might be very different indeed!

Had she really agreed to go to a strange island, with the man who just bought her car?

Wanda's head was in a total spin.

As for Sen, the poor guy didn't know what had hit him!

Arriving at the radio station earlier that day, he had one of his reporters insisting he should consider the purchase of this red convertible car that his neighbour was selling.

'If I had a driver's license, I would buy that cabrio myself.'

Gert was doing a great sales job on Sen.

'Wanda is such a lovely lady and has really looked after it well. The stories of her adventures with this car have been amazing,' he continued, with eyebrows fully raised.

'She says it's enchanted!'

'Now she's returning to Australia permanently, the price has been almost halved. Come on, convertible cars are so much fun! I just saw her at the front of her house, putting new signs in the car to lower the price. Tell your friends, she said. I'm open to any offers so long as the buyer can pay cash today. I leave Holland tomorrow!'

Gert could not have been more excited.

Normally he would have Sen briefing him on major dramas unfolding around the world and he would need to get cracking, to put a story together for their daily radio show.

This was much more fun!

Current affairs could be a little tedious at times.

So many journalists, all chasing the same leads.

This day was totally different. He laughed with Sen and they enjoyed being distracted by the lighter things of life.

Gert forwarded Sen the link to the online advertisement, Wanda's mate Denise had been running to sell the car. Wanda had driven it back across the channel for one of Denise's parties a few months earlier. Thinking being, with Dutch number plates, it should be sold in Holland. As always, Denise had been happy to help out. She was a great friend and loved having the cabrio.

'Maybe a little too much?'

Wanda was happy for her to enjoy it but couldn't help question why there had not been any takers in all that time.

Having set up an advertising agency almost two years earlier, to handle work around the London Olympics, Wanda had needed to establish an office in London. She'd been fortunate enough to rent space in the very same Covent Garden building she started her advertising career in, during the late 70s.

Good old fate yet again, playing an amazing hand to Wanda.

She even managed to recruit some of her old colleagues.

Later, clients wanted her to have a set up in Sydney too.

Most of her time had been spent in London so far and, as projects went into final delivery mode for the Olympics, public transport had become the only sane way to get around that frantic city so she hardly used her much loved car. There was also the fact that she had promised Jay and Lou, and her Sydney agency team, that she would base herself in Sydney, once the embers of London 2012 had died out.

It had been a sad day of realities, in deciding her enchanted red cabrio needed to be making its move to a loving new home.

'I could see myself driving that red cabrio,' Sen confirmed with Gert, as they reviewed the photos together smiling. 'Maybe I'll email her with a ridiculous offer and see what she says.'

As luck would have it, Wanda had stopped by her 'Bibliotheek' (library) office, when that email came through from Sen.

Free Wi-Fi and a very comfortable place to work, the library had long provided her with a home away from home. No internet connection at her Dutch house anymore and she was not up for paying high international data costs on her mobile phone. Everyone knew the best way to reach her was with an SMS or email.

Whenever she was in Holland, she loved to spend time at that library. Visits normally included enjoying reasonably priced food and beverage, provided in their cosy café. The cycle to get there was good exercise and she loved being surrounded by books. Her journey to becoming a novelist had begun in that very place. If only she could make time, to finish her first romantic saga.

No time to stop for the regular coffee and fresh orange juice that day.

Her dear friend Kiki was back at the house, finishing more signs for the car and a quick check of email, was all she had time for.

Kiki had flown across from London, to have a few days of fun in Holland and to help Wanda refresh her Hillywood home. It had been empty for some while and paying the mortgage was a struggle. Not a purchaser or renter in sight. Maybe a freshen-up would help. Now it was autumn, the sale price would be reduced too. Every effort made to get it sorted and finally off the agenda.

When Wanda moved to Holland with Jay and Lou in 2001, buying a house had been much cheaper than renting one. They shared so many happy memories in that home and all loved it dearly. A quaint corner property over three floors, that Wanda had completely renovated.

One key priority had been to create a very well placed car parking spot in the front garden area. THAT GREEN ITALIAN WAGON lived there happily for years, followed by a spell with no car, before Wanda's ENCHANTED RED CABRIO had eventually taken up residence.

Leaving Holland for the UK in 2005, the house had proven impossible to sell but at least it rented quickly back then. Wanda was happy just to have the mortgage covered.

She had also been able to capitalise on the increased value achieved, from the renovations she'd done, so wasn't complaining.

Now neither renting nor selling was on the horizon but, as with all things, Wanda remained optimistic.

She was a firm believer that everything turned out as it was meant to. So long as you were trying to impact your life and the world around you positively, things would always fall into place.

There had been every excuse in Wanda's life to feel otherwise, growing up in Sydney as the youngest of eight children. Not knowing who her father was and being shunted from place to place, in very poor circumstances. Through it all, she had always managed to find the good in whatever hand she'd been dealt.

Now it was time for her to wind things down in Europe.

Or so she had thought!

'Let's stay in touch via email and we can work out the details for my visit to your island,' Wanda continued as she walked away from the car and from Sen, feeling totally dazed.

'You need to let me know how it all goes with this incredibly enchanted red cabrio anyway!'

She smiled and hurried off, before Sen had the chance to say another word.

He soon climbed into the driver's seat and was back in the heavy Hillywood ring road traffic, watching her walk off into the busy town centre – stunned!

As Wanda paced quickly through the hustle of the shopping crowd, she dizzily remembered her conversation with Kiki earlier.

'Much less than I had wanted but he can act this afternoon. Best to just get this one thing cleared off the long 'to-do' list I guess.'

She had read Sen's email offer and spoken to him on the phone to make arrangements to meet, before calling Kiki to let her know.

Having left Kiki doing things around the house on her own, Wanda was keen to get back to her quickly. She was so appreciative of Kiki coming to help and wanted to make sure she also had some fun on this break.

A few years earlier, Kiki had suddenly lost her husband and she was still grieving. He was such an incredible human being and an outstanding musician. Wanda's eyes always watered, when she thought back to him leaving this earth. Luckily, she was able to kick straight into her memory bank and Hug would help her focus on precious glimpses of his smiling face and the many times she had been enthralled by his passionate guitar refrains.

Wanda sang in a band with Kiki's brother, way back before children and career, and she still enjoyed going to gigs. Kiki was always ready to share some decent live music. They were good mates.

'Meeting him at the post office in half an hour to do the paperwork and hand my beautiful car over. Very sad to see it go. When I get back, maybe we can go for some dinner.'

Kiki had not heard from Wanda since that morning call. Now she was back at the house and nervously blurting out to Kiki, all that had happened during her remarkable encounter.

'Standing there, holding the car documents up so this stranger I was waiting for would know it was me. Felt so stupid. Then he appeared. Oh my lordy lord!' Wanda stopped to draw breath, as Kiki dragged her to the sofa to sit and calm down. She'd been talking at a hundred miles an hour.

'Stunning! I was speechless.'

Then another deep breath under instruction.

'He came straight up to me and we just stared at each other.'

Kiki fetched a glass of water and tried again to steady Wanda. She guessed the car must have been sold but no clarification on that yet.

'I cannot believe it Kiki. He is my perfect Dutchman. All these years I've been looking for him. Then today, my last day in Holland, he appears!'

More water and a quick visit to the loo were required.

'I knew I should have gone with you,' Kiki shrieked.

'Just my luck to miss out on meeting Mr Right. Did he buy the car?'

'Yes, yes, yes. But Kiki. It has to be fate. Who would have thought my next door neighbour was working with the man of my dreams, all this time?'

It suddenly occurred to Wanda, that Gert would be able to fill her in on this magical man. He would have all the inside info. She was pretty sure they had worked together for quite some while.

'The time spent signing over the car at the post office, was all about sharing longing gazes and little car stories,' Wanda sighed and Kiki felt relief that this one could indeed be ticked off the list.

'We laughed and chatted like teenagers. Paperwork was all done, before we realised I hadn't even shown him the car.'

They paused to draw breath again. As Wanda began to laugh hysterically, Kiki started to be carried away by her infectious state.

'Then I asked him for the cash and he said it would be easier to do it by bank transfer. No way, said I.'

Wanda was forcing herself to speak more slowly, as she continued.

'We would have to drive across town to his bank, if I wanted the cash. Fine by me! More time was just what was needed. During that drive in traffic, we both did a run-down of our life in brief. We shared so many intimate and personal details. Couldn't believe it, when he said he was not currently attached. Must be some catch heh?'

As she listened to every little detail, particularly the plan to go to his island, Kiki started to turn red with excitement. They were both shaking and hyperventilating.

'Not married or even attached? And he's gorgeous? Does sound a bit too good to be true,' Kiki said, as she paused to clear her thoughts.

'Then again, this could be him. Were you really planning to be back in Holland at the end of this month?'

Wanda reminded Kiki about the trip she had mapped out with Jay.

'We found a really cheap deal for a flight back to Sydney from Amsterdam's Schiphol,' she concluded. 'That's the main reason we booked our return to Sydney from here. Jay also wanted to catch up with his friends in Holland and I thought it could give me a little more time with getting the house sorted. It all fitted in perfectly.'

'Then it's totally clear. Fate is playing an unbelievably strong hand with this Wanda. You needed to still have this house. Denise needed not to have sold the car. Your neighbour was sent to work just at the right time to see us putting the signs up.'

As Kiki detailed fate's pathway, a grin came to her face.

'You found him. He found you. This is kismet!'

The grin turned to a questioning look.

'Not an easy commute between here and Sydney though.'

Wanda went to sleep that night, flushed with disbelief.

Maybe it had all been a dream?

Yet the images of Sen were so vivid.

She guessed he must be around 6'4" tall. Longish light brown hair, with a slight curl. A strong and very upright body, with the cutest tight butt. Fug had her doing all sorts of things with that amazing body.

You could tell straight away, Sen was creative.

Casually cool in the way he dressed - a very 'in charge' sort of guy.

His confident stride and direct style, giving him a real presence. Thick eyebrows and the biggest and brightest smile she had ever seen.

As she closed down for the night, she had an incredible sense of his piercing eyes. Eyes that ventured deep into her very soul.

'Gert!' Wanda reminded herself, as she dozed off. 'He can tell me more.'

On waking the next morning, she found herself vocalising her first thoughts, to make an immediate call to her neighbour. He had introduced her to the man of her dreams. There must be loads he could tell her about him?

'Goedemorgen Gert. Just wanted to thank you for introducing me to Sen,' Wanda said nervously, as Gert's front door opened.

Gert was more than happy to relay all he knew about Sen.

He felt like he was part of some fairy tale love story.

Apparently Sen had not been himself for the rest of the day, after meeting Wanda.

Gert was sent out to do an interview but the rest of the team were sending him texts to ask what had happened with Sen.

Not one to gossip, his lips were sealed for them – but not for Wanda!

An hour passed swiftly chatting with Gert, before she needed to get back to Kiki and leave for their flight to London.

It seemed the team working under Sen greatly admired his leadership and experience, as a successful TV and Radio Executive in Holland.

So many fantastic shows to his credit!

Gert was a huge fan and could not speak more highly of Sen.

'His island' was in fact a small island in the far north of Holland - part of the Waddenzee group and nicknamed Schier.

Sen was one of six children and grew up around The Hague but he moved to the island, after meeting a girl there.

His then boss had married at the island's oldest hotel - a secluded retreat that was considered to be quite the creative haven. He had taken Sen and the exec team there, to brainstorm for the new television season. No possibility of sudden escapes, to extinguish fires back at the network.

Sen had fallen in love with a girl he met on that trip and he eventually bought a house with her but the relationship ended after a couple of years. Apparently he had found her perspective on life to be very narrow, obsessing over her son and being happy to not work. For her part, it seemed she was very vocal about telling everyone Sen carried loads of baggage from his past and made her feel shut out.

Wanda drew back a little hearing this, not wanting to believe there could be anything negative about her incredible man.

Gert sensed her displeasure and went straight to the part about Sen still feeling the island was his 'escape' so he had decided to buy her share of the house and stay.

'Umm. Escape from what?' thought Wanda to herself.

During the six years or so since, Gert had heard of a couple of different women Sen dated but he had never seen him look the way he did after meeting Wanda.

'He really likes you Wanda,' said Gert with an excited voice.

Wanda wasn't sure if this was him just being the nice guy she had always found him to be - a great neighbour and a truly kind person.

'He seems so lovely,' Wanda responded happily.

'Do you know if he was ever married? Has any children?'

'He did tell me a long time ago, that he married very young and always wanted children but sadly, they had been unsuccessful. Possibly a major factor in their eventual split. Never talked about her though.'

Matchmaking was fast becoming Gert's new talent.

He was now racking his brain, for other snippets of information to share with Wanda.

'The radio show we work on together is produced over very long days and nights. He rents a room from a close cousin in Amsterdam during work time and then returns to the island for weekends. Been trying to sell his house there I believe. We've been told our show will finish at the end of this year so I don't know what he has planned after that.'

They smiled at each other, both clearly considering whether the 'after that' might now be something that took him into Wanda's world.

She was a little surprised that Sen had not mentioned their possible island rendezvous to Gert.

'It maybe just seemed like a nice way to end our heated conversation at the time,' said Wanda, as she relayed what they had talked about.

The last thing Sen probably expected was for Wanda to say she would be back at the end of the month and happy to take up his island offer.

'Never known him to say things he didn't mean,' Gert reassured.

Wanda would just see how things went with their email contact.

If he did actually even email her of course.

Que sera sera and all that!

Whatever happened, or didn't, it had been an incredibly magical day that she would never forget.

Looking down on the beautiful Dutch landscape, as she flew high above, en route to London, Wanda recalled some of the many amazing adventures she had in her enchanted red cabrio.

Now 'he' was down there driving around in her beloved car.

The connection she felt from this simple thought, gave her goose bumps.

Where would he be right now?

Did she misread his seemingly keen desire to see her again?

Sen was all she could think of.

What an incredible year 2012 had been.

Could it really be capped off, by finding her true love and future life partner?

Wow! How could she even be thinking that way?

At that very same moment, Sen was walking away from his garage, having made sure his amazing new car was safely locked up for the weekend.

The drive from Amsterdam had gone smoothly and he had plenty of time to make his planned ferry crossing to the island. Just a short walk and he'd be on the boat. The spirit of Wanda stayed right by his side, all the way. Thoughts that had swirled in his brain, as she walked away a day earlier, were revisited with each step.

Could this woman be for real?

Why did she not turn to wave?

How could she have made such a big impact on me so quickly?'

Over and over again, he relived the way she suddenly jumped up to kiss and hug him goodbye. The stir of powerful emotions as she did. A simple hug and yet it seemed to say so much.

He hadn't felt anything close to this for such a very long time.

Wanda was enchanted. Not just the car!

He had bought a car he didn't really need and had met the most extraordinary woman. Who would have thought his Friday 14th would ever turn out like this?

Did she mean it?

Would she really come visit his island?

• CHAPTER TWO •

2012 HAD BEEN EARMARKED for any sort of role Wanda could get in London, working on the Olympics.

Topping off the sports extravaganza, would be the Queen of England celebrating her Diamond Jubilee – just like Wanda. The 60th party of a lifetime!

London had played such a significant role in the shaping of Wanda's life.

Even though she was born in Australia, she'd spent as many years in England, as she had in her birth country.

It was the city where she joined a rock and roll band; where her career in advertising began; where her failed marriage to Larry had taken place and where she had given birth to their two beautiful children, Jay and Lou.

Moving back and forth between countries, had presented challenges but it had also been pivotal to bringing up two very well-rounded children on her own and being able to enjoy so many of the wonderful things the world had to offer, whilst building an outstanding career.

Jay and Lou were just four and two, when Wanda and Larry split.

They had not long moved to Sydney and purchased a beautiful home, when the marriage failed.

Admitting their future paths lay in different directions, was heart wrenching but Wanda and Larry remained amicable. Years later, he had re-married and had three more children. Their extended family got along brilliantly and Larry was happy for the international lives Jay and Lou had been fortunate to live, whilst he and his new family stayed firmly entrenched in Sydney.

From the moment London won the bid for the 2012 Olympics, Wanda knew she had to be there for that amazingly special time.

The years leading up to it, had seen endless interesting roles presented to Wanda. She had loads of past experience with the Olympics and other major events around the world.

'Not too full on', was what she initially thought for this one, although she had not said that to anyone else.

'Would be good to have time to enjoy all the excitement of London and the 60th celebrations too.'

As the time neared, however, things had not looked so good.

Still nothing eventuating by late 2010, when her then marketing role in Sydney had come to an end. With the house in Holland empty again, before she knew it, it had been Hillywood here I come!

Lunch with ex colleague Susie, shortly after her arrival in Holland, led to a short communications assignment, with a global energy giant near The Hague. A good position to be in, for finding a simple but fun assignment around the London Olympics, she thought.

Fun had always been a priority in Wanda's life, ever since she was the one at the helm. She knew full well, that humans performed much better when they were having fun. In full time employment since she left school at 15, Wanda had proven time and time again, that fun equalled success. It also helped with leaving the childhood horrors behind.

'They offered me a permanent role,' Susie had shrieked to Wanda, as she greeted her at the cafe.

'The recruitment agency just called me. Wouldn't you know it!

I've accepted a short assignment near The Hague but I really need to get settled back into a long term situation. This permanent job offer is exactly what I want. You don't fancy taking on an interesting Hague role do you?'

'How do you know they would want me?' Wanda had replied, more than a little taken aback.

'Are you kidding? You have all the experience they want and more. Loads more than I have. They will jump at you.'

'I can call the agent right now. They expect someone to start on Monday so I guess they might want to see you tomorrow. What do you think?'

'Lou will kill me,' Wanda replied excitedly. 'That would mean not getting back to Sydney for Christmas. Seems interesting though and it might help get me set up for London 2012. What the heck. Jay and Lou are adults now and can survive a festive season without their mum for once. Let's do it!'

And jump at Wanda the Hague assignment did!

She had her Hillywood home all set up and running in no time, with the help of the Kringloop charity shop.

Felt great to be back in her cosy Dutch home.

Train journey to The Hague took an hour and a half but the money was good. It had all been a done deal, before anyone knew it.

Back in Holland again! And she was staying a while!

All very sudden and much to the amazement of her children, Wanda was taking yet another new road in her life's journey.

She had joined global headquarters for one of the world's largest corporations, as part of a team of very senior communications experts. They operated out of fabulous buildings, with amazing restaurants and meeting facilities. It was the global technology hub for the business and you could even land a helicopter out front. Often some very high level country leaders and politicians visiting so maximum security at all points.

Wanda was an experienced communicator but the learnings from this energy business, were extraordinary.

She had never heard such large numbers talked about, even in her many and varied global roles for the General.

Trillions of dollars were often mentioned in the energy world.

Technology firsts were astounding.

Subsea imaging of particular interest to Wanda but, as the end of 2010 hit, she still had nothing agreed for London and, although she made sure she completed tasks well, her mind couldn't help but be a little distracted.

Then came the lead she'd been waiting for.

'This old hotel client of mine in London is asking if I can manage their corporate sponsorship promotions, connected to a new property they're opening soon near the Olympic village,' said Wanda to her Canadian colleague Aram, sitting beside her in their Hague office.

Trying to build a new intranet portal, Aram was not about to be halted. He had promised Wanda, he would have it finished three days earlier.

The major internal communications initiative, they were working on, had turned out to be one big nightmare for all concerned.

'You know we have that meeting at 4pm and I need to demonstrate this to everyone then?' Aram had finally responded, a little stressed.

'Yes, yes. Sorry to bother you. It's just that this might be the way to go. All of those other Olympics possibilities came to nothing. I would probably need a more substantial set-up for this one though.

They will want tight controls on all the design work too. Might need to get myself some office space in London. Real money to be earned but maybe a bit more than I wanted to take on. Very exciting to be thinking about setting up another ad agency though!'

Aram nodded, trying to look interested.

'Worth at least having the conversation with them heh?'

She calmed herself and tried to play it down a little. The open plan work environment, meant that people heard every word, even though they were used to continuing with what they needed to do. Wanda had ten people within earshot. All trying to look frantically busy but she knew they were keen to know what she was up to.

Aram would finish his role earlier than Wanda. With his marriage having split very unpleasantly, he had decided to give Australia a try. Leave his cheating ex-wife behind in Holland.

Wanda helped with his plans and arranged for her big brother Joe to pick him up at Sydney airport, on arrival. Still had her home in Sydney and Joe lived there too. Having kept 'the mansion', as she liked to call it, she had decided to take in house mates. Not a full time space for Aram but he could stay, until he worked out where he wanted to live. University studies were all sorted so he was fine for his Australian student visa.

Wanda's suburban mansion with pool, would give Aram an excellent introduction to Sydney. Quite an eclectic group of house mates, with Joe being a taxi driver/owner of trotting horses and gambler. Sara - a bit of an executive misfit, with her dog Buddy. Plenty of hugs on offer there. Then there was Ben - just 30yrs old and suffering badly from his recent divorce and not being able to see his two small children. Surfing was all that kept him sane. Wanda's daughter Lou and her very cute dog Spike were also house mates at that time. No shortage of entertainment to be had with this mixed bag.

As Wanda further contemplated her move, for setting up to work on the Olympics, she drifted back to an earlier move from Holland to London, in 2005.

That time, she was leaving for Jay and Lou to start University studies in the U.K. It was just after her split with Medwin and his return to Austria, which left her in a terrible state. Their passionate Hug & Fug adventures sadly having come to an abrupt end. The mere thought of the love she had felt for Medwin, took Wanda into a euphoric state.

No regrets though. All was now as it should be.

Medwin had kept regular email contact. Always wanting to know how all the people he had met around the world with her, were doing.

In the beginning, he had called every now and then.

Wanda eventually had to ask him to stop. He was back with his wife and son and she needed to move on, as devastating as that had been.

Every downhill ski race Medwin participated in had been captured on film. Images shared with Wanda, quicker than you could say 'inferno'. Medwin in Lycra, flying down a snowy slope.

So hot!

Those images always brought back memories of incredible love making and led her to wonder, if she would ever share such intense passion again.

The Hug & Fug inner voice characters, they had laughingly created together, would live within Wanda forever.

That move, had been one of the hardest Wanda had ever made.

The right thing to do, for all concerned, but heart break recovery was deathly slow.

Jay had done brilliantly with his BA in Sound Art & Design and even come away with distinctions.

Amazing how his short period in the workforce had changed his thinking about studying. Finding something he really wanted to do was the trick.

Such a different scenario from the horrors of getting him through high school, with his learning challenges. The bleed in the frontal right lobe at birth, had definitely impacted his development.

University studies in London had proven to be the perfect choice for both Jay and Lou, even though Lou had not been so keen on her chosen course initially.

Wanda convinced her that a BA in Digital Media & Performance would stand her in good stead for future work and be a great degree title for someone looking to work in TV or Film. She stuck at it, got the degree and enjoyed the ride.

For Wanda, it had felt like a move into the 'empty nest' zone.

She presumed it must be worse for single parents.

All those years of the main focus being your children.

Then they were gone!

She had to move herself to the top of the priorities list.

Initially the trio and PJ, the pooch they adopted in Holland, lived together in a rented house in Kingston-upon-Thames but within six months, Jay and Lou had gone into house shares with fellow students and Wanda was making plans for her new 'single' life.

Scoring an executive communications role with the General's Healthcare business, at UK headquarters, meant an excellent salary and a new company car.

This in turn led to the final farewell of THAT GREEN ITALIAN WAGON. From Rome to Holland, then to a new home in London, their beloved car had served them well. Quite traumatic to say goodbye but they made sure it went to a good home.

With the high salary, came the opportunity to buy a little apartment.

Wanda's very own pad!

A time of adjustment was called for going forward but she was ready to go for it.

Cycling along the beautiful Thames River, Wanda stumbled upon the most perfect place to buy.

A brand new gated development of just five apartments; directly overlooking a weir, at the fork of two rivers; and in an incredibly special village. Beautiful communal gardens, private parking spaces and even the opportunity to moor a boat. Two bedrooms and two bathrooms, a fabulous new kitchen all fitted out with new appliances. She could choose floor coverings and would go for solid oak timber.

Short stroll to numerous village cafes, a Zone 6 railway station and even the most majestic of palaces.

Cycle paths of the flat and scenic kind.

It had the lot.

She was even able to get special permission, written into her purchase agreement, for having one small and very well-behaved PJ pooch.

No need to be alone after all, and the bike with basket trick, would see her and PJ cruising along the beautiful Thames riverside, before they knew it.

The other four apartments were soon occupied too and fellow owners got along famously.

Guardians, for this riverside gated retreat, would clearly be the elderly retired couple on the ground floor. He was French and had endless stories of his days as a flight attendant. Still owned a yacht in St. Tropez with his brother and often went down there to sail. She was terribly British and had also flown but her real claim to fame was having cooked for the Queen Mother. Such an interesting couple and ever ready to keep a close watch on things.

Wanda was one floor up and opposite her, there was an Opera Singer, who was quite charming. On the next floor, one apartment housed a Russian ballroom dancer, often away touring, and across from her, a very handsome and strong rugby player with his gorgeous blonde lawyer girlfriend.

Their little 'Waterside' development was home to a great mix of personalities!

On moving into her new pad, the thought of being wild and single, had her loveable inner voices come back to life big time.

Hug & Fug were ever present, through all the wild nights out.

Everyone seemed to be on the prowl!

The 17year age difference she had with Medwin was nothing, compared to some of the babies that often tried to chat her up.

Wanda laughed and played the game but never seemed to end the night with anyone.

Until the lovely Earl came along!

Ex-rugby player. Tall, handsome and black.

She had never been with a black man.

Super smart and interesting too.

Could it be true, what they said about black men?

They did a couple of fun 'dinner only' dates before she finally got to find out.

His amazing body shone in the moonlight streaming through to her bedroom. With the window slightly open, sounds of white noise rose up from the weir below. As he told her what he would like to do to her, in a soft and sexy voice, Fug was sending Wanda messages to stay still and let this wild man do his thing. Poetic in his description of wanting to taste every inch of her, she had no problem obliging.

As she lay naked on the bed yearning, Earl stretched his athletic body over her. Not one move needed to be made. She watched in awe, as his erection continued to grow.

Incredible! Definitely true!

They dated infrequently but always enjoyed fantastic sex.

Perhaps even more importantly, he made her laugh and they shared deep and interesting conversations, over hotly romantic evenings, that always included great food and good wine.

So…. how long did it take for the 'but' to set in?

A mere six months or so.

He was, unfortunately, still very hung up about his ex, who played silly games with access to the light of his life.

Yes, a beautiful young son. Just like Medwin.

How did Wanda find them?

At one point, she had even turned to internet dating.

Seemed no worse, than trying to work people out in busy music venues and bars.

'Maybe it would be easier to know a little about the person, before deciding to meet?' she thought.

Who could contemplate how much they lied?

A few laughable disasters but then it did seem to pay dividends.

Ooh la la! Michelle, the French Swiss man!

Hug & Fug went wild with that relationship.

He phoned her from Switzerland nightly and left everything to the imagination.

Came to the UK whenever he could, to put words into actions.

Not that many times really but the calls and messages continued.

They laughed hard and enjoyed a host of different things together. Theatre, live music, singing – and, of course, extremely passionate love making.

Chatted in bed for hours, giggling and telling each other silly stories. Missing each other when apart but never talking of either one moving country. Never any sign of 'long term' being on their radar.

He had been married to an English girl and they had three children. Wanda had spoken to the daughters on the phone. Very cute, with their little French accents.

Divorced for some years but he was still distressed about the fact his wife had run off with his best friend. They lived near each other in Switzerland and she continued to haunt him.

Always the baggage!

As University studies had come to an end for Jay and Lou, Wanda's role with the General also concluded. The CEO she worked with was made redundant.

Jay missed his siblings and father, all living in Sydney, and had started thinking that London was just too busy. His career would be in radio and there were some good opportunities already presenting themselves in Australia.

For Wanda, fate was telling her a change of scene would be good and she also needed to do some renovating at the mansion. She agreed it was a good time to head back.

Those three years in London had passed quickly and she definitely saw herself living in her beautiful Waterside pad again at some point but, meanwhile, she knew there'd be no problem renting it out.

Lou had not been so happy about moving back down under initially.

She had her very own tall black man in London and didn't want to leave him behind. As difficult as it was for Lou, if she had to choose, mum and her brother won hands down. Not to mention her dad and the rest of the family.

Discussions took place, for Lou's boyfriend to come to Sydney later for a visit. He would even look at opportunities for emigration.

'Not likely' thought Wanda.

A lovely guy but she doubted he would ever get his act together for such a move.

Shortly after the trio arrived back in Sydney, Lou settled in to a fun casual job. Bar work was something she had done during University in London. No problem jumping straight into a cool place at the beach and not too long before she started dating a work mate.

Steve could not have been more different from the guy's Lou went out with in London. Mr Nice Guy, with all the markings of success.

Lou's final split with London was made and very soon she left the bar work and had her start, working in television.

Jay landed the job of his dreams, setting up Sydney's new Black Metal Music Show for a new web-based radio station. His final thesis at University had been based on Black Metal Music.

How amazing to then land such a job!

Not that long after starting work, Jay even decided he wanted to buy his own apartment.

Wanda and Lou were astonished.

He had always said, in his very anti-capitalist best voice, 'don't ever expect me to own property or anything mum!'

Wanda gave him all the support he needed and went guarantor for his loan. A small studio was his choice, not wanting to over commit and not wanting to share with anyone. His dad Larry was both a musician and carpenter so he helped with flooring and they all painted and organised things.

Jay was set.

Wanda renovated the mansion then took an offer to lead marketing with a small Sydney software company, for a year.

The odd man amused her for short bursts but definitely nothing special happening with men, during that period in Australia.

Hillywood had been rented out finally but soon the tenants were moving on and Wanda had it back on the market to sell.

To say the Dutch property market was dead, would have been a major understatement.

Not sure what to do, Wanda had decided she would need to pay a visit, as soon as she finished the Sydney marketing role. Maybe she could find some way to get the house occupied.

How could it not sell or even rent?

Hillywood was such an international town, with loads of expats coming in all the time. European HQ for several major corporations and media capital of Holland.

The team at the Sydney software company were nice enough but the company was destined to fail and she hated working in their negative environment. It had owners who could do nothing but argue with one another. She would be very happy to get away from there and back to Holland.

Lucky for Wanda, that part of her life journey was positively impacted by a spectacular ski trip to Chile. A pity work stopped Jay from going with Lou and Wanda for that one. He really missed out.

A group of eight friends joined in the fun but more often than not, Lou and Wanda did their own thing.

Great travel buddies, as always.

The group skied together the first week, based at a cool Santiago hostel, run by an Australian. Staff knew all the best places and took them to a different ski area each day. Even as far as the very stunning Portillo.

When the others went on to Peru, Lou and Wanda ventured south on one of the super coaches they have in Chile. Luxury all the way and so very cheap. They travelled almost 600 kms for just $6. Movies and food on board. Super comfortable!

Skiing the black volcanic rocky mountains of Chillan, from their 4-star hotel base right in the centre of the slopes, the magical mountain memories were endless.

Thermal spring waters filled the hotel pool, sitting snuggly in a snow covered nook. Skiers whooshed past, as Wanda and Lou soaked up the minerals, with the welcome heat softening their tired ski legs.

Fresh mountain air filled their lungs.

The quiet of the approaching evening, was halted by sounds of laughter, as fellow skiers entered the pool.

Returning to Santiago before flying out of Chile, their visit was made complete, tasting the delights of a Terremoto.

Literally translated as Earthquake, this famous drink left many a person feeling the ground was shaking beneath them. A type of sweet fermented wine with pineapple ice-cream, served in a very large glass.

The spectacular murals of Val Paraiso, and a visit to Pablo Neruda's home, also enjoyed before departing this exciting country.

Next stop Argentina, where Lou and Wanda took in Buenos Aires and its tantalising Tango to the full.

The dance of Hug & Fug closeness and passions expressed. Bodies caught up in total embrace, as the music of Tango engulfed them.

A quick stint back at the Sydney software company, post the amazing South American adventure, and Wanda had been able to head for Hillywood.

Original intention was to stay a few weeks and sort out the house challenge but that lunch with ex-colleague Susie had changed everything.

As her brain swung back to the final moments of 2010, she was contemplating yet another move from Holland to London.

'So Aram, what do you think? Could be just the Olympics project I've been wanting,' said Wanda as she joined in with preparations for their 4pm meeting.

'Maybe that's why the others didn't pan out.

They were too small.

I've been destined to play in the bigger London Olympics pond.'

'Maybe so,' replied Aram. 'First of all I need you to OK this little puddle please.'

As they reviewed his fantastic work on the intranet portal, Wanda could only wish he might be able to support her agency business too.

'Great work Aram. How do you feel about working remotely from Sydney, if I need you for this London gig?'

'Could be very cool,' Aram responded with a twinkle in his eye.

'Might be fun to be a part of Wanda's World. Sydney, London, Amsterdam.

Look out world, here we come!'

• CHAPTER THREE •

'MUM, YOU CAN'T BE SERIOUS!' Lou had been in shock, when Wanda called from Holland to say she was taking a high powered job with some global energy giant, headquartered in The Hague, and staying on the other side of the world.

Her mum had only gone to Holland, to try to get things sorted with the Hillywood house. How could she even contemplate not being home with her and Jay for Christmas?

'Wasn't it supposed to be the children running off and leaving the parents?' Lou thought to herself. 'Not the other way around!'

She was all grown up but that 2010 Christmas, was to be the first ever, without mum.

Not happy!

After their amazing trip to Chile and Argentina, the fires of Tango still blazed. Whenever they were together, they couldn't help but launch straight into a Tango embrace, striding enthusiastically across the room. Lou had great plans for giving Wanda lessons, as her Christmas gift. Not much point in that now.

Jay was even older and very settled in his own apartment but he didn't like the idea of Christmas without mum, any more than Lou did. Even so, he tried to console her.

'No doubt it's a great opportunity for Mum. You can't be surprised at her seizing the moment. Nothing new there.'

In the end, they could only be happy for her.

A bit concerned when Wanda started talking about recruiting a couple of house mates though. It was working fine in Sydney but the mansion was so much bigger and she might not be that lucky, with getting good people in Holland.

'The Hillywood house has four bedrooms so no point mum rattling around in it all by herself I guess,' Lou was reassuring Jay this time.

Wanda's bedroom was upstairs and had its own bathroom so she could be quite separate when she wanted. She loved her top floor domain. Views of the sunrise, through the Velux sloping window, in her ensuite bathroom. Sunsets as equally beautiful, on the opposite side, from her equally sloping bedroom windows.

So quiet up there in the second floor loft conversion!

Being close to the centre, roads were tiny so no fast car noises. Most people cycled everywhere, in any case.

Giggles from passing cyclist could be enjoyed, when the windows were open. The morning flow of parents, taking children to school on their bikes, was a delight to behold. Often carrying a child on both front and back. Sometimes with a special little trailer, that sat not only the children but the family dog too.

Skype calls with Lou or Jay, happened on a regular basis so they stayed connected.

Particularly to discuss Hillywood housemate plans, as they moved into full swing.

'She is from Brazil Lou and really feels the cold. A little tough on her, to be arriving in Holland in the midst of such a full on winter,' said Wanda. 'She came with a big coat so I guess she knows what's in store. A nice thick Parka hanging by the front door too. Looks like it's going to be a cold one. Let's hope she can cope.'

Riga had been granted a Dutch work visa, based on a course of study she had completed. The opportunity was about to run out and she needed to get to Holland and find a job quickly.

Wanda only had her advertisement on the international networking site for a day, before Riga made contact. She was still in Brazil at that point but would arrive in Holland later the following week.

All was agreed online and, before Wanda knew it, Riga had arrived at the house in a taxi, from Schiphol Airport.

The second house mate came, from putting a notice in the paper that circulated the Dutch media industry. Media Park was near the house and Wanda was told people were always looking for accommodation. Robbie's mother had been in broadcasting and still had the paper mailed to her.

He had supposedly just returned from living and working overseas. Seemed like such a nice man and quite good looking. He and Wanda got on like a house on fire, when they initially met over a drink in town. Clearly, he was out to impress. No sooner had he moved in, than the stories started to not add up. Then the girlfriend started 'visiting', somehow thinking she could move in without Wanda noticing. Rent was soon adjusted and Wanda kept out of their way.

A mysterious couple indeed!

'I'm taking off for a ski with Jin and Wendy for a week so they can sort themselves out while I'm away hopefully,' Wanda confided to her good friend Denise.

She told her all about the strange house mates and their weird stories. Also how they seemed determined not to get along with each other. Denise had come around to check them out, keen to know

Wanda was at least not living with total crazies and at risk in any way.

Maybe with her out of the picture, they would find some common ground. But first to get through Christmas, which proved to be very different indeed!

Riga had decided that the cold must surely be Wanda's fault.

No sooner would Wanda walk in the door, after her long train journey home from The Hague, than Riga would pounce.

The central heating didn't get hot enough.

The super thick duvet was too thin.

The snow outside was too dangerous for her to walk on.

It went on and on …..

Wanda had gone to great lengths, trying to help Riga settle. Had taken her out and about, exploring Holland and teaching her the 'Dutch' ways.

How difficult was that?

Riga clinging to Wanda's arm, for fear of falling on the slippery roads. Train rides were OK but why oh why did Wanda not have a car?

If Riga said that one more time, Wanda would burst a blood vessel!

Tickets had been arranged for Riga and Wanda to do a special Christmas Day lunch in Amsterdam. The day before, Riga decided it would be way too cold for her to go so she cancelled them both.

Wanda's patience had come to an end.

Christmas Eve was of course already Christmas morning for Jay and Lou in Sydney. They were at their dad's. Other friends also there, enjoying a special breakfast. Wanda was online for hours with them and felt well Christmas'd by the time she'd hung up.

Early that next Christmas Day morning in Holland, she left a gift for Riga with a note wishing her well, before heading off to take the train to Amsterdam.

The gift was a hot water bottle!

Holland was having unusually high snowfalls for December.

It was a magical white Christmas!

The countryside was stunning and Wanda enjoyed a fun train ride, with fellow travellers all being in a celebratory mood.

Exactly what the doctor ordered.

Thinking about her ski trip, as she woke earlier that day, in bed alone, she missed not only Lou and Jay.

Blank stares from her bed to the bathroom sink, took her back to visions of Medwin standing there naked. He seemed to take so long with his daily rituals and she had loved every minute of it. The slight curve in his back, as muscles flexed and his spine reached from a great height, down to his tight buttocks and onwards to those solid tree trunk legs. Still so clear in her mind, even after five years.

She wondered if Fug would ever play a key role in her life again. It seemed he had abandoned her too.

Enough of that, as she suddenly jolted herself back to reality.

'Think I'll take a canal cruise to start my special Christmas Day.'

Snow covered canals, sparkled a fresh whiteness and purity as she peered out from the train. Canal cruises could be taken from directly in front of Centraal Station. Great to find others alone on that boat. One girl was in transit and decided to escape the airport and take a look around, for her few hours layover. Wanda delighted in showing her some favourite spots. Then a visit to the Leidseplein Ice Rink. Poffertjes and loads of laughs to be had there. Later, a cosy café for a nice warm mulled wine and some lekker eten.

Always someone interesting to chat with and she was in her element.

A truly special Christmas!

Boxing Day (or second Christmas Day as they say in Holland), a mid-day flight to Austria, would see Wanda bound for Saalbach-Hinterglemm.

Jin had managed to find a good pension for her, right across from where he and Wendy stayed. They went there most years for Christmas / New Year and had become quite the locals. Again, one very lucky Wanda. Her last minute booking had been turned down by so many hotels and then Jin came up trumps.

Wanda thought to say a friendly goodbye to Riga before leaving but no. Riga was determined to continue attacking.

How could Wanda leave her with Robbie and his girlfriend?

They were obviously quite mad and would be back from his family gathering in a day or two.

That was it!

Wanda very calmly told Riga she should look for somewhere else to live, while she was away. The sooner she moved out, the better!

Incredible snow and not a thought of The Hague job or her crazy housemates, helped Wanda enjoy a fantastic week on the Austrian slopes.

Jin and Wendy arranged a special New Year's Eve dinner up the mountain. Live music and great food, preceded by champagne toasts all round.

A spectacular evening!

Skiing back to the village in the dark, with the smell of burnt out fireworks still in the air.

The entire week had been totally exhilarating!

Bit of a shock going back to reality though.

'Robbie and I are getting along fine now,' said a very hesitant Riga as she greeted Wanda's arrival home.

Wanda almost forgot having asked Riga to leave.

Then it started.

It only took just five minutes of Riga's ranting to bring it all back.

'So …. how did you go with finding somewhere to move to?' enquired Wanda.

A few more conversations were needed for it to really sink in but two weeks later, Riga left.

'Just one crazy to think about now,' considered Wanda.

Did he really have shares in an oil well? Was there even one of the four cars in the garage in town that he talked about? At least the Porsche perhaps.

Then the girlfriend really settled in.

As they began to take over Wanda's home, she knew this too would have to end.

Knowing how much they disliked children, Wanda decided to let them know about the imaginary family of five that would be coming to stay for a few weeks soon.

Perhaps this would be the right time for them to travel back to their oil well.

A few weeks of extreme weirdness and then they were gone.

Thank goodness!

Wanda decided she would live alone for a while. Maybe that would help her feel more encouraged to find a new man. The infrequent nights out bopping with Denise, had so far left her flat.

Loads of handsome men at her Hague office but not one available, that she fancied. Just as well. That job was getting more demanding and she had loads to be organising, for the ad agency set-up too. Her first hotel client was already in place.

'I can't believe my luck AB! Do you really think you can swing that same office?'

Back in the late 70s, Wanda had taken her first job in advertising, working as Personal Assistant to AB. He had a thriving London agency and it didn't take long before she was client facing and writing headlines. As time passed, her ability to gain a client's trust and organise in minute detail, saw her taking the Account Management path. Years later, she became Managing Director for a different and quite substantial agency. She'd outgrown AB's bad habits, of spending more than they were earning, and decided to move her career in a new direction.

AB still remained close and they became like family over time. He had even given her away, when she married Larry. They would generally catch up for a laugh, whenever she was in London.

After her first meeting with the hotel marketing team in London, she had arranged a dinner with AB and her big brother figure was almost pleading, for a role in her new agency.

'As cocky as you know I am, I'm happy to grovel slightly, for a piece of this Olympics' pie. You know how badly I've been doing with property development. Still not clear of all the bad debts yet, you know!'

He shifted uncomfortably and she saw it was difficult for him to admit this.

'I can see some real earnings potential with this Olympics activity Wanda and I know so many people, that will give us work. You still have your job to finish up in Holland I can run the show in London meanwhile and get things cracking.'

There was no doubting AB's abilities, when it came to creative thinking.

Could he be trusted to stay on track for delivery though?

Still a full on womanizer and very much the man about town.

Age certainly did not weary him!

When he told Wanda his property connections might very well be able to get them the same Covent Garden office space, that was the clincher.

Things were falling into place beautifully and, with the Hillywood house just having her rattling around in, it also wasn't long before family and friends began making plans to visit.

'Mum. Steve and I have booked our European trip. Yay!'

Lou could not have been more excited. She loved Sydney but missed Europe terribly. Steve's father was an international pilot and yet he had not seen much of the world at all. His mum was British so visits abroad had been focussed there, visiting family. Lou had done loads of travelling and was thrilled to be able to share her knowledge for their planning.

'I'm coming over earlier mum so that you and I can spend some quality time together beforehand,' said Lou with an excited high voice.

'Where shall we go?'

'Steve will arrive in Holland just in time for Queens Day. Can't wait to share that with him. He's been reading up on it but I don't think he really gets just how huge it is.'

A slight change in Lou's voice, before she continued in a mildly pleading tone.

'Pity you don't have a car mumma. Would be so great to be able to drive Steve to the all those special places, public transport can't reach. Have you thought about getting one?'

Clearly that would soon become a priority.

Within a day of Lou arriving in Hillywood, she was online hunting for the next car that would take a lead position in Wanda's life.

Cars had always been central to the adventures that made up Wanda's passionate journey.

So many 'favourite' and very special cars, all with their own stories to tell.

Her first ever, was a red convertible!

Having reached the required age for a driver's license, Wanda had saved up A$300 for that car. She'd been working for over a year full time by then. Did really well at high school but the need to help support her single mum and siblings, meant leaving school at fifteen to get a proper job.

Wanda was never out of that special first car.

It felt like the home that she never had!

Built in 1956, it had little arms that came out from the sides, to indicate when turning left or right. Cream leather seats, that were as new as the day they were fitted. She loved that rich leather smell, as she nestled in to drive. Or often just to sit and listen to the radio.

A motorbike rider until then, both on and off road, due to learner licenses being available at a younger age than for a car. Her first teen boyfriend shared that love of bikes and they hit some wild and rugged trails together. Two years older, he always had a bigger and faster ride.

Not a chance of surpassing her red convertible though. No matter what car he bought, during their six years of dating.

'I know you are busy there at work mum but can you just take a quick look at this amazing car I found on line. I sent the link to your business email.'

Lou was feeling very happy with herself.

It was a red convertible!

Not quite the same as mum's first love but she knew straight away, they could have loads of fun in it.

Wanda had two days of important meetings in The Hague, then she would break from work for the week's holiday with Lou.

'Price looks great, if it's in as good condition as they say. Low kilometres for the age. Some other similar ones at much higher prices. Owned by a man living just the other side of Utrecht,' Lou continued.

She had it all worked out and had even called Denise, to ask if they could borrow her car to go take a look.

'OK. Sounds great! Well done. I'll get home as early as I can so we can go give it a whirl. Thanks bubs,' replied Wanda.

Buying a car had not really been on Wanda's radar, strangely enough.

Quite a first but, with her plan to be working in London soon, she had been happy to stick to public transport for a while.

Didn't take much to convince her how much more fun she and Lou could have with a cool cabrio though.

Wow! Was the first thing that came to both their minds, as they later pulled up at the hot little red number.

It was even better than it looked and sounded in the ad.

They were wrapped!

'I hate having to sell my amazing cabrio,' the young man said almost tearfully.

'With my wife pregnant, we need to go 4-door and serious.'

A little negotiating and arrangements for insurance, then they all ventured to the post office to sign things over.

Wanda and Lou were thrilled to take possession of their convertible. This car had 'exciting new adventures' beaming out at them, from the word go.

Brilliant!

It was the first time Lou had driven a left hand drive vehicle but she was an excellent driver so no problem at all. That said, Wanda took it slowly driving Denise's car so Lou could settle in and follow.

Just one more day on the train to The Hague and then Wanda and Lou could leave on their trip.

Lou spent that day getting the car ready and picking up maps for the Rhine Region.

Nothing booked. The plan was, to have no plan. They would set off in their red cabrio, in the direction of the Rhine River - only a few hours drive from Hillywood and just let their journey unfold.

So many beautiful little villages to see along the way.

Looping back through the Moselle Valley was a distinct possibility.

It was Spring!

Normally still quite cool in Holland but this day was extraordinary.

Hot and sunny!

They had passed by Cologne and were beside the majestic Rhine, in no time at all.

Car went like a dream!

'Could the ride be any smoother mumma? Glides along the road so beautifully.'

Lou was indeed very pleased with her find.

'That looks like a great place to stop for lunch.'

She spotted an old riverside inn, with a balcony looking directly onto the river.

Sun streamed down and temperatures soared.

River waters below moved and sparkled, brighter than the brightest of stars, as they sat for ages, watching massive Rhine River barges and cruise boats pass by.

With slow cabrio cruising alongside the river next on the agenda, it was time for the roof to come down and some basking in the full glory of the sun, as they took in the majestic Rhine. It was a road they had travelled before but this time, they would stop to explore.

Spotting a medieval castle surrounded by grapevines, Wanda and Lou ventured up the hillside.

'He said they're doing a re-enactment of this traditional ceremony to thank good spirits for helping to protect their Rhine trade,' Lou happily relayed to Wanda, on returning to the car.

'We can park over there.'

The man, who gave his approval for the cabrio to park near the entrance, soon presented himself with a troupe of actors, dressed in period costume. A magical sight, as they pranced close by and waved scented lanterns in the air - flute and lyre accompanying their singing.

Wanda and Lou moved away from the car, to view the terraces and picturesque valley below. Hearing the ceremony, they turned excitedly.

At that very moment, the troupe was perfectly framed with the car to their side.

Rays of sun struck the heavily polished car bonnet in such a way as to make it appear to float – all perfectly timed to the lantern waving.

Wanda and Lou looked at each other with stunned expressions!

They were clearly seeing the same thing and Lou's quick thinking, even captured it on camera.

'Enchanting!' exclaimed Wanda.

From that day forward, this special car was forever to be known as their ENCHANTED RED CABRIO.

The enchantment continued, with a magnetic energy engulfing all who shared adventures in this special car.

Soon after Wanda and Lou returned from their Rhine trip, Steve arrived in Hillywood. He had already heard loads from Lou, about the enchanted happening.

Initially he found it difficult to believe but he was certainly entertained by the story and excited to be with Lou in Holland. She was his first real love and everything about her enthralled him.

Landing on the eve of Queens Day, made everything seem even more amazing. Steve was happy to think anything was possible. A little sceptical about the car's enchantment perhaps but certainly impressed by the incredible castle photo.

Commencement of Queen's Day festivities, for Lou and Steve, had been the night markets in Amsterdam, with a group of Lou's school chums.

Steve had no problem wearing the orange t-shirt, sitting on the bed as his arrival gift, and could not believe the sea of orange they melted into.

Imaginations ran wild, as every man, woman, child and pet joined in right across Holland, to toast the house of orange and their royal heritage.

Orange wigs, clogs, jewellery, clothing, bikes – even orange musical instruments.

Live music around every corner and the tantalising smell of poffertjes.

Up bright and early on the actual day, to explore the fun in Hillywood, then back to Amsterdam later in the day, to join more of Lou's mates. By the end of Steve's second day ever in Holland, he was hooked. It had turned out to be everything Lou told him it would be …. and more.

'A tough act to follow but tomorrow we hit the road for Antwerp and Bruges.'

Wanda was saying this quite casually but Steve was beside himself. He'd forgotten just how close everything was in Europe and the thought of visiting Belgium so easily, made him tingle all over.

'We might just drive home late, rather than book accommodation. Should only take a couple of hours to get back. Wait til you taste the waffles with strawberries and hot chocolate sauce. Zo lekker!'

She knew Lou had briefed Steve on a little Dutch.

Lekker (yummy) being one of the main tools for communication he would need.

'Quite happy for you to do some driving on the wrong side of the road, if you're up for it?'

Steve's initial apprehension soon vanished, once behind the wheel of their enchanted red cabrio the following day.

'As soon as I gripped the steering wheel, I felt it,' he said. 'The positive energy was so calming.' He had waited, until they were all relaxed with waffles in Bruges, before telling his tale.

Earlier, they had stopped for morning coffee in Antwerp's main square – Grote Markt. Golden spires, on the magnificent Flemish Renaissance buildings, glistened in the sun. Wandering the old town's narrow streets, a brief visit to the music museum and riverside castle, were unexpected delights.

On arrival in Bruges, they went straight for bike rentals, to take in all the sights like locals - the only way to really see all the quaint squares and canals. This fairy-tale medieval town, of tiny cobbled roads, was more than spectacular!

Whenever in Bruges, Wanda would recall her romantic few days with Tim the fireman so long ago. Wondering what might have happened, if she had made his dream come true and married him?

Driving home very late that night, with Wanda and Lou fast asleep, Steve felt strangely attached to the enchanted car and totally elated with his first driving experience, on the roads of Europe.

The trip he and Lou were to start, in a couple of days, would mostly be by bus. So many awesome destinations mapped out and several months of being alone with Lou. He could not think of a more perfect scenario.

And yet, he couldn't help but wonder....

How would any travel experience ever surpass the incredible feelings he experienced that day, driving this magical car?

Departure day soon arrived and, as Lou and Steve boarded their tour bus, Wanda's excitement for their journey was marred only ever so slightly, by the fact she would miss them dearly.

Plans had been made for her to join them in Krakow and maybe in Nice too, if she could manage the time away.

Everything was hotting up for the Olympics and she was astounded by the enchantment surrounding her life on all sides!

Seeing her daughter so clearly in love, she couldn't help but wish that she too, might find her special person.

Their enchanted red cabrio had definitely added some magic to Lou and Steve's relationship.

Maybe it would do the same for Wanda!

• CHAPTER FOUR •

'JAY. THERE'S AN EMAIL FROM SEN!' Wanda couldn't believe her eyes, when she read its content.

She'd been daydreaming a little, after an upsetting call with Lou.

Nothing seemed to be changing in Lou's relationship with Steve and she was at her wits end. When they returned to Sydney a year earlier, after all those months travelling around Europe together, he had moved straight back in with his parents. Lou, on the other hand, had bought her own apartment and hoped he would want to move in with her.

Staying over a couple of nights each week was enough for him but not for Lou. That caused an initial split back then but it had only lasted a day. They loved each other and wanted desperately to make things work.

The year had passed with numerous discussions of being at different stages of their lives. It also saw Steve trying to get his family to be more inclusive with Lou.

Finally she had to admit to herself, that they were miles away from being on the same page.

She was a couple of years older than Steve and ready for more. He did not want to leave the comfort of his harbour-side family home – and there was nothing he could ever do, to have his family open up fully to outsiders.

After all those years in their very committed relationship, the way forward was not looking good for Lou and Steve.

Wanda had simply listened, feeling her daughter's pain.

Lou hadn't made her mind up fully yet. She loved Steve but was not seeing the future she wanted.

'What does Sen have to say for himself this time then mum?'

Jay managed to drag himself away from the computer game he was playing, to give Wanda the attention required.

They'd been out exploring the hills of Lisbon all day and a little gaming was called for, as they relaxed back in their room.

Riding the funny old trams around the maze of roads, that dipped down as much as they dipped up - a roller coaster of multi-level streets and alley ways had been theirs to discover.

Lisbon was fascinating!

Wanda was now back in the moment and talking like a child, who just found the hidden candy.

'He asked if I was still going to be in Amsterdam at the end of this month and would I be free to come to his island!'

The grin she was wearing stretched from ear to ear.

'Woo hoo. Go for it mum!'

Jay had made it clear to Wanda, that it was about time she had a special man in her life. As soon as his mum told him about Sen, he responded that he felt this would go much further than she could possibly imagine.

Even though Jay had not yet met Sen, the cosmos was sending him strong messages that Sen was the one.

'That earlier email was so casual. Just talking about the car and how well it went. Not a mention of what he had said re the island visit. Not a hint of anything to do with me coming back to Holland. Never mind the fact he hadn't mentioned it to Gert. I have to admit, I was a little doubtful.'

Thinking back on it now, Wanda realised she had also been casual with her response to Sen's first email back in London and even waited quite some days to send the reply. Client meetings had been a good excuse too. A.B. making sure he got as much of her time as possible.

Sen took a few days before making that first contact so she had played it a cool.

When the much awaited email had arrived, she was done with the anxiety and expectation.

That was Wanda all over.

Growing up with constant disappointments, she had trained herself well to expect nothing. That way she would never be let down.

Sen had said very little and Wanda responded likewise.

It hadn't stopped her thinking about him constantly though.

Had they really only spent under an hour or so together?

'Don't play all the silly games mum. You are way too old and wise for that. So is Sen I guess. Be honest and get in there. You are both on your own and free agents, from what you told me. He finishes his job at the end of this year and your agency is going great guns, even without you in the picture on a day-to-day basis, so the world is yours for the taking.'

What Jay said was, of course, all true.

Wanda replied immediately to Sen's email and confirmed their arrival back in Holland, plus the scheduled flight out of Amsterdam for Sydney a few days later. She made it very clear, how much she would love to spend that time with Sen and visit his island.

The 'getting to know each other' plan was then quickly agreed, with notes flowing thick and fast – albeit rather short.

Wanda talked about the fun things she was doing with Jay each day, on their Diamond celebration travels. Sen talked mainly about what he was covering on his radio show and the dynamics of his team. He had travelled to several places in Europe with his work but not really done much on the personal travel front.

Tales of Lisbon excited him. Particularly the stories of the haunting sounds of Fado music, that Jay and Wanda enjoyed.

An online friend of Jay's had suggested a Bairro Alto cave. Quite the perfect place to absorb this important element of Portuguese culture.

Sen had been a little surprised to hear from Wanda, that they were staying in a youth hostel.

Something Wanda often did.

They always seemed to have prime positioning and Wanda enjoyed being able to mix casually, with the explorers of the world.

Priced right too – even for a private room.

Having looked Wanda up on the main business networking website, Sen knew she had a high flying international career. He would ask her more about that when they were together. Guessed she must have stayed in some pretty fancy places around the world. Funny she was in a youth hostel now but he totally got what she was saying.

Some of the English was a little strange in Sen's emails.

Wanda recalled thinking how well he spoke the language, during that time they spent together, but naturally it was always different, when it came down to writing. She guessed he must be using an online translation tool. They often got the wrong end of the stick.

Funny to read sometimes but she loved the way he expressed things.

On their last night in Lisbon, Wanda and Jay were eating outside at a café. The man sitting next to them was chain smoking and with every mouthful, smoke was being sent directly towards Wanda.

A thought suddenly occurred to her.

'What if Sen is a smoker Jay?'

She reminded Jay of the men she had initially been attracted to, who turned out to be smokers.

It was as if a sudden barrier dropped, when they lit up.

No way could she ever be with a smoker.

She had not even tried a cigarette. Not even pot. Not ever.

The mere thought of being around someone smoking, put her totally off. She would need to email Sen and ask.

'Mum. You can't be serious. If he is the man of your dreams finally, would you really not move forward just because he smokes?'

'Totally!' responded Wanda and Jay could see she meant it.

No wonder she was alone. Way too fussy.

This guy could be Mr Perfect in every other way but she would dismiss him because he smoked. Crazy!

'Lies and smoking. Two things that cut the magic instantly for me Jay. Can't do anything about it. I have to ask him. No way I could spend three days in a strange place, with a guy who smokes. Better to know now and be done with it.'

Wanda spent ages crafting that email.

She wanted the message to talk more generally about the challenge she faced living in Holland, with so many people smoking. It had been almost impossible to go out for a night and not go home smelling like an ashtray. Her dearest friend Denise had tried to stop so many times. She had even lost a close friend to lung cancer but still, that had not been enough to give her the willpower to stick it out. At least she was always very careful not to smoke in the house and moved away from Wanda, when the craving took hold on their nights out.

'I realise that I don't even know if you smoke,' the email concluded.

A response was not forthcoming that day, nor the next.

'How cool was Lisbon mum? Thanks for this incredible trip. Did you say this flight to Stockholm lands at 2pm? I told Eran I would message him as soon as we land. He might come into town tonight.'

Jay had discovered a second cousin from Scotland, who had married a Swedish girl and was living just outside Stockholm. They had a little girl and he was eager to meet up.

As much as Wanda tried to keep her mind on their travels, she kept drifting off to thoughts of Sen.

It amazed her how clearly she could still visualise him.

The constant replay of that tall handsome man, walking into the local supermarket in Hillywood.

Her heart pulsing so hard at the thought, that he might actually be the one she was rendezvousing with, to buy her car.

The amazement when his broad smile was directed to her and his eyes beamed with a shared delight.

Such electricity!

'Mum. Are you there? Off in Sen land again? We've arrived.'

Collection of luggage - and then a taxi ride to the harbour. Wanda a little dazed throughout.

'Another cool hostel! Well done mum. Check out the views. The old buildings are all so ornate. Love it. Sen will email and all will be well.'

Wanda was not so sure.

He must be a smoker and is not responding because he thinks there's no point in carrying on the discussion. Wanda had been very clear she could never be with someone who smoked. She would most likely get some sort of email to let her down gently, at some point.

'Right Jay. Let's head out to explore and have some dinner, as soon as we get our bags into the room.'

Wanda needed to snap out of it and get back to her focus on fun. She always figured if you were having fun, things would go well.

Explore they did. Found a cool bar with live music and some great food. Loads of laughs and good people watching. Quite perfect!

'I heard back from Eran. Meeting us at noon tomorrow. His wife can't make it but he's bringing their little girl. I looked up where they live and it's quite far out. Think they're coming by train so a bit of a journey for them.'

Jay was really looking forward to meeting this newly discovered relative and so was Wanda. He was Larry's cousin's son apparently.

Firing up the wifi once back in their room, both Wanda and Jay decided to hit their laptops and see what was happening in the world. If Lou was on line, they might call.

Another email from Sen, finally!

Wanda was so nervous she needed to take several deep breaths, before opening it.

He did smoke!

A couple a day - normally when having a drink or late at night, after he finished his radio show. So infrequent, the thought of it now made him realise it was plain stupid and that this could be the right time, to just give it up altogether.

Wow!

Wanda was astounded. He must really be keen.

He wanted her to come to the island and would make sure he did not smoke. In fact, he would more than likely just stop immediately and not even wait for her arrival.

The feeling that came over Wanda was quite wonderful.

She read it again and again.

It made her head float and shudders went right through her body. Sen had taken his time responding so the words could be exactly right. And they were so right. Honest and caring to the point where they left no doubt in Wanda's head whatsoever.

She found herself not just believing in what he said but believing in something much deeper.

The certainty of her emotions was overwhelming.

He *was* her Mr Right and she felt deep down inside, that they might well spend the rest of their lives together.

Flushed in that knowledge, she closed her laptop and fell fast asleep.

Breakfasting in the hostel dining room the next morning, a fleet of incredible tall ships were on view directly across the street.

Jay and Wanda had ventured behind the hostel the evening prior, to explore the amazing old town. Knew the harbour was right there in front but had not seen these incredible ships. They must have sailed in during the night.

Across to the far side of the harbour, they could also see a giant cruise ship.

Such a striking panorama of water and seafaring vessels!

Wanda had read about the thousands of islands in the beautiful Stockholm archipelago and they would seek out a ferry or two, for getting to the nearest ones, to get a feel for it all. Several major ferry companies served countries around the Baltic Sea. Time was limited for this visit so Eran advised on how best to prioritise.

The day spent with this new found relative and his beautiful two-year old daughter, could not have been more splendid.

'There they are mum,' Jay cried out, as he spotted Eran pushing a pram across the cobbled streets. He had seen photos and recognised him immediately. The likeness to himself was uncanny.

'Good grief. You guys really do look alike,' exclaimed Wanda as she approached.

They were not far apart in age and had similar builds too. As the day progressed, they even seemed to share close similarities in personality.

'All you need is the Scottish accent Jay and you two could easily pass for twins. So great to be shown around by a local. Thanks so much Eran.'

His wife was Swedish and he had a good command of the language - full of really in-depth historical knowledge too.

Changing of the palace guards and walking the Monteliusvagen path, were favourites for Wanda. For Jay, it was the specialist music and gaming shops that Eran took him to. Then they all enjoyed looking down across the water to City Hall and Riddarholmen, discovering the charming old houses of the city.

'How good has your beautiful daughter been? When we get back to Australia, we will find something very special to send her as a little thank you for such a fantastic day.'

Wanda and Jay hugged them both warmly, then stood waving, until the train for Eran's long journey home, departed.

That night they met with an old colleague of Wanda's for drinks.

The next morning a tour of the Royal Opera House, followed by a special luncheon classical performance. Dating back to 1773, the

Kungliga Operan had been commissioned by King Gustav III, who had been a great patron of the arts.

Most impressive!

Dinner in a Viking cave, with minstrels to entertain – their gift shop providing the perfect souvenir for Wanda to take to Sen. A most useful and very relevant cheese slicer, sporting a carved wooden handle with solid stainless steel slicer head, shaped like a Viking horned helmet.

Their last day in Stockholm, was spent on the island of Djurgarten – Royal lands that had been kept for the people, since the 15th century. Museums, galleries, cafes, a fun park and the most stunning animal sanctuary imaginable.

'Such a short ferry ride and it feels like we've stepped back into ye olde world of Swedish folklore. These wooden cottages of Skansen, will lead us up through the forest. Today they have traditionally dressed performers and a food market of taste delights. We can quickly look in on the Junibacken fairy-tale land. Want to make sure we see all the animals, at the highest point of the island too. Great views from there. Way too much to take in with just one day. How incredible is this place?' Wanda was reading the information handed out on the ferry. 'I'd really like to see the area where they held the 1897 World Fair but I don't think we'll have the time.'

Reindeer and elk proved to be the stars of the hillside.

Wanda and Jay could have watched them for hours.

Definitely a place to come back to.

Initial email content from Sen had suggested he might pick Wanda up from Schiphol airport. Now, on the night before her scheduled arrival, he was saying he would meet her in Groningen, the day following.

Was he having second thoughts?

The excitement Wanda felt about being with Sen as soon as possible, suddenly seemed to not be equally shared.

'What could have happened in these past couple of days?' she wondered anxiously.

She had emailed constantly about fun things in Stockholm. He responded appropriately, to sound interested. Now he was happy to wait an extra day before seeing her and without any comment on why.

Such a spirit dampener for Wanda but she tried to be calm.

'Oh well. That will give me a chance to catch up with Denise and see what's been going on with the house.'

It had still not been rented.

The train from Schiphol was always the easiest way to get back to their Hillywood home so, what did it matter if Sen didn't collect her from the airport?

That first night back in Holland, Sen phoned Wanda for the very first time.

His voice was not as she had recalled, from the brief time they shared together, two weeks earlier.

This was not the voice she heard in her mind, when she read his emails.

Why did he sound so hesitant?

Maybe he had met someone else in those past couple of days but still felt obliged to continue with the island visit.

Or maybe it was the simple fact he needed to speak in English and was struggling with the language.

'Must be quite different, not having the time to review words and craft what you really wanted to say,' she thought.

He briefly told her about a video he was making, for the ferry company that took people across to the island. The CEO had called a meeting at short notice. He would see him on the ferry the next morning and then drive to Groningen station to collect Wanda. Very sweet to say in 'her' enchanted red cabrio but no 'sorry', for not sticking to the original airport pick up plan.

Wanda didn't ask questions.

The conversation was so stilted. It left Wanda uncertain about everything.

When the call ended, she could not remember saying anything at all.

Mumblings about the flight perhaps.

Made some strange comment about the island.

Left it saying she would text him to confirm, that she made the train time he suggested. That was about it. The fantasies of spending the rest of her life with this man, seemed to all but disappear.

Doubts that she should even go, had been squashed by Jay but it was all becoming a little bit weird for Wanda.

She didn't know whether to cry or be mad.

Denise had convinced her she had nothing to lose. At the very least, she would get to see this beautiful island and more than likely get laid by a very handsome man.

That simple thought, had Hug and Fug jumping through hoops in Wanda's head.

She recalled the intense emotion in that farewell hug.

The body and the attitude - he was sure to be good in bed!

How many times had she imagined being up close and oh so personal with Sen.

Nervous was a definite understatement, as the next day unfolded. Sleep had eluded Wanda and the early morning cycle ride, did nothing to help calm her anxiety. Even the text from Sen, to say he was looking forward to seeing her soon.

Her internal fluttering could not be eased.

Every piece of clothing she had with her, had been mixed and matched, to plan out what she would wear at every moment of the island liaison.

Constant visits to the loo, continued throughout the two hour train journey from Hillywood to Groningen.

'Silly school girl behaviour,' she kept telling herself. 'The guy has clearly gone cold on the whole idea. What the hell am I doing? I'll be stuck on this tiny island, in the middle of nowhere, with a man I don't know, who does not really want me there.'

Jay had dropped his bags at the house the night before and headed straight into Amsterdam. Old mates were gathering at one of their favourite watering holes and a few days of outrage had been planned. He had gone off a happy chappie and would meet Wanda back at the house, on the day of their departure for Sydney.

Finally Wanda arrived at Groningen station. It was the end of the line for one hell of a train journey and Wanda had, by that point, convinced herself it might also be the end of her imagined romance.

The wind howled around the entrance to the station.

Wanda could easily see where cars would need to stop for pick-ups.

Should she send a text to say she was there?

Didn't want to seem too pushy.

Perhaps it was better to just wait. He would text her if he needed to.

So many people being collected. They came and they went but still no car and no Sen to be seen.

Maybe the train had arrived early.

As her frozen bones started to seize up, she contemplated a quick coffee inside somewhere warm.

Just then, her phone sounded for text arrival.

'Sorry. Meeting just finished. On my way. Maybe it takes an hour. Hope you can have a coffee somewhere there.'

She could have cried.

'How could he have me waiting at this cold station for half an hour already and now tell me he will take another hour? This guy has got to be kidding. Clearly not interested in getting off to a good start. I should just get back on the train and let it all go!'

The conversation she was having with herself was not a pleasant one.

Tears welled in her eyes.

A dizziness came over her and she felt totally alone.

• CHAPTER FIVE •

WANDA'S HEART WAS BEATING so fast, she thought she might explode! Seeing her enchanted red cabrio, heading towards the station entrance, had been the weirdest of experiences.

The last time she'd been with her beloved car, it was her doing the driving.

After handing the keys to Sen, she had not looked back and yet, most of her waking hours since, she had longed to see this incredible man. She wondered if he was being infected with the enchantment of her cabrio, as much as she had been. She needed to be with him and to know, if what she had felt so deeply about him, was shared in some way.

Could the energies she experienced with her special car have played tricks on her, that hour or so she spent with Sen?

Had the emails exchanged since, only been an amusement for him?

Why would he not agree to this crazy woman spending a weekend with him?

She was attractive and made him laugh.

Could be, that he just saw it as a fun liaison with the possibility for some good sex.

Maybe she created the man of her dreams in her head and he was but a figment of her wild imagination. She had desperately wanted to believe he was the one.

At least he did actually exist so that was a good start.

Odd to see her cabrio, suddenly in front of her again. She still loved it totally and found it difficult to think, it was no longer hers. It was being driven by the man she had thought so much about those past two weeks. He was quite real but she doubted her view on shared intensity of feelings, was actually the case.

If it had been, no way would he have changed plans at the last minute. No way would he have kept her waiting all that time, at a cold railway station.

This was the man she was fast becoming very disappointed in.

An entire hour, sitting in the station café, and there had been just one final text from Sen, to say he should arrive in ten minutes.

That had been twenty minutes earlier.

'Unreliable,' she told herself.

The mere thought, sent her reeling back to memories of ex-husband Larry.

She often told people, after her marriage to Larry ended, 'if I had to say but one word, to sum up why we split, that would be unreliable.'

Larry was such a charming and likeable man. Always obliging and instantly replying with a yes, whenever asked to do something.

No trouble at all.

The second time you asked; the third; the quick yes, without a blink of the eye. Eventually, people stopped asking. 'He means well,' often heard as they gave up.

Trusting people to do what they said and when, had always been important to Wanda - a foundation stone to any relationship, whether personal or business.

She always stood by her word and had made a choice, not to ever allow herself to get close to others who did not.

If there had been a train heading back to Hillywood, she might well have taken it.

Having vented her displeasure to Denise on the phone, Wanda had decided she would be better off doing some stretches and trying to get herself to calm down. A.B. had also called her to see how it was all going but she hadn't told him about the no-show. Way too embarrassing, being stood up like that.

Deep breathing always helped.

Yoga moves to loosen up and allow blood to flow to the extremities.

A coffee and read of the paper were also good distractions.

She told herself, life could be worse.

Mixed emotions flooded through Wanda, as Sen finally pulled up.

He stepped from the car and gave her the longest hug, lifting her up into the air. Even in her highest shoes, she was still only up to his chin. In the lifted position, they were cheek to cheek and she could feel his heart close to hers – both beating at a high pace.

All so very real!

She was back in the 'perfect Dutchman' zone and all uncertainty was gone.

'I can't believe I kept you waiting all this time. Will you ever forgive me?'

He pleaded, looking into her eyes, with total sincerity.

Wanda was jolted by that spell he cast on her, when they first met.

Every inch of her sparkled, just being with him and hearing the sound of his deep and sexy Dutch voice. The desire was back in full swing.

She convinced him she had been fine. The café was beautifully warm and it had been nice, to be able to relax and read the paper.

It seemed the only way to go!

What was the point in letting him know how disappointed she had been?

He seemed genuinely sorry and she hung off his every word.

They would now have quite some hours, before the next ferry to the island, and Sen had plans to take her for lunch, at one of his favourite canal cafes on the way.

She would make sure she enjoyed every minute of it.

Conversation was excited and bubbly.

All the while, Wanda kept thinking 'How gorgeous is he!' Pinching herself to make sure she wasn't dreaming.

It was impossible to stay angry at him.

Enchantment was all around, as they cruised along the small country roads, in the cabrio that had brought them together.

Maybe she was actually dreaming. That was exactly how she felt.

Light headed and a little giddy. Her sense of reality, having been pushed to one side, whilst the body floated on a different plane.

In a short while, they were at the canal café, in a stunningly quaint village.

So romantic!

Several small boats parked in front of the entrance. A sign above the door, confirmed its fish specialty and dating back to 1826. Being at a lock gate, bookings were a must in the summer. People would take hours to dine and enjoy the passing parade of watercraft. Not so, that autumn day. It was super quiet so Wanda and Sen had no trouble getting a table.

'I hope you like fish?'

Wanda nodded enthusiastically, questioning whether she had actually told him that it was her favourite food.

With so much to talk about, all her anxieties faded fast.

The video had been well received by the boat company's CEO and Sen told her every little detail, about the filming and editing so far.

'Very smooth with the waitress,' thought Wanda as she agreed she was happy for him to order for them both. She had sensed he liked to be in charge, the first time they met.

He went on to tell her how much he loved to cook and that he hoped she wouldn't mind being waited on in his home.

Brilliant!

Wanda had no problem putting a tasty meal together but she would be more than happy, to have this amazing man looking after her.

Time passed quickly, as they talked and laughed non-stop.

'We really need to get motoring now. It's a little later than I thought.'

Sen would not hear of Wanda contributing to the bill. This weekend would be his treat. He wanted to make up for the low purchase price, he negotiated for her car.

As Wanda stepped outside the café ahead of Sen, she almost ran into a couple of heavily dressed cyclists. Apologising for being in her way, she could hear they were from Scotland.

Such a small world!

Larry was from Aberdeen and so were these two lads. Not so small a world, that they actually knew his family though. Sen was happy to share some local cycle path knowledge with them and they all enjoyed a laugh about the flat state of Holland, compared to the hills of Scotland.

They soon realised they'd been chatting way too long.

As Sen moved to open the car door, one of the lads commented to to meet them.

They really did work well together and the fit was clearly evident.

Sitting side by side in the cabrio again, Wanda was acutely aware of the aura that connected her with Sen. Was it just the unique energies of the car? The two of them were very much at one with the universe and a sense of peace came over her.

Not having slept much the night before, she relaxed into a gentle doze.

Sen felt a great comfort, in the knowledge that she was confident enough with him, to close her eyes quietly. Staring across at his sleeping beauty, it seemed all was very right in his world. She looked every bit enchanted.

He couldn't believe she actually did turn up for this visit to his island.

So glad he didn't let his nerves get the better of him, he felt a certainty of them being very right for each other and wanted her more than anything.

Not a great deal further to the ferry but they only just made it in time.

'That was close. Three hours to wait, if we missed this one.'

No cars allowed on the island and the garage Sen kept the car in, still left some distance to walk to the ferry terminal. By the time they put the roof up and made sure the cabrio was comfortably stored away, they had to dash for it.

The swift walking pace soon needed to become a run, as a crew member waved at them to hurry.

You could see the island from the terminal but the crossing took 45mins, which allowed for coffees to be enjoyed in the cafeteria.

Shallow waters of the Waddenzee, left a small channel that needed to be manoeuvred to reach the island port. Travelling far left, before being able to cut back to the right, the boat had to make its path through the waters, with quite some precision.

The sky was a spectacular pink, as the sun began to go down.

Sen was a great storyteller and took Wanda up to the deck after coffee. Standing on the open top of the ferry, a gentle breeze caressed and slightly chilled their faces. As he relived historical elements of the island's past, squawks from seagulls, added to the atmosphere. Wanda nestled under Sen's strong arm and again decided to pinch herself, to make sure she wasn't dreaming.

Totally mesmerized, she felt as though she was watching a movie, with her as the leading lady - the strong and oh so charming suitor, at her side.

Germany was close by and the island had once been part of their realm. Sen spoke of the impacts of the war and eventually moved on from history, to tell her what originally took him to the island.

She didn't let on that Gert already filled her in on that brainstorming visit and the ensuing relationship.

'Good to hear his thoughts on the split with that woman,' she had decided.

So many years had passed and he clearly had no regrets about that coming to an end. Initially he was happy to stay on the island but the past couple of years had seen him decide, he was keen to escape.

Umm. There was that word again. Gert had mentioned that Sen thought of the island as his 'escape' and she had wondered 'from what?' Now he was talking in the opposite context. It was the island he wanted to escape from.

Just like Wanda to overthink everything!

Sen went on to tell her about the trouble he had selling his house.

So it wasn't just Wanda not being able to move her Hillywood home. The property market, all across Holland, was at a complete standstill.

At least Sen had a couple, who were keen to buy his house, just as soon as they sold their own.

Several buses awaited the ferry's arrival.

As they boarded, everyone seemed to know Sen.

It was a small island community, with a population that tripled during the summer months. Coming to the end of that but still quite some tourists about.

Entering Sen's home for the first time, Wanda felt a little uneasy.

Beautifully furnished and decorated, as she had expected.

Large framed images adorned the walls, most of which had stories. They were either from his own photography or artworks his brother had created.

Several photographs from places he had visited with Deta. She worked in television too and was the partner he had stayed reasonably close to over the years. As he relayed that story to Wanda, she had to admit to a slight feeling of jealousy.

Not like her normally.

Sen enjoyed photographing into glassed areas, for interesting reflections, and it didn't take Wanda long to see he was with that girlfriend, in a couple of the shots. Not sure she liked having to see that constantly. When Sen talked about that relationship, it became clear he was happy they still had contact.

No knowledge whatsoever, of the wife he had been to school with and married when he was just 21 years old. Might have been different if they had been able to conceive a child but that was not meant to be. When he talked about that marriage ending, he seemed quite glad it had.

It was a very long time ago that he had been with Deta but they had bought an apartment in Amsterdam back then and set up home for several years. Might even have married, if she had agreed to have a child with him. The age gap was 17 years, same as Wanda had between her and Medwin, except that Sen had met Deta when she was in her early twenties and not ready to settle down and have a family.

The house tour continued, with a quick look at the enormous back garden and then up to the first floor.

'This is my bedroom and next door is a guest room. Mind those steep steps if you want to look further upstairs. That top floor goes into the roof. Kids love it up there. It has a little office space and another small bedroom.'

He looked a little shy and nervous, as he continued.

'I made up the guest room so you have options for sleeping.'

Then to distract her from talks of bed.

'Do you like the rain head shower I added over the bath? '

It was a small landing area and all rooms could be seen easily, without moving.

Nodding her approval, and making some bland comments on how nice everything was, Wanda had difficulty focussing on anything other than where she might like to sleep.

Been a while since she had sex and now she was feeling like an inexperienced school girl. Maybe she should just take the guest room and keep things on a 'friends' basis.

'I thought it might be nice to go out for dinner tonight so you can see some of the island. A few minutes to walk to the end of the street and be at the oldest hotel in the village.'

'Ah. That's where the brainstorming session was,' thought Wanda.

'The main restaurant is really popular so I took the liberty of making a reservation. Tomorrow we will have time to shop and I can prepare dinner at home.' Sen was in total control.

'If you would like to cycle, we can rent a bike for you in the morning. People come from all over Europe to explore the nature we have here. You will love it.'

Wanda had done a little homework.

She read that birds migrated to Schier in the thousands. Alternating forest, beach, dunes, pond, creek, polders, marsh and mudflats, made this national park area one of the finest in the Netherlands. Measuring just 4kms wide and 16kms long, dedicated cycle paths reached every corner. Colonies of seals were often to be seen on the sandbars or close to shore. The wide beaches provided the perfect hard surface for sand sailing and kite flying. Charming cottages dated back to 1720. The tiny village had a dozen or so cafes, boasting full terraces as soon as the sun showed itself.

Conversation over dinner mainly covered their families.

Sen was one of six children - four boys and two girls – and he was the fourth born. His father had passed away some years ago. Dad had been a carpenter and he and his brother ran a workshop making doors and doing special joinery. That factory had been their father's and they were obliged to take it over from him. The work gave them both enough income to provide for their families.

Living space was attached to the factory and Sen recalled how pleased he was, when his father and uncle finally sold the business and they could move. Some of that money had also gone into the purchase of an old Dutch yacht, which the six children and their parents spent a large part of their lives on.

Sailing was a passion of Sen's.

He had a plan to buy a boat to live on, when he finally sold his island home. Taking paying passengers for cruises, around the seas off Holland.

Saw himself as a bit of a loner these days.

The radio show he worked on was scheduled to finish in a couple of months.

If only the two women that were buying his house, could complete the purchase by then. Still no buyer for their house so not looking very likely at that point. It had been over a year, since they gave him a small deposit to hold the house.

'I think we must be the last ones here.'

They had talked so intensely, it escaped their attention that the restaurant had emptied and it was almost midnight. Wanda was a little intoxicated, both from the wine and from being in Sen's company. She felt certain everyone must be able to read her mind.

Could they really know what lustful thoughts were spinning through her head?

The waiter definitely looked at her with a grin.

Fug had not let Hug get a look in.

No soft and cuddly thoughts for her.

The raunchy little Fug had been filling Wanda's head with images of Sen naked and what they might do to each other in bed.

Intense looks had passed between Wanda and Sen the entire night.

They must surely be the talk of the island by now.

Floating was the sensation that came to mind, as Wanda walked arm in arm with Sen, to make their way home down the darkened street.

Chatter turned to silence, as the anticipation of what might happen took them over.

All thoughts of the past couple of weeks went spinning through Wanda's head.

That incredible but oh so brief liaison, when Sen bought her car, had left her convinced she had found the man of her dreams.

Subsequent emails that passed between them, during her travels with Jay, had ended in disappointment with her Mr Perfect. When he changed his plan to pick her up from the airport and was then so late arriving at the station, she starting thinking she had it all wrong.

During the course of dinner, Sen explained how he had not wanted to bring her home to a messy house. That was why he changed airport pick up plans. He had been staying with his cousin during the week, for easier access to work, and recalled what a state he left the house in the weekend prior.

Then the CEO called the meeting about the video production and it had all fallen into place.

Not that he had ever dreamt he might be close to two hours late in picking her up from the station. For that, he had apologised furiously, over and over again.

Of course there was still the possible issue around smoking.

No sign of any cigarettes so far though.

He loved music and told stories of younger days, when he played in a band. Very interested to hear Wanda had done the same.

Sen on banjo and guitar. Wanda singing.

Perhaps a nice little duet in the making?

Once inside the front door, Sen grabbed Wanda in the biggest and deepest of hugs.

She was happy to have cuddling back into the agenda.

Again she was lifted off the ground and into the tight hold of his arms.

'To the sofa or upstairs?' he whispered.

'Think I'm more than ready for bed!'

As Wanda spoke those words, she wondered if he would usher her to the guest room and they both gave a quick nervous giggle.

Stepping up one stair, Wanda turned towards Sen.

They were face to face, at equal height now.

She kissed him gently on each cheek, as he stood motionless.

The kisses moved to his nose.

To his forehead.

To his lips.

His warm, soft and very large lips teased, as he snatched tiny nips around Wanda's face, in response.

No need for any conversation.

The heavy breathing said it all.

As their bodies connected at heart level, Wanda returned to her unsure state. She became very aware of one massive erection taking hold of Sen. He was almost two metres tall and she began to think he might have a penis of equal proportion to his height, even though the hands and feet were not unusually big.

Always the detail, in her busy little head!

It even occurred to her that she had given birth to two children so was well stretched in the vaginal zone.

'Should be no problem,' she tried to reassure herself.

Kisses became more intense and the sexual fire was well alight.

She loved to kiss but had, in recent years, found the man was either too slobbery or too rigid. That perfect soft and loving kiss had eluded her for so long.

Different with Sen - it could not have been more emotionally charged or perfect.

76

Soft and sensuous, arousing every fibre of Wanda's being.

'I need to visit the loo so I will be up in a moment.'

Sen was leaving the final choice of room to Wanda, as he made a dash for the toilet.

Continuing up the stairs on her own, she stood on the landing, peering into both bedrooms and questioning herself yet again.

Hug telling her to just enjoy the kissing, cuddling and island discovery.

Fug making it very clear she should not miss this opportunity for what could be, at the very least, some fantastic love making.

No way the 'friends' stance would last the weekend.

'Go for it girl.'

She had been longing for Sen ever since they met. Now she had just this weekend to see if he was really Mr Right or not. Just two nights to explore the passions she had imagined in detail.

There was no time to waste so why on earth was she hesitating?

True – she would soon be back in Australia and that was almost 17,000kms away from this tiny island - but Sen was very open for change. He already talked about his job ending and sounded flexible on the boat purchase idea too.

Who knows?

Maybe he would consider a move down under!

Right now she was more interested in getting down under and dirty with him. Under those bed covers and seeing if their bodies gelled, as much as their minds and souls did.

The choice was made!

A quick visit to the bathroom to freshen up and she was soon in his bed.

'So glad you decided on this room,' he said grinning like the cat that got the cream.

'Much more comfortable in here!'

• CHAPTER SIX •

ELECTRIC CHARGES crossed between Sen and Wanda the entire night.

Sparks overwhelmed them both and neither one had managed much sleep. It would only shorten the precious time they had together this weekend, anyway.

'Was it really now time to be thinking about that bike ride?'

Wanda found it difficult to believe her body could stand it.

Early morning sun had been streaming in for an age already and they had made love twice, since that day's first light. The clumsiness of their first encounter, the night prior, had gone. That sense of desperation to connect, no longer overshadowed the release of their emotions.

Driven by passionate kisses and a little too much alcohol, foreplay had been cut short, as soon as they hit the bed that first night. No sooner had they been horizontal, than Wanda was confronted with taking in the largeness of Sen's penis.

Happy to have this precious closeness and yet in quite some distress, at the thought she might not be able to cope with his size, it took Wanda back to her first ever boyfriend.

That beautiful young man, who shared her love of motorbikes and had been with her, when she bought her first ever car - the special red convertible. Dating him for six years, from the young age of twelve, petting and kissing was as far as they had ventured to express their affections. Reaching eighteen years old and trying finally to have intercourse, Wanda's physical pain had been too much to stand.

Doctors and books were sought out, to learn whatever tricks they could, but the mind was too blocked and they eventually had to end things. He had been so distraught, that he considered ending more than just their relationship. Luckily, that didn't eventuate but they did need to live in different states, to get their new lives on track.

'Two children and several partners since so it must just be the cogs needing oil, from not being used for a while,' she considered, on feeling the size challenge.

Pity there was no oil to hand.

Note to self – bring a fun lubricant next time.

Sen seemed to enjoy the tightness and came much quicker than he had wanted. Not long before his tantalising tricks then brought Wanda to a climax. Reeling from the impact, she melted further into his embrace and, as she nestled in, Wanda could not think of anywhere else on earth she could ever rather be, than safe in his loving and very strong arms.

He most definitely had not gone cold on the idea of them being together and it even seemed he shared her fantasies for their future. Any doubts she had over the past couple of weeks, vanished completely.

Talking for the larger part of that night and into the morning, they reminded themselves how lucky they were to find each other. Fate had played more than a strong hand and their lives would be changed forever.

Wanda explained her Hug & Fug inner voices to Sen, which provided him with the launching pad to go straight into expressing the raunchy thoughts he'd had about her, since they first met.

Sen laughingly blamed Fug for what he said was the hardest erection he ever experienced. The fact it could come back again so soon after orgasm, amazed them both.

He was insatiable and it was all Fug's doing!

'Still so much for me to learn about you Wanda. I want to know every crevice of your body and how it works. Share your deepest thoughts and know exactly how you feel about everything. The love making will become even stronger, as we learn about each other and relax in the knowledge that we want only to please one another.'

Wanda's eyes watered and she whimpered a gentle sigh of satisfaction.

Nothing seemed to be left out, as Sen went through details of his life and the different girlfriends he had. Not even the period where he joined a commune and lived in a world of shared partners and mixed parenting.

That had created more questions in Wanda's mind, than it did to help complete the Sen story that was unfolding.

He seemed fine with her simple questioning but she still found the commune thing a little strange and felt awkward asking, most of what she was actually thinking.

Sen had been doing a radio story on the commune's activities and, as he got to know some of the people living in it, he'd become drawn to the creed they lived by.

Couples had taken their young children into the commune, with a view to them being educated by the much broader perspectives and knowledge of a group of different adults. Parents relinquishing their strict partner stances and taking up equal positions with the 'singles' in the community.

Sen was a qualified school teacher, who had failed his marriage and not been successful with bearing children. He came from a large family, where he felt his parents did not connect with their children, as well as they might have. This new concept was incredibly appealing.

Sharing sexual partners and delving deep into the whys and wherefores of relationships, had also attracted him. It was part of the hippy world of free everything, where the first objective was to question the 'norm'. Too bad for Sen that he fell in love with one of the mums. That was totally forbidden. He had invested all his money, purchasing one of the houses for commune living, and been totally caught up in the doctrine.

Later, he realised there was really just one strong leader, who called all the shots.

This guy was more controlling and dangerous than anyone he had ever known.

It also became apparent that the children were concerned, about not getting quality time with their real parents. They were also confused by the outside world's reactions and had become traumatised, by what went on in the commune.

Sen wanted out.

Easier said than done!

Still working in radio, he could at least move away from the commune during the day. Eventually he met and fell in love with Rianne. This had given him the impetus needed, to finally escape from the group.

They lived together for several years and she supported his efforts, with disconnecting from the commune and selling that property.

Sen went into details of other relationships, to the point where Wanda became a little overloaded.

'Might be a bit too much information for our first weekend together,' she had thought to herself on several occasions.

Trouble he had with the law. Women he had only gone out with briefly and what sort of crazy behaviour, had led him to not wanting to go any further. The bad financial state he had been in.

It was clear he wanted it all out on the table.

Sen could not be more serious about Wanda and he needed to know that she would take on board, all that was good and bad in his past.

Wanda told him all about her poor upbringing. Not knowing who her father was. Being dragged from pillar to post, growing up in Sydney as the youngest of eight. Her mother doing unskilled jobs, to keep them all fed and clothed. The roof over their heads, changing constantly.

He was keen to know every detail of her past relationships. Why her marriage failed? What ended things with others since? How did she feel about the future?

Future?

The mere mention of the word, gave Wanda an incredible feeling that, whatever the future was going to hold, she would be sharing it with Sen. The romance that she had imagined, was now very real.

'So! How do you feel about that bike ride?' Sen realised the time had come to lighten things up.

'Let's do it!' Wanda responded, secretly feeling a little like she'd been rammed by a charging bull.

'A quick shower first.'

Maybe that would help to soothe the groin!

As they discovered the natural landscapes of the island, Sen was impressed that Wanda could actually ride a bike.

So was she, the way it felt sitting on that hard bicycle seat!

He was also pleasantly surprised by her ability to speak Dutch. When he introduced her to people, she had no hesitation in responding to them in the local lingo.

Sitting outside one of the cafes in the sun, drinking lattes and eating applegebak, Wanda looked and sounded every bit the Nederlandse vrouw.

'It's a text from my friend Tod. He'd like me to pop over this afternoon to help with something on his computer. Do you mind if I leave you to rest a while later?'

Sen could see by the tired look on Wanda's face, that she did not mind one bit. He knew how exhausted he felt and expected the newness of everything, combined with no sleep, would have made Wanda feel even more so.

Tod was an older islander friend, who had helped Sen with much of the renovation work at his house. Not terribly well educated and what you might call 'rough around the edges' but he had a heart of gold.

When times had been tough for Sen, he had even worked with Tod mowing lawns on the island.

Anything to keep some money coming in.

Paying out his girlfriend, for half of the island house, had come at a time when TV and Radio work had dried up for Sen.

Depression kicked in and Sen had been in a very unhappy place. Tod gave moral support and helped him through it all. Repaying his friendship was important.

Wanda admired that. Her friends had always been important to her too and she cherished the great friendships, she had around the world.

Having some space to herself Wanda did a quick few emails to let

Jay, Lou and Denise know how well things were going. She also checked in with her agency offices, then hit the sofa and was fast asleep in no time.

Waking almost two hours later, Wanda was a little surprised to find that Sen had not yet returned.

What to do?

Almost another hour passed. No text. Nothing!

Perhaps a little television.

Eventually Sen appeared at the side window, as he parked his bike.

No sooner had he opened the front door, than Wanda could smell cigarette smoke and beer. As he moved in to hug her, she could not help but turn away.

'So sorry. You can smell that I had a drink and a smoke I guess.'

He was at least being honest.

'Tod was in a bad state. His son got arrested for being in possession of marijuana and he needed me to try and help get things sorted. The son is living in Utrecht and is a constant problem for Tod. Once we had done what we could, I felt I could not turn down his offer to have a drink with him. Unfortunately Tod is quite the smoker so it was difficult to keep saying no, as he kept lighting one after the other. My phone had gone dead so I couldn't text.'

The phone was held up to demonstrate.

Tales of Tod went into his split with his islander wife. Her move to Germany with their daughter. His son deciding to fend for himself. The daughter later marrying a black Nigerian and him trying to make his way in Germany. The two grandchildren they had given Tod. Trials and tribulations of son, daughter and ex-wife all wanting his financial help on a regular basis. Him only surviving from his carpentry, lawn mowing and newspaper deliveries.

Poor Tod!

'He is very keen to meet you so I hope you don't mind that he is popping by later, for a couple of beers with us. First thing I need to do is shower and clean my teeth. I really want to hug and kiss you but I know you won't come near me smelling like this. If it helps at all, I really did not enjoy the cigarette even a little bit. So happy that you have motivated me to stop.'

On that note, Sen smiled and headed to the bathroom.

The experience was not a pleasant one for Wanda.

'What if he was unable to really stop smoking?' she quizzed herself.

'No point in focussing on anything but the positive,' she finally got her head back to where she liked it to be. 'He has made it clear that this is what he wants. I believe in him with all my heart. As Jay pointed out, I'd be crazy to turn down Mr Perfect, for just the fact he had an occasional smoke.'

Wanda could tell herself that until she was blue in the face but she knew for a fact, that she could never be happy with a smoker. There was also quite some unease, with the fact he had left her alone in his house all that time.

The smell of Sen's cologne entered the room way before he did. Wanda melted into his arms and lost all negative thought immediately. They snoozed in front of the TV hugging, with kisses interjected at regular intervals.

Seeing Tod arriving on his bike, they were up and pulling themselves together to greet him. No knocking on the door required. Tod would always just enter the unlocked front door himself.

Wanda greeted him in Dutch, having already been warned that he spoke no English. Three kisses to the cheeks, as required. She was surprised by his appearance. A thick beard and skin resembling that of a crocodile. Large red nose, with pits you could almost park your olives in. Not overweight but this was clearly an unfit man. Alcohol and cigarettes had taken their toll. Looking very much the tramp and clearly wanting to check Wanda out.

Wine was served for Wanda. Beers lined up for the boys.

A lekker plate of snacks soon put together by Sen.

Trying her best to participate in the conversation, Wanda found herself mostly nodding and smiling – unable to keep up with the pace of the discussion.

Tod was clearly interested in a variety of worldly matters and this was a key factor in the friendship developing. He would drop free copies of most daily papers to Sen. Current affairs and being in touch with all the news, was really important for him.

Sen had already told Wanda, that he often spent the entire day just reading the papers. Keeping up with what went on in the world, was also something Wanda liked to do but not quite to that extent, although she did appreciate that Sen's radio show required him to be knowledgeable on all the latest happenings in the world.

When Sen left the table to get more beers, Wanda made an effort to ask Tod about something and he seemed to speak more slowly for her. He was interested to hear about Australia so that gave them subject matter to work with. Both appreciated the other trying but both were also very relieved, once Sen returned and jumped back into the conversation.

Nice to meet Sen's friends but the stay was perhaps a little too long for Wanda's liking and, as much as she tried to go with the flow, she hadn't relaxed with it.

'Couldn't really ask him to leave. Hope you didn't mind?'

'Of course not,' Wanda replied, smiling uncomfortably.

'Now I can prepare us some dinner. You must be starving.'

Indeed, she really was rather hungry by then. Offering to help out in the kitchen, she was told there was no need and she should just make herself comfortable.

All well and good but it felt strange to sit watching TV, while Sen was busy with everything. Wanda would much rather be in there beside him, chatting and helping wherever she could.

That was not how he liked to cook.

He needed the kitchen to himself and was very particular about his food preparation. She felt excluded but sat quietly, waiting for his culinary delights.

If they were going to spend the rest of their lives together, she would have to accept his ways. Learning to be the person your partner needs you to be, was a little foreign to Wanda but she was more than willing to try this time.

'Wow! How beautifully presented! Seems a pity to eat it and disturb such an amazing work of art.'

Very impressive!

Colours chosen carefully and laid on the plate totally synchronised.

Meat sliced equally.

Vegetables and salad, all adorning a splay of sauté potato.

Not only looking like it was ready for the photo shoot - it tasted delicious too!

Amongst all of his incredible talents, Sen was undeniably a fine cook.

They enjoyed the scrumptious feast, in front of the Dutch News –

like an old married couple. Comments made on what was happening in the world, interspersed with Wanda's compliments on every morsel. Sen lapping up every bit of the praise and enjoying the banter, just as much as the food.

Falling into bed, not long after Wanda had washed up, they both breathed an enormous sigh of contentment.

Was this really only the second night they had slept together?

Wrapped in a warm embrace, there was nothing in their immediate world that did not feel right. They seemed so perfect for each other, in every way.

Wanda had only to get close to Sen's hot body and she became instantly aroused. Longing began for her, as soon as their eyes met and she took in the depth of emotion on his face. Gazing at his large soft lips and knowing that his sensuous kiss would melt her heart totally, she could make love with him at any time.

They chatted and shared thoughts, on how a movie they watched after the news, might have been improved. Laughing as their creative brains churned out ideas, for making it more entertaining.

Wrestling with the bed covers playfully, Sen crept down to suck Wanda's toes.

Kissing his way up her body slowly, until he found her soft warm centre, it was time to make up for the lack of foreplay the night before.

He talked about her beautiful body, with such a sexy tone to his accent, flicking his tongue onto her skin strategically, at frequent intervals. Eventually it was gently caressing her clitoris, with absolute tenderness.

Wanda ached with desire and understood he wanted her motionless, for as long as she could stand. As her body tightened and her back arched, she became helpless to hold on any longer. Peaking with a deep pleasure and signalling for Sen to enter her, he instead moved back up to hug position and whispered softly.

'I think I might have pushed your body a little too hard this morning and last night so I'm very happy to just hold you now and fall to sleep.'

Tears welled in Wanda's eyes, as she came back from her heaven on earth and considered her incredible good fortune to have found this caring, gentle and very sexy man.

As her watery eyes met Sen's cheek, he hugged her even more tightly.

Intensity of touch, sent shivers through them both, as they gradually fell into a deeply satisfied and exhausted sleep.

The following morning, began with an instant charge of emotions.

On waking, Sen was immediately activated by Wanda's leg that was wrapped across his body. She began to sense the hardness of his appendage. Passion overwhelmed them. Moments later, they were connected as one, deeply sharing a slow and loving pulsation that took them to orgasmic heights in unison.

Moans of ecstasy were followed by more soft tears of joy, as they held on to each other for dear life, realising that they must soon leave the island.

They had been to the moon and back and never anticipated how truly desperate they would feel, when it came time to part.

Wanda suddenly remembered she hadn't given Sen the gift she bought for him in Stockholm.

'Can't believe I forgot to give you this - had to kill a shipload of Vikings to get it!'

One most interesting cheese slicer was soon cutting the sad state that had begun to engulf them. He loved it, of course, and they were happy to be able to inject a little laughter, into their highly emotional state.

Bags were packed and waiting at the door.

They had decided the night before, that they would breakfast on the boat and stay in bed for as long as they could.

Wanda jumped straight into the shower and soon Sen was in the bathroom with small crackers and slivers of cheese.

'Had to quickly put it to the test. Works perfectly. Definitely worth that Viking assault!' His humour was well placed, bringing them nicely back to the now.

Standing on the ferry deck, watching as the island became smaller and smaller, Wanda was convinced this would not be the last of her time with Sen on his island.

She had planned to locate herself more permanently in Sydney and give stronger support to her ad agency team there but her London office still had loads of client activity too so she could easily justify travelling back and forth.

The book she was writing neared completion. Hopefully that would mean a publishing deal and global promotions.

No shortage of reasons to be back in Europe.

Not that she needed any other reason, than to just be with Sen!

She recalled how clear Kiki was, about fate having played her a strong hand and how the series of events that led Sen to Wanda, were so definitely Kismet!

Back in the enchanted red cabrio again, that same mystical aura wrapped itself around them, as it had on the way there. A peaceful vibrant energy, that made them acutely aware of being exactly where and yet they should be.

Sen suggested they listen to one of his favourite radio shows, for their journey to Hillywood. Music, from the seventies and eighties, would provide a light touch to this ride that would end with goodbye.

Coffee break conversation was dominated by all the great things Sen had heard about Australia - Sydney in particular. It was somewhere he had wanted to go, for a very long time.

Wanda's excitement, at the thought of showing Sen her Sydney, was clearly evident. She dared to dream, of the life they could live together there. At the same time, telling herself she had no problem being wherever in the world made sense for both of them - so long as she was with Sen.

Seemed a bit wrong, to actually say this to him at that point though.

In a matter of hours, she would have left Holland. Maybe this would all end up being tagged, as one of those fantastic 'holiday' romances.

Once she was back in Sydney, and Sen was in his Dutch world without her, things might be quite different. As emotionally charged as they both were right then, it could all change.

Wanda knew that Jay was eagerly awaiting her return, in the Hillywood house. Not so much to be seeing her again and heading back to Sydney but rather, to be finally meeting the much talked about Sen.

Jay's 'out there' self, had seen great things in the stars for his mum, with this exciting new man.

Hitting it off immediately, Sen talked of radio show production production needs for that day, whilst Jay recounted his different involvement with radio – right back to his time as a youngster and the community show he put together in Sydney.

It warmed Wanda's heart, to see the two most important men in her life, getting along so fabulously!

Wanda felt confident that Lou would be as equally positive, when she met Sen.

So weird that her grown up children were working in radio and TV and now she had fallen for a man, with exactly that background.

As much as everyone was enjoying being together, it was soon time for Wanda and Jay to be on their way to Schiphol Airport.

Sen was already late for his first meeting too.

'Let's get those bags into this enchanted red cabrio and get you to that train,' Sen's effervescent and in-charge voice commanded. The little quiver in his chin, giving way to signs of not actually wanting this to be the case.

An immense wave of sadness came over Wanda, sitting for what might be the last time, in the convertible that was now his car and yet, very much their car.

If Lou was not meeting Jay and Wanda in Kuala Lumpur for a family holiday, Wanda might well have considered not taking that flight.

'Leave him with memories of happy smiling faces,' she told herself.

'This is no time for sad behaviour. Stay upbeat and positive.'

Always the glass half full attitude for Wanda!

She smiled much too widely, as she thanked him for the fantastic weekend.

It was he who should thank her, he insisted.

Hugging intensely, after making sure all the bags were on the pavement, Sen made the station drop as swift as possible.

This time Wanda stood and waved, as he jumped back into the car and drove off into the distance.

Jay gave a quick smiling nod to Sen and saw that familiar daze creep over Wanda.

'Come on mum. You'll be together again soon. I just know it.'

As he juggled all the bags, he accepted his mother would be of little use, for some hours. Once on board the train, he gave her a reassuring hug.

Staring out the window, reliving every small detail of the weekend, a yearning came over Wanda that was making her stomach turn.

She wanted Sen more than anything else in this world.

It was a deep gut-wrenching desire that she couldn't recall ever feeling before.

There was absolutely no doubt at all in her mind that fate meant for them to work out, how to spend the rest of their lives with each other, wherever that might be.

As the moments became large blocks of minutes, they were soon checked-in for their flight and in line for customs clearance.

Haunting doubts started washing over Wanda, like a swarm of attacking bees.

Could she be sure that Sen was really feeling as intense as she was?

This was all so crazy!

Three days after a couple of weeks of emails and an hour of enchantment.

The emptiness in the pit of her stomach, made her feel like she might faint.

Why was such abrupt caution, dominating her thoughts now?

Was it just her protection mechanisms kicking in?

She had come to the realisation a long time ago, that she would never find any truly special man to share the rest of her life with so why would she set herself up to be majorly disappointed?

Reviewing all the break-ups he'd told her about and the commune period in his life, span around in her head. She questioned his ability to really stop smoking. Reminded herself of the times he had left her waiting on her own. His clear need to be in control so often. Could his depression illness come back again?

Escape kept jumping into her mind.

Could that be all that Wanda actually represented?

A way to get off his island finally!

• CHAPTER SEVEN •

'MUMMA! TOO LONG SINCE I SAW YOU!' Lou ran into Wanda's arms shrieking, demonstrating to all in the arrivals hall exactly how a truly loving daughter should greet her mother. Jay jumped in for a three-way hug. They were all over the moon, to be back together, and had great plans for an exciting few days in Kuala Lumpur.

Wanda stories about Sen were fast and furious.

The look on her beaming face said it all and there was no doubt in Lou's mind whatsoever. Her mother was smitten!

Surprised at how positive Jay was about Sen, Lou could not stop herself thinking that this might present some major challenges for her mum.

The saga with Medwin, had taken her so long to get over and Wanda's pain had been felt deeply with Lou. She had hated seeing her mum so upset and sad.

Likewise for Wanda.

She shared every ounce of pain Lou felt, with the serious doubts about the relationship with Steve and his family. As much as Wanda liked Steve, she totally understood why Lou was thinking about calling it quits, even though they shared loads of happy times, in their four years together. The way forward wasn't clear but Lou was still giving it her best shot.

She'd been so happy, when Wanda said she would be making Sydney her permanent base again. Intensely disliked living in a different country from her mum. It would also be great to have her near, if she did end up splitting with Steve.

Lou sometimes helped out in the agency's Sydney office and knew how excited Pan was about Wanda coming back to live. He was running things fine but he just loved being around her and knew the clients did too. Lou also knew how much Wanda wanted A.B. to feel, he was totally in charge of the London office. He needed to prove he was capable of making the agency a success this time. Leaving him to run things, showed just how much faith she had in him. He was like a brother to Wanda and she was proud of how he had managed things so far.

Now this guy Sen could be shaking things up.

Holland was supposed to be coming off the radar, albeit for the Hillywood house still to be sold.

One less country to deal with - it had to make life easier!

'Oh well. No point stressing over it,' Lou thought to herself. 'They're on the other side of the world from each other now. Anything could happen.'

When Jay and Lou had a quiet moment alone, he told her about the questioning that had plagued Wanda, for the first half of the flight. She'd made herself sick, thinking of every reason in the world, why it wouldn't work with Sen. Jay hadn't said a word. He knew she had to work through all her thoughts herself.

Then she watched a chick flick and it turned everything around.

Lou immediately wanted to know what the movie was but Jay hadn't bothered to ask. He just observed, as his mother sat there on the plane, in floods of tears. Then she grabbed his arm and fell asleep on it. When she woke up, she told him she felt absolutely clear. Sen was the one. He was her Mr Right and she wasn't going to blow this.

Who cared if she was an escape for him?

He was an escape for her too!

Escape from wondering, if she would ever find a loving partner, to join her for the rest of her life journey. She was blessed with loving friends and family but nothing could compare to sharing your life with a well matched partner.

He might have challenges but who didn't?

She certainly did.

Nothing truly amazing was ever meant to be easy.

Her confidence shone brightly. It would all be worth whatever pains it took.

But for now, she wanted to focus on their special Malaysian holiday!

Bukit Bintang shoe shopping was always a priority for any visit to Kuala Lumpur. Swimming and lazing by the pool, at an ever so inexpensive 5-star hotel, definitely important to the agenda. This visit, they also had plans to take in the monkey steps and Batu Cave temples. Of course Jay had identified record shops and gaming stores to be checked out too.

No fixed Batu Caves bus trip for them.

They would take the train and do their own thing.

One of the biggest Hindu shrines outside of India, these limestone caves were said to be around 400 million years old. Sacred families of monkeys line the 272 steps that lead up into the caves.

As luck would have it, the trio's visit was highlighted by a musical worship ceremony, taking place in the main Temple cave.

Deeply moving!

In one perfect email from Sen during the KL holiday, he made it clear he didn't want to interrupt their family time. He and Wanda could Skype, once she arrived in Sydney. He missed her so much and was cherishing memories of every moment they had spent together.

Wanda replied to let him know she was feeling the same but kept the bulk of the content about what they were doing in KL.

The relief she felt, knowing their emotions were in sync, was enormous.

She would have liked to speak to him straight away but, he was right, better to be with her children completely, at that point.

Their few days holidaying together, would soon be over.

'The car is downstairs to take us to KL Central Station mum,' Jay was answering the room phone, just as the porter arrived to pick up their bags.

KL Central's train service to the airport was by far the easiest, cheapest and fastest way to get to the airport. Certain flights even had bag check-in at the station.

Lou reached into her beautiful large designer handbag, to grab her wallet and settle with the driver on arrival. Jay made sure all the luggage was out of the taxi and accounted for.

As the trio walked up to the counter to buy their train tickets, Wanda was front and centre, with Lou immediately to her right and Jay to the left. They were all leaning in to hear details of platform and time, as tickets were bought. Once downstairs on the platform waiting for their train, Lou went into her bag to get mints.

Sitting the handbag on her lap, she suddenly gagged in horror. A straight cut, half the length of the bag, was now evident.

Wanda was beside herself!

'Someone has seen you paying the driver and worked out where you put your wallet back, into the corner of your bag. An incredibly sharp knife quickly cuts the bag to try and steal the wallet. The bag was over your shoulder and we were all busy with ticketing things at the counter. What if you had moved or Jay had seen someone? Must have been so sharp, to cut through the fabric like that and you not feel anything. Your scarf, and all the other rubbish in there, foiled the plan. Nothing missing but imagine if you moved into the knife. Urgh! I dread to think what could have happened!'

On arrival at the airport, they reported the incident to transport police. The bag was ruined and it had been an expensive purchase, on a visit to Paris. At the very least they would get a formal report, to use for the travel insurance claim. The form was duly completed but none of them had seen the culprit so it was not of much use to the police. They would add extra surveillance to the taxi arrival area at KL Central. The officer made all the right noises, to show he cared, but there was nothing more to be done.

A whirlpool of emotions hit them all, during that flight back to Sydney. Still shaken by the bag incident and thoughts of what might have happened, with some crazy person wielding a sharp knife.

Lots of new things awaited them all.

Wanda had house mates, to get to know in the mansion. They also needed to bring in someone else, with Lou having bought her own apartment and moved out.

The biggest thing Wanda now contemplated, was what the Sen effect might be?

Where would lady luck's dice land this time?

The Agency's initial flow of work, for the London Olympics, had been so well managed, that clients had wanted her to create a presence in Sydney too. Much of the work, they still handled, came from clients with offices in both cities. A.B. and Pan had great teams in place and did brilliantly without her. They always said that she was their secret weapon. Great to be able to bring her in, when that extra bit of something was called for. They knew she was fine with jumping on a plane, if it was justified and were happy to keep things going without Wanda so she really could be based anywhere. That said, Pan was going to be seriously disappointed if she didn't stay in Sydney this time.

Writing her novels, could happen in any location too.

She was a totally mobile and very global person, with the world at her feet. That proverbial 'oyster', was still there for her taking and it seemed Sen was the pearl.

The biggest thing for Wanda had been living in the same country as Jay and Lou. They all felt much happier, when they had easier access to each other. Even so, her children had made their adult lives a success and could easily cope without her, on a day to day basis.

She had to be her own most important priority now and that first call with Sen, once they landed in Sydney, pointed her life in a totally new direction!

'I've spoken to my boss and it's all agreed. Two weeks leave can be covered with other staff. I want to come and see you in Sydney, if you will have me?'

Wanda didn't hesitate to respond.

'I'm so happy that you would do that. All I can think of is being with you. As much as I also love being near my kids, I now can't see my life without being right by your side - whether it's in Sydney, in Holland, London or anywhere else in the world!'

A silent pause was followed by a massively deep breath, as Wanda took but seconds to make her decision.

'Such a long way for you to come here, only having two weeks you can stay. If the show is still finishing in a couple of months, maybe it would be better if I came back to you and then we could make proper plans to come to Sydney together, in the New Year.'

Sen was astounded.

'Is that possible? I can't believe what I'm hearing. Would you do that? You just arrived back in Sydney. Don't you have commitments? I want us to be together more than anything but the most important thing for me, is that you are happy.'

'Being with you is what will make me happy. I have no doubt that we are meant to be together forever. Lou has her birthday in a few days so I will stay for that. There is one client meeting I really should attend in Melbourne too and then I can fly back to you.'

A spontaneous energy flowed between them and nothing was going to keep them apart.

Wanda had searched the world for her perfect man.

She would do whatever it took, to help realise the full potential of this relationship.

'I can still take the two weeks off. You could fly to London from Australia and we can meet there. Have a week or so doing fun things you told me you like to do. Maybe go to the theatre and see some live music. Catch up with some of your old friends and visit your agency. Then we can go to my house on the island. Two weeks to just concentrate on us and getting to know each other better. We can make plans for our future life together!'

Wanda sobbed with happiness and a calm quietness came over them both.

After sharing another brief silence, they reminded themselves how amazingly lucky they were, to have found each other.

Happy tears muffled Sen's voice a little, as he continued.

'You are an incredible life force Wanda. From the moment we first met, I knew we were being offered a uniquely special opportunity, to become part of each other's lives. There was never one shadow of a doubt in my mind, even though I could see we would need to jump some hurdles. How do you think your family will take this news?'

Sen had a confident feeling that Jay would have no problem with his mum returning to Europe so quickly but he wasn't sure about Lou. He had spoken only a few words to her on the phone and could sense she had reservations about him. Not so much directed specifically at him but more to the possibility of her mum being taken away and let down by love again.

Lou had been very polite, saying she looked forward to meeting him some day, but Sen could tell she was worried.

He understood what a close relationship she had with her mum and guessed she might also be a little afraid of that being impacted. Not that he would ever dream of coming between them.

Sen knew how strongly Wanda felt about her children and totally accepted that they were a big priority in her life.

'Maybe tomorrow we can have another call, when you are with Lou. Then I can chat with her more and give her the chance to ask me any questions she might have. We can share TV production stories too. It will be interesting to hear what she is working on in Sydney.'

It was incredible that Sen shared such common ground with Lou and Jay, through their chosen careers.

The more Wanda and Sen talked, the more strange co-incidences they discovered.

Wanda's work with the energy giant in The Hague, had taken her to the very suburb that Sen grew up in. His mother still lived just around the corner from their buildings. Wanda had taken the train each day, to a station immediately opposite the Teachers College that

Sen studied at.

Back in the days of THAT GREEN ITALIAN WAGON, Wanda's office with the General had been just around the corner from where Sen lived with his then partner.

All those years, it seemed they may have even frequented the same small bar and café.

Had they ever shared glances or perhaps even said hello?

They thought not.

Fate had been saving them for the right time and the right place.

Sen had been way too caught up with his work then. His private life had always come off second best, when choices needed to be made. Now he was older and wiser but he had almost given up, on ever finding the woman of his dreams.

Then there she was – selling him a car!

'I still can't believe how we met Wanda. Gert insisting I should take a look at your convertible. It really could not be more enchanted! I love that car but most of all, I know that I'm falling in love with you so very deeply!'

Wanda's immediate reaction was to say 'ditto' but she stopped herself just in time.

That 'Ghost' moment, would have most likely not been understood.

'I think it was love at first sight for me.' Wanda gulped with surprise, at having made such an honest admission.

'Jay is so very right. I'm just too old to be playing games. If I waste one minute of this, I will be doing myself a great injustice. I am totally convinced that we can be incredibly happy, sharing the rest of our lives with one another.'

As Wanda recounted tales of Sen to her friends and family, they too were in awe of how this chance meeting came about. The smile it brought to people's faces, added to the sense of enchantment about that beloved convertible.

This gorgeous man seemed to be Wanda's for the taking.

No ex-wife or children to consider and his job about to come to an end.

The fact he was already keen on Australia.

It all added beautifully to the possibilities.

'He seems really lovely mum. Funny to hear him talk about the TV shows he was Executive Producer on in Holland. Did you know he won a Rose d'Or?'

Indeed she did.

The chat Sen had with Lou, had done the trick.

Lou was quick to tell Wanda, how delighted she was for her to have this special man in her life. Her mum's happiness was of the highest importance and the look on Wanda's face, when she talked to Sen, beamed exactly that.

Pan didn't quite share Lou's positive attitude towards this new flame.

He'd been expecting Wanda to finally get into the Sydney hot seat for The Agency but that was now looking much less likely.

He had taken the Sydney office from strength to strength. All she had to do was front up to clients and come up with a few clever ideas. Most of that so far, had been done from the comfort of her Covent Garden desk in London.

Admittedly, most of the work for Sydney came about in the beginning via London clients, for the 2012 Olympics.

Execution was left totally to Pan to manage and, although he had been fine with that, his little dream world had looked forward to the day when his Wanda would be a daily feature in his life again.

They went back some 20yrs or so, to when Wanda was Account Director for a Japanese agency in Sydney.

Wanda and Larry had moved from London to Sydney with their two babies. Their marriage was on the rocks and the move had been a last ditch effort to save the day.

Didn't work!

Soon Wanda was being chased by an advertising agency, where Pan worked as Creative Director. They desperately wanted her to lead the account for a big time camera company she had done so well for in Europe.

The head guy had been transferred to Sydney, on his way back to retirement in Japan. He couldn't believe his luck, when he heard Wanda had moved back to her home town. No effort was to be spared, to get her onto his advertising for Australia.

Wanda and Pan had hit it off immediately. They could not have been more in tune. Almost being able to finish sentences for each other. They knew exactly what the client wanted and could deliver it with real zest. Fun and laughter always at the top of the priorities list.

When Wanda asked Pan if he would like to be her man on the ground in Sydney for The Agency all those years later, he jumped at it.

He also got along famously with Aram, when Wanda connected them. Soon that dynamic duo were joined by Ernest – another ex-colleague of Wanda's, from her days with the General.

She couldn't believe her luck, at being able to bring together the best in creative, web and finance so easily. They were also happy to take the profit ride with Wanda and didn't get paid until she did. Wanda was more than happy to have them share in the rewards and made sure The Agency only took on work that paid well.

She was very clear with any new business, that she did not have the capacity to carry debt so some clients were even paying up front. They were getting great work and could totally rely on The Agency to deliver what they needed, when they needed it. Service was always speedy and professional so they had no problem covering costs ahead.

Not too long afterwards, Sydney office also had the opportunity to take Nicole on board as an intern. An amazing graphic designer and so enthusiastic. The daughter of very close friends of Wanda's and quite brilliant.

Lucky to the core! That was Wanda.

They all worked closely with the guys in London and both office teams complimented each other perfectly.

A.B. seemed to feel he was the unstated second-in-charge to Wanda all round and made it quite clear to Pan, when he came on board. He was, after all, the first person to join Wanda with The Agency and London was the originator of business initially. He considered himself to be older and wiser and clearly leading the creative charge.

As the owner of the first advertising agency Wanda ever worked for in London, back in the late 70s/80s, A.B. felt he had been the one who taught Wanda all she knew about the industry.

She had been his PA way back then.

Not really wanting a full time job, because she was singing in a rock band, she had only gone along to meet A.B. to check him out.

Close friends worked for this concert promoter client of his and they insisted she should meet the very flash chap, who did their advertising. Driving his Bentley and always looking like he just jumped out of a fashion magazine. Continuous stream of gorgeous women, hanging off his arm. Very smooth and sophisticated.

After A.B. had sent that agency of his bankrupt, he went into property development. Later going bust with those endeavours too.

Not terribly good with money but always an amazing creative.

Wanda had moved on to run a larger successful agency in London but stayed very good friends with A.B. He was like family and even gave her away, when she married Larry.

When she contacted him to see if he wanted to lead the creative charge for The Agency, he was ecstatic!

His marriage had ended and the three children were a daunting challenge to keep supported. The faith Wanda expressed in him with this new enterprise, would be more than earned. He was determined to shine this time.

And so he had!

Very quickly appointing Cindy to keep him, and pretty much everything that went on, in check. She had worked with him and Wanda in the early days too and really had a sharp mind for keeping production flowing.

Then the most incredible copywriter ever joined – Paul. Great at what he did but insecure with his sexuality, he idolised A.B. and so far, that had only proven to be of benefit.

As business grew, the very charming Yuki joined the team, to help manage clients. He could speak not only Japanese but also fluent French, Dutch and Italian. English too of course.

Wanda originally thought work would dry up, post Olympics. She had talked about closing London and moving whatever activities remained, over to Sydney.

Clients in Europe were, however, not slowing down at all so she had decided to just maintain the status quo, albeit with her being based in Sydney.

Each office seemed to stand on its own merit and she could just float around the world as required.

With Pan at the helm in Sydney and A.B. heading things in London, as long as she made a call every now and then to clients, Wanda seemed to keep them happy.

She would give her tuppence worth of brilliance to each weekly work in progress meeting and make sure team dynamics stayed strong.

No prizes for guessing where Pan got his name from!

One of the most talented creatives ever but he was always drifting off to fairy land. And he even looked a little like Peter Pan.

Now Wanda had relayed her story of Sen fully to him, Pan seemed even more distant.

'I'm always just at the other end of a phone or email Pan.'

Wanda's efforts to appease him, made little or no impact.

'I'll do the pitch in Melbourne before I fly back to London and you have my almost undivided attention for the next week or so.'

Pan gave a hearty laugh.

He knew full well, that there was no such thing.

Multi-tasking was OK but Wanda was ridiculous.

Lou seemed to be the only one who could keep up with understanding what she was on about.

Pan was a pretty close second and they did have very similar creative brains but 'undivided attention' would never be on the cards.

When she announced to Pan that she started writing a novel, he could not have been less surprised. Her brain was a hive of activity and nothing seemed to be slowing down in her old age. Stories flowed like water down a mountain stream. Maybe that was why she was so good at concepts and headlines. Clients loved her. She had never ceased to amaze Pan, how well she could sell in an idea. The thing was, she believed in the idea and the clients knew it.

Passionate to the core!

'Pan darling. You know how it goes with me. Fun has to be the priority and when life throws a big opportunity at you, the only option is to grab it with both hands and run. That's how we got this advertising ball rolling again. London Olympics fun was at the top of the agenda and the clients just followed. We did such a great job, that their Australian counterparts wanted us too. Et voila! Lucky for me the ever so talented Pan wanted to have some fun with this too and he was available. I could never have done any of it without you. But you know that!'

Pan and Wanda shared a warm hug. She had introduced all of the team to her beloved Hug & Fug inner voice characters and they too had adopted them.

Quite a special thing for The Agency.

Pan tried to rationalise his feelings about Wanda not making Sydney office and his team her priority, by drawing upon Hug to try and get her to feel sorry for him.

What was it with his thing for Wanda?

He had been gay for longer than he could remember and in a longstanding loving relationship, with a very cute young man from Korea.

Why was he so jealous of A.B.'s relationship with Wanda? And now this Sen person?

Wanda didn't know that he also knew about the fling she had with Ernest, when they worked together at the General. A moment of drunken outburst from Ernest revealed to him the Singapore hotel tale, some while back apparently. Never mentioned again of course and certainly not affecting anyone's working relationship.

Pan almost wished he was straight sometimes.

He just wanted to get closer to Wanda and yet he didn't know how or why? Fug put some wickedly raunchy ideas into his head every now and then.

When it came to Aram, it seemed Hug was the one that would lend a helping hand. He was still raw from his divorce and not sure whether to move back to Canada. His ex-wife stayed with the guy she had an affair with back in The Hague and the whole nasty business, made him very sad at times. Nicole would often provide a nice shoulder to cry on, with some loving hugs.

Ernest was a randy old bugger so he and Fug were besties.

'Less of the old,' he would say!

The women loved him. Never married and was still playing the field heavily. No way he looked his age. Mr Smooth had done well for himself and drove a flash car. Lovely apartment overlooking Sydney harbour and always dressed impeccably, with his constant stories of new romances, always keeping everyone entertained.

None of the team could believe how radiant Wanda looked, when she talked about Sen. It had been a long time since they had seen her quite so happy. As much as she always made a point of enjoying life to the full, they all knew she craved the love of a special man.

Now it seemed she had found him and they could not have been happier for her.

Conspiring to get him to move to Australia, would become their most important mission!

CHAPTER EIGHT

THE SMALL HOTEL WAS PERFECT. All they would need for a few days of serious reconnecting.

Wanda had a night to herself before Sen would arrive. Having picked up a rental car at Heathrow, she'd taken a quick lunch stop with a good friend in Richmond and then driven straight to Southend-on-Sea. Not somewhere she had been to before so the lunch stop was focussed on directions.

'Bit of a strange location for such a romantic occasion isn't it Wanda?'

Her friend was definitely a 5-star woman and thought something on Park Lane might have been more appropriate.

Sen had booked the cheapest flight to London he could find, not realising it was actually to a town in Essex.

Wanda decided to enlighten her friend and justify his choice.

'They just opened up this tiny airport for the Amsterdam run. Great prices and the train stops right by the terminal so the access into Central London is really easy. Good to know heh?'

A quick stop had also been made at The Agency in Covent Garden, on her way from the airport, and A.B. was stunned to see the unannounced Wanda.

'This Sen must be one hell of a man. Nothing else could have brought you back onto our London turf so quickly. Jay and Lou must be in shock!'

Wanda had given him a quick rundown on things, during her stay in Kuala Lumpur, when he needed her nod on something going to a client. She played it pretty low key about Sen though and certainly didn't give him the feeling, she might be of a mind to head back to Europe so quickly.

Things had clearly moved along at a great pace since then.

'I guess Jay and Lou are a little uncertain what might happen next but I honestly believe they're excited for me. Let's just hope it has the happy ever after ending we would all love.'

A quick twenty minutes of scanning some things with A.B. and Wanda was out of there. She was not about to let work get in the way of one of the most romantic liaison of her life.

Wanda had been as surprised as anyone, when Sen told her where he was flying in to, for his trip to rendezvous with her in London.

Being the great traveller she was, and with the aid of the amazing world of online search tools, she soon discovered the unknown airport was on the edge of a large seaside town, with quite some things to explore. That would do nicely.

The room she booked, at the quaint Bed & Breakfast, had an incredible view right out across the Thames Estuary.

She was pleased to find it lived up to the website entirely and they had scored the best room in the house, upstairs and with a beautiful bay window.

No need to even leave the comfort of their large bed, to enjoy the uninterrupted views across the wide waterway. Large container ships and an assortment of yachts and boats, all parading on this unusually warm and sunny afternoon.

It had been a great choice.

Sen would love it!

Having a night to settle in before he arrived, gave her a chance to work the room out and create the love nest she wanted, never mind recover a little from the long flight back from Australia.

Nice bath products in the ensuite.

Good bottle of wine at the ready.

She remembered how he liked a nice shaved pubic zone so that was also on the agenda. The first time for her, outside of the required childbirth cut back.

Her little Fug inner voice had been pushing for her to buy a sex toy or two but she thought that was all way too early.

A sexy bottle of 'tingling gel lubricant' on the bedside table should be fine though.

Fruit and tasty snacks to go with the wine.

Clothes all arranged so she could get ready quickly when needed.

Hated to be the one holding things up, when they did decide to venture out of bed. Liked to plan what she might wear in advance and be confident that she would look good.

Yet, it was true.

She did expect to spend quite some time exploring Sen's body further and felt it highly likely they could be spending most of the time in that bed with a view!

Exploring her own body too, for that matter.

This time, she knew what to expect and would be prepared for that enormous 'weapon of oh so much pleasure' of his.

The lubricant packaging promised increased sensuality.

She certainly intended to put that to the test.

After several texts, Sen finally called from Holland.

'Things are crazy here. Off to the studio soon for a late night.'

Wanda knew about this session already. Lots had to be juggled for Sen to take the two weeks off so he had to agree to produce this last radio show before disappearing. This was the reason he couldn't make it over, on the night of Wanda's arrival from Oz. She had been happy to have time to herself and get a good night's sleep so no problem there.

'Hope you manage some decent sleep before your 10am flight in the morning,' she responded. 'I'll be at the airport to pick you up.'

She had gone on and on about how happy she was with the hotel and that she hoped he would be too. Bit of a nervous conversation on both sides.

'So excited to be seeing you again soon. Can't wait!'

Her heart was racing at the mere thought.

Sen was excited too.

He had found it difficult to think of anything else but seeing Wanda and was very clear this was going to be a pivotal time in his life.

Nerves really kicked in, as he told himself to be sure he didn't mess it up!

The flight landed on time that next morning and passengers were soon crossing the tarmac to the small terminal.

Wanda kept looking for Sen in the rental car's rear view mirror.

She had texted him to say she would wait outside.

Passengers could pretty much walk straight off the plane, then out onto the street and she could stop right in front.

The weather turned nasty that morning.

A very different day, from the one prior.

October was nearing its end and a wintery wind blew fiercely.

'There he is,' Wanda muttered to herself.

Sen was wearing a big ski jacket so he was well prepared for the change in weather and was every bit as handsome as she remembered.

On getting into the car, he removed his outer layer to reveal a smart grey jacket over a white shirt. Jeans and stylish shoes completed the picture.

Wanda felt the urge to pinch herself yet again. Could they really be together forever? Was he just as keen as her? Or could it all be a dream?

Wanda had a smart jacket on too, complimenting a sleek skirt and skimpy top. Shopping in Kuala Lumpur had included the purchase of new shoes. Particularly high so that she could be taller for Sen.

Height and comfort. She couldn't believe her luck.

The shoes she wore that day highlighted her great legs perfectly and were a pleasure to walk in.

Being that little taller, was a definite advantage.

The quick scan from Sen, as he jumped in the car, ended with a definite look of approval.

A standard three kisses to the cheeks exchanged, as Wanda was about to be moved on by a parking attendant.

'Great that you chose this airport to fly into. I never knew what treasures were being hidden up here in Southend. The Thames Estuary is captivating. Always loads of activity on the waterways. A few other interesting things we can consider checking out too. Their Pier is the longest one ever made. A small train still takes you to the end. They used to unload ships here and, with the tide going way out, the super long pier had to be built. An old favourite band of mine is also playing here tomorrow night - Level 42. If you're interested, we can see if they still have tickets.'

A little hyper at this stage, Wanda blurted everything out uncontrollably.

Sen took it really well and responded with equal enthusiasm.

'It all sounds great. Happy to do whatever you like. The view from our room sounded good too. Maybe we can check that out first.'

Wanda was driving by then so not in direct eye contact with Sen but she could sense his energy and feel his wide smile.

They both had huge expectations and were clearly pleased with what they saw so far but what if the memory of that weekend on the island, had been built up out of all proportion?

Quite some pressure for things to be perfect and the butterflies inside them both were going totally crazy.

Wanda had travelled all the way back from Australia this time.

She was really putting herself out there and now her mind was in a total spin.

'He wants to go straight to the hotel. Maybe he just wants to get clear of luggage and know where he's based. I hope he likes it. Think I left everything prepared and welcoming. Can't wait to get my hands on him but I don't want to look too needy. Don't want to play any pretend games either. Pretty clear he has me just where he wants me. What if the gel doesn't do the job? Hug and Fug were going nuts!'

The journey was literally ten minutes and Wanda was doing her tour guide thing and pointing out landmarks, yet her thoughts were running wild, under the exterior that was trying to be jolly and calm.

Of course Sen loved everything. The view was just as he had imagined.

In truth, he wouldn't have minded landing on the moon, if it meant being with Wanda again.

Once they were in their room, Sen grabbed Wanda in the tightest of hugs. No words were spoken. He lifted her onto the bed and cradled her in his arms, for what seemed an age. Fug had been in his ear for days, teasing him with a wide range of fantasies about Wanda but now it was Hug at the forefront.

'I never ever want to let you go,' Sen finally whispered softly into Wanda's ear. Deep sighs of satisfaction followed from them both, as Sen ran his fingers through Wanda's hair and gently caressed her cheeks with his large soft lips.

'I hope you never do,' replied Wanda.

'I have no doubt whatsoever, that we'll be together forever.'

Holding each other tightly, for what seemed an age, chatter stopped and they sank into a contented bliss. Feeling only their hearts beating and hearing nothing but their deep breathing, tremors of desire began to take over.

Slowly they began to undress one another, until they lay naked side by side.

Looks were intense - gazing deeply into each other's eyes.

Happy tears welled, as they moved that gaze around their yearning bodies.

Gentle strokes of the skin, mixed in with soft kisses, all directed to arouse.

'I wonder if this gel really does make you tingle?'

Wanda enquired in her most sensuous yet playful voice, as she pointed to the bottle on the bedside drawers.

Sen had seen the lubricant and immediately noticed the word 'tingling'. A word he knew and was most pleased to anticipate. His muscles flexing of their own accord, as soon as he read it.

Wanda placed a few drops gently onto the tip of Sen's magnificent penis and used one finger to rub the gel in a circular motion. It worked a treat and it was all Sen could do, to not come right there and then.

Lovemaking moved into top gear, as foreplay took them both to the edge.

Wanda was on top of Sen and no sooner feeling him perfectly fitting inside of her, than she was quickly moving to orgasm.

Sen lifted her and stood to hold her shaking body, as she wrapped her legs around his waist. He moved so deeply into her, that he could almost imagine himself projecting out through her belly button. Moments later he released his juices fully and their connected bodies became one, in every sense.

Maintaining a tight hold, as they came back from orgasmic heights, he gradually placed Wanda into the bed.

No way either one of them had any intention of releasing their hold.

Life could not be more perfect and neither one could dream of ever wanting for more than exactly what they shared at that moment.

The depth of their emotions softened them into a gentle sleep.

Wanda had travelled back and forth across the world and the time differences and intensity of her actions, finally hit.

Very little sleep for Sen, in the lead up to them being reunited, so he too, was happy for his eyes to close.

Waking together, after an hour or so out cold, it took a moment or two to stabilise.

They kissed and hugged and spoke of the elation they felt being together. Unbelievable how totally 'right' their bodies now were for each other. No issues with size or concern for the possibility of not pleasing each other fully.

Their hearts, minds, bodies and souls, seemed completely synchronised.

They were falling deeply in love.

In her inimitable way of bringing things back to having fun, Wanda jumped out of bed and laughingly jolted their reality.

'I guess we've missed lunch. Perhaps a glass of wine and some nibblies, before we venture out for some dinner?'

Sen could see that she had thought of everything.

Even remembered what sort of wine he liked and bought similar snacks, to those he had provided during the island weekend.

Two nights and days of sheer ecstasy followed.

Walks along the beach. A train ride on the longest pier in the world. Laughs all the way. Sen almost knocking himself out, boarding the tiny train. Then sticking his head inside the large historic bell at the end of the pier, to provide a perfect snapshot of one tall Dutchman, with a very strange upper torso.

Bopping away with the hordes of dedicated followers of Level 42.

Singing with the locals, as they rocked along to a band in the small pub near the hotel.

Exploring the delights of the full English breakfast, included at the B&B - Wanda going for the lot and Sen opting for the special smoked haddock instead.

Sex in the shower, over the chair, by the window, on the floor …. and even in bed. Positions explored and teasing with feathers, tongues, orally and any way it came. They were opening up fully, with their only desire being to please and allow themselves to revel in their new life together.

When it came time to leave Southend, Wanda put on her best tour guide hat and took Sen for a little sightseeing drive, as they made their way to her friend Ken's Thames Barge.

For the remainder of their week in London, they would become Thames River dwellers, on the shores of Battersea.

A visit to the docks of Dagenham and the Olympic Park; past the Tower of London and over Tower Bridge. Along the embankment, passing Big Ben and The Houses of Parliament.

Soon they arrived at their Thames destination.

Sen had visited London on a few occasions but listening to the stories Wanda shared, as they passed incredible landmarks steeped in so much history, his eyes were seeing things in quite a different way.

Wanda was ever the tourist. No matter where she was. Whether she was a resident or just visiting. She adored exploring and always found new and exciting adventures to be had. Present her with new laneways to discover and she was as happy as good old Larry.

A quick drop of the bags, then out to Heathrow for the rental car to be returned.

Ken was most impressed they worked out they could get directly back to the barge, with just one bus. He would have a lovely dinner prepared and await their arrival with bated breath. Couldn't wait to check out this incredible Sen. The man who had captured Wanda's heart so instantly.

He had never had any doubt that cabrio of hers was enchanted but who would have thought it might lead her to the love of her life? The man bought her car and now they had plans to live out the rest of their days together!

How enchanted does it get?

'You will get on with Ken like a house on fire.'

Wanda often quizzed herself, after giving out stupid English expressions like this.

Did Sen know what they meant?

'The barge is so beautiful. From the turn of the century. Not motorised anymore. One of the largest on this river I think. Fabulous living room on the upper deck area, with French doors to the deck. Down a small spiral iron staircase to the central living space, with dining, lounge and kitchen in the centre of the boat. Front end for the master suite, with a further room that has bunks and a freestanding iron bathtub,' Wanda sounded just like an Estate Agent.

'To the opposite end of the boat, there is the second sleeping cabin. Two double bunkers head to tail and another bathroom. We'll be in there. You will need to watch your head in bed, when you sit up. All over the boat in fact but you're the experienced sailor so no need for me to tell you that. Not much room for suitcases in our sleeping area either so we will need to leave bigger bags on the upper deck I guess.'

She really could babble on sometimes.

Often Sen didn't quite know what she was talking about and wished she would speak to him in Dutch. All the same, he was just happy to be with her and knew they would get by with the languages. He loved the way she was always so enthusiastic about everything - such a positive and energised person. Just what he needed, to get him back on top of the things that had so often dragged him into a depressive state.

Ken and his wife Clara and their two children, were very close to Wanda and her kids. They went way back.

Clara and Wanda being old mates from the 80s, they had met during her early days of working in A.B.'s advertising agency in London.

A.B. had a mate who dated Clara for quite some time back then.

They all found it particularly amusing that A.B. was now working for Wanda, in her new agency. He was down to his last proverbial dollar, when Wanda offered him the role.

'Low tide tilting challenge so just be careful your food doesn't fall off the table,' Ken said in his truly droll American accident. His humour was deep and more often than not, came without a matching smile. He had a delicious meal prepared, by the time they arrived at the barge.

'Feels OK once you sit at the table,' Wanda responded. 'It's the walking about that gets me. My head knows which direction I want to move in but gravity has a completely different view.'

She was now demonstrating an over-exaggerated body lean.

'This has to be the worst tilting I've ever experienced on here Ken. Quite funny really. A bit like being on one of those magic mirror things, with moving walkways. In those fun houses, you get at amusement parks,' she said laughing and demonstrating how the walkways moved.

Wanda had stayed on the barge several times.

One of her most memorable, being during the Queens Diamond Jubilee flotilla along the Thames, earlier that year.

Lou was with Wanda for that and they had cuddled up in the same double bunk she and Sen would now make theirs.

What an incredible day that had been.

Around twenty guests partying hard on the barge, with flags flying everywhere. Access via an official printed pass that local area controllers issued. Strict security controls to go through.

When the Queen's barge cruised past, everyone grabbed whatever they could get their hands on, to wave furiously.

The shoreline was teaming with people vying for the best vantage point. Boats tightly packed on the water, all filled with party goers.

What a spectacular celebration!

An historic time for Great Britain!

Still having a very active monarchy, with a Queen that continued her rule for 60years. A Queen that was still very much loved by her people.

The buzz of excitement that day, was felt not just in London but throughout the UK and, indeed, around the world.

Thrilled to be part of this momentous occasion, people united to have street parties and celebrate in any way they could.

Those that were privileged to be front and centre on the Thames, were in awe of the procession that lay before them.

With over 300 royal, military, commercial and pleasure craft, the pageant on the water, was the biggest ever.

More than a million people lined the river banks, whilst over 11 million watched on television across the globe.

Members of the Royal Family boarded The Spirit of Chartwell, directly across the river from Ken's barge.

The Queen, Prince Philip and their two popular grandsons, stood on the upper deck of the vessel, under a gilt canopy decorated with red drapes, in the most elegant style of royal barges from the 17th and 18th centuries. Thousands of flowers and plants, added to its beauty.

The magnificent fleet of seafaring vessels were a remarkable sight.

Onlookers were entertained by a variety of live music coming from many of the different boats, as they passed by, and the procession went for well over an hour.

Wanda's 60th birthday had taken place just a few days earlier.

Celebrations were non-stop, for both Wanda and the Queen.

The day following the boat pageant, a concert was held in front of Buckingham Palace. London was jam packed and full to the brim! People began to set themselves up in nearby parks and Pall Mall, in the wee hours. Many others deciding they would just watch it all on TV.

Not so for Wanda and Lou.

They wanted nothing more than to be right there, in the thick of it. They had been partying for a least a week and this concert would be the icing on the cake.

An enormous stage had been specially constructed, completely engulfing the majestic Queen Victoria statue that sits on the roundabout, directly in front of Buckingham Palace gates.

With the dynamic line-up of performers including Robbie Williams, Paul McCartney, Tom Jones, Shirley Bassey, Elton John, Grace Jones, Annie Lennox and more, it was the party to beat all parties.

A-list UK celebrities for the most part but Australia did get a look in, with Kylie Minogue, who is pretty much an honorary Brit anyway and a couple more.

Wanda and Lou managed to wind their way right to the front of the crowd on Pall Mall. The sound was so clear and the atmosphere was on fire!

Speaking of fire …. Wanda was now bringing her thoughts back to the barge right there and then …. being with the man of her dreams, feeling like the gazes they had been sharing all night, could surely light any spark.

Dinner was finished and Ken needed to be up and out early for a business meeting the next morning so he was off to bed. They were happy to head to bed too.

'Tomorrow you guys are heading for the Tate right?' he enquired finally.

'Yep. We're thinking to just stroll along the Embankment and make our way to Tate Modern. Might see if there is an afternoon show at Shakespeare's Globe on the way. Possibly pick up some theatre tickets, at the half- price ticket booth in Leicester Square. Should we let you know what's available, in case you want to join?'

'Can't I'm afraid. Dinner with the IOC chaps. Maybe Thursday night, when Clara comes in from Oxford.'

Wanda was more than happy to contemplate being off to the theatre twice that week. This had always been one of the biggest drawcards to London for her.

'Are they happy with how London 2012 went?' Sen enquired.

He knew Ken was in charge of a sports travel company that looked after VIP groups, for major events all over the world. Wanda had done quite some work for them too.

'Everyone has been pretty much OK with everything. Always things to learn of course. Tomorrow night is more about checking out who needs to suck up to whom, for Russia and the next Winter Olympics.'

A short chat over politics and they bid each other good evening.

'Slaap lekker!' Wanda called out to Ken from the bathroom.

The gentle rocking motion of the barge, proved to be a soft aphrodisiac.

Complimented by good food, good wine and great company, all elements would come together, to provide a perfect launching pad for a night of passion for Wanda and Sen.

'If you sit on the edge of the bunk, I can rub your back and shoulders a little,' Sen enticed.

Lost in each other totally, the lovemaking was tender and sincere.

The sleep that followed closed all sounds to the world out completely. As Wanda and Sen held each other tightly, waves of happiness took them into a soulful peace.

Morning light soon streamed in through the small porthole window.

They were both still fixed in the hug that had taken them into their deep sleep.

'Normally I am such a restless sleeper. Tossing and turning all night long. I can't believe how I have not moved one bit. Could there be anything more wonderful than being able to sleep for an entire night, in the arms of the man you love so very much?'

Sen smiled broadly and gave a deep sigh of contentment at Wanda's remarks.

'Ik hou van jou zo veel,' he replied, as he intensified his hug.

The UK holiday was filled with everything Wanda and Sen could ever possibly want from life.

They laughed hard. Enjoyed some fantastic live music and went to the theatre twice. Visited the galleries and museums. Dined with friends and learned so much about each other.

There had only been one occasion, when Wanda had felt perhaps a little destabilized.

During their visit to the Tate Modern, Sen took loads of photos of Wanda reflecting in different items of glass. She thought back to the uneasy feeling she had at his house, when she saw the framed enlargements of similar photos Sen had taken.

That time with Deta.

Somehow, when he had spoken of her, there seemed to still be a twinkle of sorts in his eyes.

Did he have that same twinkle for Wanda?

Would he maybe replace some of those reflective images in his house, with new ones of her? She was not the jealous type so why did she feel uncomfortable when Sen talked about Deta? Did she have anything to fear from the contact Sen still had with her?

• CHAPTER NINE •

'YOU MIGHT BE IN HOLLAND FOR SOME MONTHS! ' Lou exclaimed down the line from Sydney. 'Here we go again,' she thought.

Not that she was at all surprised really.

Her mum had been pretty clear, that Sen needed to be her main focus at that point. Lou agreed, she should totally commit, if it was going to work, but she hadn't quite thought through the time factor. Somehow she had convinced herself that her mum would have everything sorted and be returning with Sen in a mere matter of weeks.

Scary enough that Wanda had said she would be fine with living wherever worked for her and Sen but what if that actually meant staying in Europe long term?

Lou wanted her mum to have a loving partner to share her life with but she had hoped that could be in close enough proximity, for her to be included.

Now her career in television production was getting off the ground in Sydney, she didn't fancy moving between countries again. As much as she still loved to travel, she wanted them all to make Sydney their home.

Wanda and Sen were still buzzing from their romantic UK rendezvous, as they settled back into Holland and set about planning their future life together. Everything pointed them to Australia but early indications, showed they would have to manoeuvre their way through a mind field of emigration obstacles first.

As they researched all the different possibilities, they discovered loads of horror stories of months turning into years and then still not eventuating in the permanent visa being granted.

It seemed Australia was making it very difficult for people to set up home there.

Easy enough to get a visitor's visa though – just fill in the online form et voila!

That was it!

They would make Sen's first visit down under, a trial three months and he could see how he felt about living there permanently.

Fate was taking them down the right path yet again.

A big thing to move to a country, with a language that's not your mother tongue so a three month trial would be perfect. His English was first rate but it was still difficult, living with all the nuances.

Meetings could be set up with possible employers, during the visit. Hopefully one of those might cover him for a sponsored long term work visa.

He couldn't have been more excited to give it a try but you just never know.

It was settled.

They would make plans to fly to Sydney late January, once Sen was clear of his current job and they had time to get things sorted with their houses. Having that agreed, they could concentrate on the myriad of things to be done before they could actually relocate anywhere.

The Hillywood house was still not rented or sold and the buyer for Sen's house, continued to elude him. This meant they could live in both homes and be close to Sen's radio job during the week, then return to the island for long weekends.

How lucky were they?

Everything was fitting into place very nicely indeed.

The amazingly enchanted red cabrio would carry them back and forth between their two homes and would support them well, in their new shared life. It never ceased to amaze them that they might not ever have met, if Sen hadn't bought Wanda's special car. This was a tale they would not tire of telling - always guaranteed to evoke a smile and excited stares from the eyes of the listener!

Having lived on Schier for almost eight years, it was rather a surprise to find Sen still had so many moving boxes unopened. Almost as big a surprise to him, as it was to Wanda. Putting it mildly, there would be quite some sorting out to do.

'Some of these things look valuable!'

Wanda was being her positive self and ignoring the horror of finding yet another stash of boxes, in one of his many super large kitchen cupboards.

'We might just have an absolute Pandora's Box of incredible treasures here!'

Things that were not ever to be parted with, were put to one side. Items of possible value, that Sen was happy to sell, were listed in detail.

A neighbour of Wanda's had a little business, buying and selling antiquities. She knew he often did house clearances and made a decent enough living, with the small percentage he kept for himself. Sen would speak to him about partnering to value and sell whatever made sense.

'Perhaps we can take these LPs to one of those specialist vinyl record stores in Amsterdam?' Wanda continued. 'I should let Jay see the list of what's there too. He just loves old vinyls and has a fantastic collection but that would mean getting them to Sydney, if he was to have them.'

Jay had been collecting vinyl records for as long as she could remember.

'There are also some designer label pre-loved clothing stores we could try in Amsterdam, for your Boss suits that don't fit anymore, if you like?'

She had to be careful not to sound like she was telling him what to do and not be her often too-organizing self.

Sen's bookcase covered floor to ceiling in the living room, with around three metres in width. He was sure some of those might also fetch a reasonable amount.

They would take their time getting it all organised.

Just take baby steps and fit clearance calmly in, to the daunting list of tasks to be undertaken.

No rush.

Going to Australia for three months initially, would give Sen the chance to make sure he loved it as much as they both thought he would.

It was important for fun to stay a priority.

Wanda had arranged a time to skype with Lou, to tell her the news. Knowing they'd be back in Sydney at the end of January, would make all the difference. The open ended thought of things taking months, had been difficult for Lou to take.

An hour before the allocated call time, Wanda heard her computer signalling that Lou was already on the line.

'Mum we broke up!'

The sobbing made it difficult for her to say.

'Oh bubs. Very sad. You tried so hard to make it work.'

Wanda felt Lou's pain deeply and wished she could be there to provide that shoulder to cry on. Hug was wrenching at her heart strings desperately.

'It was so awful mum. Steve couldn't stop crying. We were both just howling messes. Do you thing I did the right thing?'

That call was one of their longest ever.

They talked through it all. The ups and the downs that led to the final demise of Lou and Steve's relationship. Fantastic times shared travelling the world. All the good things that made up their four year journey, mixed in with a reality check on what would never have been right. Timing played a big part. Steve was just starting a Graduate position and not in the same headspace as Lou. Those two years in age, that she was ahead of him, seemed to make all the difference.

Lou was busy with a new television show and leading a full on life so Wanda had a feeling, there would be a swift recovery. This was not out of the blue. A year earlier, Lou and Steve split up for a day and the things that brought that about, had not changed one bit.

Onwards and upwards for her beautiful girl!

Wanda thought highly of Steve and knew he would do well in life. She sent him a nice email to wish him happiness and said he would always be welcome, if he ever wanted to visit.

Life was changing drastically for Lou and for Wanda.

Exciting times!

Sen's radio show was going well and there was even talk of it being extended. Regardless, he told them he would be finishing up at the end of the year, as already planned. They were happy for him and envied his possible migration to Australia, enormously.

Only a matter of weeks before he would finish but that didn't stop him from still giving 120% to his work.

It didn't take Wanda long to realise, that was to the exclusion of all else and that he was a little obsessive about what he did. Not at all happy with management and suffering continued stupidity from junior interns, he was very vocal about the lack of funding the show received and its detrimental impact on production. Even so, as soon as he walked in through that radio station door, he was on.

No little text messages to Wanda and definitely no chatty calls, to share how the day was going.

Wanda understood very quickly, that it was going to take some time for her to work out what her role needed to be, in this new partnership.

Never mind.

She intended to have the rest of her life to learn.

Often she didn't know when to expect him home and, when he did arrive, he would be tired and on edge. She wanted to have dinner waiting for him but knew how much he loved cooking and used that as a tool to wind down. When she spoke, it seemed she said too much. She was way too talkative anyway so convinced herself she would need to hold back and let him have his peace.

'Put a sock in it!' she told herself on many occasions.

It had been such a long time since Wanda lived with a man.

'You know how I can rabbit on,' she confided to Pan, at the end of a skype call to go through work-in-progress.

'I need you to help, by reminding me that I should let Sen be the one in charge of things in our personal lives. He can be so sensitive and you know how I can just blurt things out. I need to change my behaviours and you can point me in the right direction. You get me and love the ratbag I can sometimes be.'

Pan was only too happy to help.

How great to think he was special enough, to add this sort of value to her life!

Might be a little easier, if he had actually met Sen but what the heck.

Language was generally not a problem between Wanda and Sen but it became clear he did take some things Wanda said, the wrong way at times. He could easily shut down on her totally and take himself into a solitary state, where she felt helpless to know what to do or say.

Could Pan help her to recognise his buttons and not push them?

When Sen began to be aware of Wanda's discomfort and feelings of being shut out, he too decided to make a concerted effort to change things.

'We have an amazing singer on the show next Friday.'

He was truly excited that Wanda might enjoy this entertainer and that it could help her to feel more a part of what he was doing.

'Maybe you would like to spend the evening seeing the show come together? I'll be running this one myself, with our studio guy being on holiday.'

Wanda jumped at the chance and loved him deeply, for this caring gesture.

'Come to the office in the afternoon and I can introduce you to the team. We can grab some dinner from the cafeteria and then go to the studio together.'

That was better.

This would be an important step in the right direction.

Not that Wanda was sitting at home twiddling her thumbs, with nothing to do.

In between exploring visa pathways for Sen and people he might try to meet up with in Sydney; keeping her two agency offices and their clients happy; managing her different properties, family and house mates; she was also trying to finish writing her first novel and play travel agent.

A very full life indeed but she loved it that way and felt totally blessed.

Sen's birthday would be January 1st and she had convinced him to go skiing, after a fifteen year lapse - brave man.

He really must love her!

They would fly to Switzerland, the day after he finished work and be away for New Year's Eve too. She wanted it to be perfect so needed to plan it all carefully. He was happy to let her take charge with that and recognised, when it came to travel, there was no match for Wanda's experience and enthusiasm.

Later that same January, they would make their first trip to Sydney together.

Always one to stop over somewhere en route, Wanda checked out every conceivable option for what might be new and exciting locations for them both to share.

South Korea came up trumps on both airfare and fun!

Wanda always enjoyed planning trips but this time she was not her usual bubbly self, for some reason. Sen came across as being happy with what she suggested and yet she was having nagging doubts about so many things.

Particularly over the personal challenges she and Sen had to face.

If they were to feel truly connected for the long term, Wanda and Sen would need to adjust their thinking and behaviours significantly.

Wanda could be a little stubborn and sometimes just a bit too much to take but she was able to let annoying moments pass. Sen seemed to stay angry and sulk for ages.

It's not easy to fully share your life with someone but she figured, at their later stage of life, they would know the pitfalls and should be smart enough to work out how to avoid or at least work with them.

Sen had gone to great lengths, to explain his history of shutting people out and showed deep concern for his past inability to stop this happening.

They had discussed some of the difficult periods with work and relationships that led him to become clinically depressed years earlier. Anxiety often still presented itself as something he had to deal with and he'd only stopped medication, after meeting Wanda. Also quit smoking, was drinking a lot less alcohol and ate much healthier food too.

Great achievements, in such a very short space of time!

He wanted this new world with Wanda to work more than anything and was as determined as anyone could possibly be, to make a success of things.

Wanda was as equally determined and had so much admiration for what he had done. She loved him deeply and knew he loved her too. If only she could be as successful as he was, at improving so many things with life habits.

Making their relationship as great as it possibly could be and living their life to the full, was of the utmost importance to her and to him.

Motorway driving was a good example of an anxiety challenge, they could deal with jointly. Wanda loved to drive distances and was happy to take over, when they were about to get into the fast lanes.

As good a driver as Sen was, he had a mental block when it came to motorways.

On the other hand, Wanda was not so happy with small country roads, which Sen loved, so he was more than happy to cover that part of the driving. It worked well both ways and shared driving was a good simple demonstration of how they could achieve the best end result, whilst supporting each other.

With the novel Wanda was writing, they began to make plans for it to be part of a series of books that would lead content for a TV show and a plethora of other interesting things.

This would be an amazingly exciting enterprise for them to work on together and their creative juices went wild, just talking through all the possibilities.

The world was theirs for the taking!

For Wanda, true personal partnership had not been something she had ever felt she fully achieved. Often it seemed she was way too unsympathetic, to work with her partner's needs - instead, just seeing those needs simply as short comings.

Why was she ready to give up so easily?

'If it's not fun, I don't want to be in it,' she'd say when it got tough.

Never looking back on things negatively but definitely never going back.

When she was done with things, she was very clearly 'done'.

Her marriage to Larry for instance - bringing two young children into the world isn't easy. His life as a musician made it even more difficult and she was also running an advertising agency at the time. Tolerance had been in limited supply for Wanda. She wanted perfection and had not been able to accept the changes that took place, when the initial feeling of being 'in love' evolved and emotions got buried with the demands of parenting.

Strengthening a long standing relationship, to find an enduring 'true love', required a great deal of effort and she had not been successful in making it to the desired end result yet.

The split with Larry had been devastating but she had at least been glad they were able to maintain a good relationship ongoing.

Surely that should be considered a win – right?

Maybe she was just too independent.

Or was it all about self-preservation?

Her poor and disjointed upbringing, had left her with an innate sense of having to protect herself against let downs and false expectations.

Scars from a tough childhood maybe?

Not something she ever cared to dwell on. As far as she was concerned, she led an amazing life and was never short of feeling loved and cared for in some way. Very grateful for her selective memory, not going back much further than her teen years, when she was more than capable of taking charge of her own wellbeing.

When the going got really tough on a close personal level, Wanda more often than not, just got going. She'd give all solution pathways a good shot but if results weren't forthcoming, she didn't see the point. And yet, she was the very best friend anyone could have. Always there when needed and totally willing to help out in any way, she treasured her many friendships all over the world.

Wanda had moved in with Sen just a month after meeting him and she hadn't hesitated to quickly fly back to the other side of the globe to do so.

Any chance she might have acted in haste?

Already she was feeling left out of his world and uncertain of how to move forward in the best way. Having to think about when to speak and when not to speak, was really not a good feeling – and that was just the tip of the iceberg!

Pan certainly had his work cut out for him.

Sen thought some of the past strains he suffered with girlfriends, had most likely come about for much deeper reasons than he was yet to learn.

Simple things like a knee jerk reaction to pull away, when a body part surprisingly touches you. Feeling left out, when a group of people get chatting excitedly. The need to be recognised for every little action and thought.

He had spoken of how he felt his parents never understood him fully.

In fact, not many people had.

It seemed they often did not take what he said seriously enough and didn't pay him an appropriate level of respect or acknowledgment, for what he had achieved.

Wanda felt that the commune thing had a lot to do with what he saw as failed parenting in his own upbringing.

He still seemed distressed, when he talked about that part of his life. It made Wanda feel uncomfortable to quiz him on it so she never quite got the full story.

Whilst at the island house one weekend, Sen announced his dear friend and ex TV producing colleague Alec, was visiting for the weekend. His family gathered each year, at the main hotel. Sen was arranging to meet up with them for drinks. This was the guy who had first taken him to the island, when he met that girl and decided to stay.

Sen was in the back garden, when a knock came to the front door.

'You must be Wanda,' this extremely forthright and attractive looking man was quick to say, as he checked her over thoroughly.

'Umm. More mature and still very attractive. Might actually work this time.' Wanda smiled in response and took Alec through to find Sen.

After a brief chat, they all agreed on a time to meet.

Wanda had an instant feeling she was going to like this friend and his wife turned out to be even more delightful.

Having already had a couple of Sen's family make cryptic comments to her at a birthday gathering, Wanda understood what Alec meant. He had quickly assessed, she might be more capable of rising above possible issues. More than some of the younger less experienced partners, that had gone before.

Wanda made sure anyone sharing such thoughts, knew immediately, that she was in it for the long haul with Sen. She had more than her fair share of skeletons in the proverbial closet too, which she hoped he could learn to cope with.

They were both all grown up and had pasts but were now focussed on their future, which would most definitely be nothing less than exceptional!

As Christmas approached, Wanda was uncertain of her place in helping to arrange festivities in Holland.

'Best to leave things to Sen I guess,' she confided to Lou on a call.

Wanda would be more than happy to go along with whatever he wanted to do.

Back in Sydney, Lou and Jay were again not happy that mum would be on the other side of the planet for another Christmas.

Lou needed to play host to some distant family that were scheduled to visit but she was more than happy to make them feel welcome. These guests also knew Larry so would participate in the Christmas morning celebrations at his house.

Lou would also be doing something for all the house mates at the mansion to get together so there would be no shortage of celebrations.

Wanda and Sen could join them on line from Holland.

'We fly to Switzerland December 29 but I will be working on the show 27th and 28th so we need to be back in Hillywood early 27th.'

Sen's eldest brother called him to see if they could celebrate Kerst (Christmas) on the island and they were soon crafting a spontaneous plan, for a family get together.

Only a few days until Kerst and before they knew it, Wanda and Sen were hosting a full house on Schier. Another brother had decided he would come with his family too. In total, there would be eleven joining in the fun!

'I guess you've done this before so will know how to sleep everyone?'

Wanda thought it was all a great idea and Sen didn't seem at all fazed.

'Ja. Geen problem.'

Sen was confident that his eldest brother would run the show efficiently. He would travel to the island with them, in their enchanted red cabrio. |

Shopping to be done that evening, at the island supermarket.

He would be orchestrating menus and delegating tasks, as required.

Wanda and Sen were to create a couple of lunches and consider shopping for those. Easy!

Big brother would do the rest.

It turned out to be one of the most special Christmas gatherings Wanda ever had the pleasure of sharing.

Everyone dressed quite formally for the amazing Christmas Eve dinner, very festive in their colour choices.

Wanda wore a short red dress with white silky top.

Jackets for the men…. and a couple of bow ties on show too!

Big brother had even printed up menu cards, to get everyone's taste buds going.

Sen's beautiful table decorations were complimented by Wanda placing little gifts from Australia at each setting. Things she had purchased 'just in case'.

Games, music, dancing and a great spirit of family.

Delicious and delightful!

Walks over the sand dunes. Visits to cafes.

On a long skype call with Lou and Jay, most of Sen's family had a quick chat and everyone communicated brilliantly, with both English and Dutch.

It was an amazing few days and Wanda felt very at home, with Sen being the most relaxed she had ever seen him. He chatted about anything and everything, making a point of spending quality time with each person.

Games and conversation took precedence over watching television, which Wanda loved. She couldn't help but think how much she would prefer that, when it was just the two of them. So far, they always seemed to eat dinner in front of the TV.

Breakfast was different. They sat together at the dining table for that, although Sen did often read the paper.

Little quirks of living together.

How big they can sometimes seem!

'You can read the paper too can't you?'

Pan's advice was so simple.

Of course she could.

Then there would be no challenge with feeling ignored at breakfast.

'And you like TV so just make the most of a relaxing dinner in front of the box, with the man of your dreams. You guys spend so much time together. There must be plenty of opportunity to have decent conversations.'

He was right.

Wanda reflected on the great chats they had in bed and how those often started or ended with making love. Never any problem when it came to romantic encounters.

She was a lucky girl!

They left the island before the last of the family. Just two days of work for Sen and that would be it. He would finish his job and they'd be off to Switzerland skiing.

New Year's Eve followed by birthday celebrations.

It would be fun fun fun all the way!

Snow had been falling non-stop, in the Alps, and the week ahead was forecast to be sunny. They were both feeling incredibly happy and totally blessed with good fortune. A fantastic Christmas, with Swiss adventures to follow and then, hot on the heels of that, they would be heading for Sydney via Korea.

Could it get any better?

The flight to Zurich was smooth and swift. No problem finding the right train platform and soon they were on the mountain express for Engelberg.

Magnificent scenery the entire journey and a smiling face to collect them on arrival, their B&B immediately reminding them both of the Pippi Longstocking house. Sitting high at the top of a snow covered lane, this extraordinary property boasted spectacular views to the entire ski field. They'd been allocated the best room in the house and had no need to even sit up in bed, to enjoy the incredible outlook.

Another B&B success story in the making!

That week in the snow could not have been more perfect.

Sen bravely taking on whatever slope Wanda led him to, apprehensive after such a long time away from skiing but soon relaxing back into it like a pro.

The sun shone and snow glistened out of a deep and solid cover.

Wanda was a confident skier but more than happy to take it easy and just make sure Sen felt comfortable and had fun.

Lots of café stops and a visit to the Igloo bar all helped.

New Year's Eve turned the stunning village into a fairyland of lights, as fireworks burst forth from all points surrounding. It was as if the different areas across the Alps, took turns to set off their displays.

A choir sang in the distance and people wished each other well for at least an hour, sharing glasses of champagne and whatever else they had for the park picnic.

The magical evening concluded with B&B guests wishing Sen a happy birthday.

Wanda gave him an extra special massage, with the new oil she'd given him.

They then made love passionately, as they stepped into the new year that would take them onwards and into their fantastic new life journey together.

Not one uncomfortable moment between them for that entire trip.

Not even when Sen kept receiving text messages from girls wishing him happy birthday. Not even when one of them was from Deta.

Everything was so right with their world and they were deeply in love.

Arriving back in Hillywood totally elated, Sen was soon asked if he would cover a few days for someone off sick at the radio station. No problem. Wanda had loads of things to be getting on with and would be happy to have some time to herself.

She was on top the world, with everything as it should be.

'They doubled the budget for the car launch and want us to pitch for a corporate responsibility campaign too. All on the back of that idea you came up with Wanda, to use that shot in negative. Clever you!'

A.B. was shouting down the line to Wanda, more excited than he had been in ages. The rest of the team were cheering and woo hoo-ing in the background.

So….things were seeming to get even better!

'Wow. That's fantastic. Well done team. This is a WIP to remember. Drinks on me when I'm next there.'

No way they were letting her off that lightly this time.

She would be at that client meeting in London mid-January or there would be hell to pay.

'They really want to see your face at this one Wanda.'

Cindy's tone sounded like war could break out if Wanda didn't show.

'We've scheduled it to fit in well before your date for departure to Sydney.'

A.B. continued, feeling really uncertain she would make the effort.

'Clever me? I don't think so.' Wanda responded.

'You were the one that kept that transparency on the board A.B. I may have added the tag line, when I saw it, but I know you had the idea boiling already.'

Now he was really getting nervous.

'Don't worry guys. I wouldn't miss it for anything,' she reassured. 'The date works perfectly so a big thanks for making it happen. I might even bring you some Swiss chocolates, if you're lucky.'

Wanda was so excited to share the news with Sen, she called him at work.

The response was not what she expected and her heart and soul plummeted.

Clearly she had interrupted something important.

He thought there must have been some emergency but no ….. just news from The Agency.

He sounded like a jealous school boy.

Wanda just wanted to cry.

Getting better was suddenly getting a whole lot worse.

Where to go with this one?

• CHAPTER TEN •

'NOT A CLOUD IN THE BLUE AFTERNOON SKY, as the short flight from Schiphol took Wanda across to Heathrow for her client meeting. The single clear view, to the coastlines of Europe and the UK, highlighted just how small the distance was between them. So close in mileage terms and yet, still so very much apart. It was not until Wanda lived in Holland, that she realised the UK was, in reality, not truly 'in' Europe. That tiny channel kept them disconnected and they were very happy to keep it that way.

Her mind drifted through events that shaped the history of lands and sea below and she recalled the road trip she and Lou had taken from London the previous June, in their enchanted red cabrio. Having moved back to Waterside, after finishing The Hague role early the year prior, that cabrio was well accustomed to being on the wrong side of the road and they had exciting plans to give it a run back on home turf, as part of Wanda's diamond birthday celebrations.

Things were going nuts in London, with the countdown to the 2012 Olympics but Wanda was determined to take time out from The Agency to spend with Lou. She had flown all the way from Australia, to party hard with her mum.

And party they did!

On the back of all the Queen's Diamond Jubilee fun, Wanda's own birthday dance fest had been a total blast. Friends gathered at the local cupcake store, she had taken over for the actual evening of her birth, to catch up before the nightclub was ready for them. Lou worked behind the bar at this Kingston nightclub, during her years in

University, and still saw a few familiar faces. The average age of most club goers, remained in the early twenties. Wanda and her mad mob of friends fitted in like worn out gloves but the music being pumped out, was from their era. The kids loved it and knew all the words. So did Wanda's gang. The place was rocking and no-one got off the dancefloor until the wee hours. Numbers played no part in who was to have the most fun that night. 26 or 60? Not one soul cared!

Hitting the road for a week of new adventures, Wanda and Lou made plans to finish up in Brussels for Lou's flight home to Sydney. Found a fantastic airfare from there and it came with super easy access. Discovering places they had never been to, was the order of the day. Except for their last two nights in Paris, which was an old favourite and a must do for Lou's shopping list. Cabrio cruising, along the Champs Elysees, would fit well into their agenda.

They were no strangers to travelling around Great Britain and Europe but researching was a definite forte and they had no problem making it interesting.

Itinerary agreed. Accommodation all booked. Cheap and cheerful was fine by them. Didn't really matter where they went or what they did. Being together would mean loads of laughs, non-stop singing and plenty of hugs. They just loved spending time with each other and their enchanted red cabrio was all loaded and ready to rock and roll.

First stop was a town with a Dutch sounding name – Overstrand – and the Edwardian Mansion they dined in for that first evening, was famous for the fact that Winston Churchill had stayed there.

All those years of running the Lotus Cars advertising, and making so many trips to their Norfolk factory and test track, and yet Wanda had seen very little of this corner of England.

White sandy Norfolk beaches and dunes endlessly stretched for miles and had definite similarities to the Dutch coast. The sound of seagulls shrieking over wind noises and the chill of icy waters, even in summer time – it was all very familiar.

Wanda's dear friend Bea hosted them for one night near Peterborough and had arranged concert tickets, as her birthday gift. The Eagles tribute band was as popular as the boys themselves and had sold out the large civic centre auditorium for several nights. Lucky them yet again. Best seats in the house!

Take it Easy was not an option.

Everyone was up bopping by the second number and a fun night was had by all. Rising early the next morning, they had driven straight down to Folkestone for the Chunnel crossing. Such a novelty, to drive your car in a train through a long tunnel. Their first night on the European mainland was at Le Touquet's Beach, a short drive from Calais. An *encroyable* discovery! The French call it Paris by the Sea. *Magnifique*!

Venturing further south, *apres le petit dejeuner par la mer*, they were soon on the Normandy Coast and taking in the different commemorative sites that suffered the horrors of WWII. Saddened to read the many plaques of tribute to lives lost.

Arriving in Dieppe, they became aware of significant events that had taken place earlier that week, in memory of the D-Day landing of 24,000 allied troops. A major turning point in the war but oh so many fatalities and the mood for that afternoon became deeply solemn.

Important not to forget these ugly times but when do we learn?

Lou sent photos to Steve. He was intrigued by all things WWII and they had been unsuccessful in making it to Normandy, when they did their big trip together.

A few hours driving, to get to their next accommodation, so they kept to the main road. The French countryside B&B for that night and the next, would give them easy access to the piece de resistance of their discovery mission.

'Oh my goodness mum! Look at that, way off in the distance. Could that be it? I feel like we're about to become part of a Harry Potter film shoot.'

Quite some kilometres still to go, the flat countryside had begun to reveal to Lou, silhouettes of the most remarkable Mont Saint-Michel. A Gothic island abbey, built by Benedictine monks in the eighth century, it sat high up on top of a rocky tidal island and marked the boundary between Brittany and Normandy.

This small mountain reached to 92 metres above sea level, with a circumference of 960 metres. Castle-styled entrance, was via a long mudflat causeway.

It was said that the Archangel Michael himself, told the Bishop to 'build it and they will come.' And so they did. Pilgrims and tourists numbering in the region of three million visitors each year.

Wanda and Lou felt so ignorant to never even have heard of it.

UNESCO classified it as a World Heritage Site in 1979 and this outstandingly unique fortification-styled village, was totally unique. A masterpiece of medieval architecture, lined the tiny cobbled laneways that wound their way up to the pinnacle. Each doorway leading to a new part of the maze of quaint cafes, shops, hotels and bars. Small parks giving a green feel to the clutter. The climb to the very top, being rewarded by spectacular views, never to be repeated - tides transforming the land and sea scape twice daily.

A full day exploring was not enough. This would most definitely require a return visit or two. The lavish Abbey alone, warranting a day completely to itself.

Lou and Wanda were acutely aware that there were so many amazing places and stories for them to still discover around the world. They would make it a life endeavour, to seek them out and would enjoy every minute of it.

Two nights in a tiny room in the Latin Quarter of Paris followed. The sun was in full summer mode and cabrio cruising was sublime. Shopped til they dropped; cycled along the Seine and around the Louvre and Place de La Concorde; and did loads of people watching from *tres chic* cafes.

A great many happy memories were shared from past travels – with each other and with different people. Paris was somewhere they had both visited often and it always managed to captivate their imaginations and remind them how blessed they were, to be able to soak up its spirit once again.

Too soon, they were approaching Brussels International Airport.

Not such a sad farewell really. Lou understood that Wanda would be returning to Sydney to live, soon after the Olympics were done and dusted.

The saddest thing was that Wanda would carry on up to Hillywood and leave their enchanted red cabrio with Denise, to be sold.

They loved that car so much and spent much of that last day of driving reliving the adventures they had in it. At their lunch stop, they toasted their beautiful cabrio and thanked it for making so many moments, that extra bit special.

It still gave them a strange sense of connected auras, when they were in or near it.

London would become crazy town and the best place to sell their beloved car, was Holland. Dutch number plates still adorning its shining bumpers.

Denise was happy to help out, as always. Wanda would have one night with her – no doubt out bopping and singing somewhere. Then she would fly back to London.

'We'll be landing at Heathrow shortly. Please fasten your seatbelt, stow your tray and put your seat back in an upright position.'

Staring blankly out the window, the announcement jolted Wanda back to the now.

The Agency meeting in London...Cindy had everything arranged. All good!

The client had insisted on an early start so Wanda was flying over the night before and combining it with a celebratory team dinner.

Sen was helping out with a radio show until late that evening and was fine with her enjoying this visit without him but she was missing him severely.

The vibe of London usually hit Wanda, from the moment she stepped off the plane. Not so this time. All she could think about was Sen and the time they had spent in London together, a few months earlier. That unbelievable closeness they shared. Finding out they had so many things in common, with similar values and passions. Everything about them fitting perfectly, especially their bodies.

Being there without him, made her feel only half present somehow. The emptiness slowed her pace and made her disoriented, to the point of almost getting on the tube going in the wrong direction.

As she arrived at The Agency in Covent Garden, A.B. sensed immediately that something was very wrong.

'Are you OK Wanda?'

He was busy gathering things into his bag, in readiness for their early dinner, but dropped everything and sat her down on his office sofa.

'You look like you just travelled from Sydney, not just from an hour's hop across the pond.'

Trying to lighten her up wasn't working.

'I shouldn't be here,' she stammered.

He couldn't remember the last time he saw her so upset. The eyes were starting to water and she looked like she could faint at any minute. Water might help.

'It's all too much for him and now I see it is for me too.'

A.B. figured it was best to just let her rant and see if he could fathom what she was on about, once the verbal diarrhoea concluded.

She told him every detail of the roller coaster ride she was on with Sen. Clearly there were some major challenges. A.B. knew Wanda could be difficult but some of the things that went down, sounded way out of line. The moody sulking thing was never going to be something Wanda could take. Sen seemed like such a nice guy though.

'It's all too much,' she repeated.

Eventually she calmed down a little and explained what she meant.

'When I met his mother, loads of things fell into place. Having expected her to be a little distant and not really affectionate, I was completely surprised. She's approaching ninety but still as bright as a button and fully engaged with what her six children, their partners and children are up to. Knows what's going on in the world at large too and has such a plethora of interesting things to talk about. Doesn't mind me struggling with bad Dutch and does her best to say the odd thing in English too. She couldn't be more loving and yet Sen seems to be happy keeping some distance from her. They talk non-stop when together and she often calls for long chats but he has no problem with not having contact either. Other siblings live near her and see her regularly so there could be a chance he feels he's not needed. When he told her of our plans for skiing and for trialling a life in Sydney for a few months, her eyes almost popped out. Of course, she was happy for him to have the experience and would miss him but it was more than that. The way she quizzed him on how we would live and what he thought of being so far away from his homeland. I see now that she was getting at how difficult it all might be for him. Even though he has led an extreme career in television and radio, the past few years have taken him to negative and sad places, that I think might have limited his ability to take on too much at one time now. And there's me, used to flitting from one country to the other and busier than the busiest queen bee you ever saw. He must be reeling!'

She told A.B. about the sarcastic comment, when she mentioned coming across for this meeting and celebrating the success. Within minutes, Sen had called Wanda back to apologise and tell her how happy he was for her to enjoy this. Later explaining, that she caught him just when someone in the radio station had let him down. It was a bit of a reflex action. He was genuinely sorry and came home that night with flowers and long hugs. All had been well for the few days since and he'd been researching things they might do in Seoul on their 4-day stopover, headed to Sydney. When things were good, they were fantastic together.

Wanda realised now that she was totally overwhelming him and that, in turn, she was also being overwhelmed. It put her on edge and made her overreact to things.

She had to slow down her pace and learn the importance of doing nothing.

'I have to make this one work A.B. This sort of opportunity doesn't come your way often in any lifetime and I'm on the last third of mine.'

She went on to say that all she wanted, was to lead a peaceful and caring life with her beautiful Sen.

'He's so passionate and amazing. Every time I look at him, I just want to melt. We have the resources to travel when we like. So many friends and our wonderful families. He never had children so we can focus on mine for our future generations and hopefully become loving grandparents together some day.'

Suddenly it was all very clear to Wanda.

She would back totally away from The Agency for the next several months and leave things in the more than capable hands of A.B. and Pan. Clients would be told she was taking a sabbatical. Simple as that!

Establishing a calm and secure future with Sen, was the single most important factor she wanted to concentrate on, over the next several months. If he didn't like living in Australia, they could consider other options. So much wrapped itself around that possible relocation to a new country. It was more than enough for any new relationship to have to deal with.

Keeping their creativity alive, could be achieved via everything they ventured into together with publishing. They could have so much fun with all of that. It wasn't like they needed to prove anything to anyone or had a desperate need to earn.

So many people their age, were at a loss to know what they might do in their prime. Not so for Wanda and Sen. They would be creating til the bitter end!

She could write her romance novels and he could work up television show formats and other brilliant ideas, as well as delving into unchartered publishing territory.

This should be all about them enjoying each day and nothing more.

Now it was A.B. who was looking a little faint.

'I could try to say something to change your mind but I know you too well. Don't worry. I'm with you Wanda. You can do this. What's the point of having worked hard all your life, if you don't seize the moment when you can. Let's wait until after the client meeting tomorrow, to tell the team.'

He was up on his feet and checking his hair out in the mirror.

'A night of fun celebrations for us now my sweet!'

While he gathered the troops, she sent a quick text to Sen and told him she was dropping back from agency activities. She loved him dearly, needed him more than anything and missed him terribly. His return was in Dutch and as happy and emotional a text, as she had ever received from him.

Sen called her just before sleeping that night, just as she too was about to close her eyes. They chatted for ages and shared greetings of love and good wishes for sweet dreams. Finally concluding with a reminder about his best mate Ty having invited them to a party at his house, the following Saturday.

Ty and Sen went way back over thirty years or so. They met living on the commune but had only struck up the close friendship, after leaving it. Wanda had been with Sen once, to the lovely Amsterdam apartment he and his wife Veet had. They were nice enough but she had really felt scrutinised and gathered Ty wasn't at all happy, about her taking his best mate off to the other side of the world. He had said that evening, that they would have a party in the New Year and it might be a nice chance for Wanda to meet some of the commune 'kids'. Ty and Veet had tried hard to conceive children but with no luck. They treated these 'kids' as if they were their own family. Wanda wasn't sure what that was actually founded on but sensed there might also be some sort of connection, to what had happened with the children during those commune years. They were all of a similar age to Wanda's own children and a couple already had babies. Ty and Veet looked after two of the babies on a regular basis and loved every minute of it.

Wanda was pleased to fit into Sen's life in any way he wanted. His family could not have been nicer and the friends and colleagues she had met so far, were all extremely pleasant. It would be way more difficult for him to fit in with everything in my life, on the other side of the world.

Sen was at the airport with their enchanted red cabrio and Wanda rushed into his waiting arms. Hug was at one with Sen, as he lifted her into the tightest hold ever. Their first night apart and they had both hated being away from each other.

Kissing lingered on, as though they were reuniting after a long absence, then eventually they relaxed into the car - again connected by its enchanted aura.

Wanda shared every detail of what happened that day and how well the team had taken her decision to go on sabbatical.

Earlier that morning, she had called Pan to let him know. He was a little sad initially but he got it.

These were not just co-workers. She gave thanks for having such close and trusting people on her side, who really cared about her wellbeing. No doubt at all that they would do a great job running things.

She had also called Lou, who was beside herself with joy.

This sounded much more like her mum and Sen might end up making Australia their permanent home, if they could work out the visa thing.

The new man in Lou's life was also revealed!

Alex was his name. They'd been working together on a popular TV show, for some months and had hit it off straight away but only recently actually dated. Wanda could tell Lou was really keen and it made her so happy, to know the recovery from Steve was complete.

Sen told Wanda he had words with his demons, while she was away, and felt confident they would keep a lower profile. He knew he had issues to deal with but, as long as he had the love of Wanda, he could conquer anything.

During the flight back to Holland, Wanda had put together a mental list of all the things she could strive for with her behaviours, to make her life with Sen a happy one. She knew the only person you could ever change, was yourself.

The reason was always 'you', when it came to analysing where relationships met challenges. She was not a perfect person and neither was Sen.

They didn't need to be.

Anything worth having long term, always had to be worked at.

She was going to find her way to being a better her.

After a delicious Sen meal they relaxed in hug position, to watch the news on television. Wanda had her leg wrapped across Sen's lap and he was gently rubbing her thigh – encouraged by Fug more and more.

Not quite what you might call foreplay but to Wanda, this was enough.

Goosebumps were taking over, as she reached across Sen's waste, to find a large bulge pushing out of his jeans. He was as turned on as she was.

A simple look into each other's eyes and they could wait no longer.

Sen lifted her with sudden strength, to carry her off to bed, only reaching the first floor landing, before he had to stop and make love to her there and then, on the stairs. Heated passion ruled the moment and their lust was quick to overpower.

Small carpeted stairs provided just enough grip and space, to fulfil each hot desire and they were sweaty masses of pleasure, in a matter of minutes.

The night of Ty and Veet's party soon arrived. Wanda knew all eyes would be on her so she had taken great care to choose an appropriately striking outfit to wear. Cold outside but it was bound to be hot in their apartment. Boots with a shortish skirt, smart jacket and shirt should do the trick. Not too short. Not too smart. Not too casual. Sen was wearing jeans with a white shirt and navy jacket. He always looked so smart. The tall slim stance was a great asset.

'So you plan to take Sen away from us and hide him in Australia heh?'

Nothing like getting straight to the point!

That was fine with Wanda.

She laughed and so did the person asking.

Everyone was friendly and general conversation was light. They were pleased for Sen to have such an exciting adventure.

Ty served quality champagne. Nothing but the best would do.

Veet had prepared delicious snacks and was busy looking after everyone and perhaps a little stressed. They had taken care of one of the babies that day and her back was suffering from the lifting.

Soft classical music provided a pleasant background that people could still talk over. Catching up with the latest news, it seemed to Wanda that the 'kids' might not actually see that much of each other.

One couple were due to have a baby in the coming months and did not have a car yet so a plan was made for them to borrow their enchanted red cabrio, whilst Sen was in Australia for the three month trial. They would arrange appropriate insurance and take good care of the car that they knew meant so much to both Sen and Wanda. It would give them a chance to see if they really wanted one or not.

It was agreed that they would meet at Schiphol, prior to the flight that would take Sen and Wanda to Seoul, in a week's time. That would give them a nice easy ride to get their luggage to the airport, then keys could be handed over with instructions and the young couple would take the cabrio home.

As it happened, this was easier said than done.

Things had been going so smoothly, in that week leading up to their departure.

Sen found a great place for them to stay in Seoul and had researched so many cool things for them to see and do. Wanda had only been there once before and not for very long. They were excited to learn a little about South Korea and even practiced a few basic words like thank you and hello. Their flight would leave early evening so no need to get to the airport too early. Excellent.

The big Schier sort out had gained some momentum and drops had been made to records stores and pre-loved clothing shops. A neighbour would be watching over things while they were in

Australia and making sure the heating ran for a short while each day. Frozen pipes were always a worry in winter.

It looked like the Hillywood home might have a couple of paying house guests, during their absence too. Wanda had run a small advertisement in the local press and two different people took a room each.

One would only be there a few days during the week. He worked for one of the big multi-nationals in Hillywood but lived in Groningen so would be spending his weekends there.

Great to have the house occupied and keep some money coming in towards the mortgage and running costs.

A neighbour would keep a watch over things and make sure it was all looked after. She'd sort out cleaning and wash and change beds if necessary. Lucky Wanda yet again!

It would be cold in Seoul so a few wintery things needed to be packed but most of their time would be spent in the hot Australian summer. A couple of weddings to go to and clothing for those had to be included. Sen made sure he put in the new boxer shorts that had been sent for his birthday, from Wanda's niece and close buddy Elle.

Replicating the Australian flag and fitting very snugly, they could possibly double as swimmers - a little more coverage than speedos and not as bulky as boardies.

Farewell visit had been made to Sen's mum two days earlier, catching up with a sister and brother at the same time. All overjoyed for Sen's impending adventure and in awe of how his life was twisting and turning.

Totally ready, packed and sorted the night before and a nice quiet dinner at home, after cycling into town to meet with Denise and some friends for a little farewell drink, all seemed in order.

Then it started!

Snow was dumping on Holland, like an avalanche had moved the entire Alps to fall on The Netherlands. Records were being broken and it would only get worse.

Wanda and Sen woke the morning of their flight, not being able to see out of the Velux windows that sat over their bed. As they tried to open one porthole a little, it became clear that the thickest of thick snow was weighing it down like a ton of bricks.

No way would that window budge.

Moving to the small side window, Wanda could not see one of the many cars she knew were parked outside their house.

'Unbelievable!'

Sen wasn't quite as awake as Wanda and gave her an enquiring glance.

'Look at this darling. It's so beautiful but I've never seen so much snow! Wonder if it's affecting things at the airport?'

Their plan was to leave the house around 4pm and take an easy drive to Schiphol.

Rendezvous for car hand over, at 5pm and it normally took half an hour to get there. As the weather worsened, they decided they might need to reconsider timing.

Reconsider timing!

Airlines were reconsidering whether to even take off or not.

They would leave at 3pm and take it very slowly.

On checking with Korean Airlines, they had been told departure was expected to still take place – and on time.

Sen spent an age scraping snow off the cabrio and getting a path cleared for backing out of their entrance. Cars had been driving on their street so it looked like they might be OK.

Loaded and ready to go, they made one final check to the road service website, to make sure the motorway was clear.

All systems go!

Getting to the motorway from their house, normally took 5 minutes. This day it took them half an hour. They couldn't fathom why so many people would venture out into the thick snow …. go figure.

'We'll be fine my love. I have no problem going as slow as we have to and there's plenty of time. Just as long as we don't get any crazies on the road.'

Wanda had spoken too soon!

• CHAPTER ELEVEN •

ANXIOUS PASSENGERS FILLED cafés and airport benches everywhere, as the departures and arrivals boards kept changing to flash 'CANCELLED'. Not so for the flight Wanda and Sen were to take. It stood alone, in keeping to the same expected time for take-off.

Still shaking, from the drive through the bleakest of wintery storms, Wanda was happy just to be inside the building. A near miss, on the motorway, had been way too close for comfort.

'How we didn't skid into that line of cars to our left, when that idiot suddenly appeared from the slip road, is beyond me. Our enchanted red cabrio must have been looking after us again. I just went with it but remember a feeling of uncontrolled sliding and expecting to hear an almighty bang, at any minute. That guy had not even realised he was entering the main flow of traffic!'

Wanda had kept her reactions to herself when it happened.

No point scaring Sen too.

Now she was releasing the shock and talking too fast.

'His wipers were not coping with the heavy snow and I just think he couldn't see anything. I accelerated ever so slightly and luckily added just enough momentum for us to slide clear of him. Incredible!'

Fear factor, had Wanda gripping the steering wheel so tightly, the pressure on her hands was enough to have them still ache, almost two hours later. Finally arriving at Schiphol, after a long slow crawl, she'd taken quite some time to calm down enough to even let go.

Sen loaded their luggage onto a trolley and sat her quietly inside, while he went off to facilitate the car handover.

'That was some excellent manoeuvring but all quite frightening. Lots of time for us to chill now. His last text said the train finally came so it looks like we may have accidentally synchronised our arrivals well. Meeting me at the car. So many trains stopped with this weather, it's a miracle either of us could get here. They don't live far so hopefully his ride home should be OK.'

Most people had already checked in for the flight to Seoul and they were clear to go straight up to the counter. No problem getting their extra legroom seats and solid confirmation they should depart on time. Was this all for real? How could their flight be so different from so many others that were cancelled?

Fully expecting the situation to change, they had just made themselves comfortable with a glass of wine, when the departures board signalled go to gate.

Not delayed one minute and soon they were up up and away.

'South Korea here we come!'

Arm in arm, with Wanda's head resting on Sen's shoulder, the thrust of take-off was powerful but smooth. Still no sign of any impacts from the outrageous weather.

'How lucky are we?'

Wanda whispered, as she gazed into the eyes of her beautiful man.

Lucky indeed!

It was all working out super well and soon she'd be showing Sen off to friends and family in Australia. She had calmed down from the traumatic drive and was blissfully happy.

A quick nap and they were both ready to enjoy excellent inflight hospitality. The Korean attendants could not do enough for them. Service with a smile and comfort all the way. Sen was adventurous with choosing Korean options from the menu. Wanda played it safe and kept to the familiar. Her priority was to plan the order of movies to be watched. Light and entertaining for her. Great Expectations first she thought. Then perhaps Lincoln followed by Parental Guidance and Skyfall. Sen would be looking for the deep and meaningful, plus anything leaning towards current affairs.

Korean hospitality continued, post landing in Seoul. Unbelievably friendly and helpful people. They had chosen a reasonably priced hotel, in the downtown area, and an airport bus delivered them to the doorstep. Not many speaking English but the attitude towards visitors, was totally positive.

Interesting magazines in their room, promoted some beautiful locations around South Korea. They would have loved to get up into the mountains or down to the islands but not this trip.

Mixing it with the locals, next morning they visited the ice rink in a square at the front of City Hall. A group of protestors quietly stated their case, as they circled the square holding banners high.

The new City Hall was built directly behind the old one, with an urban spatial theme that used glass, metal and greenery, to achieve a 'no axis' feel to its industrial lines and shapes. Aimed at replicating mountains and valleys, it undulated around a vast atrium. Absolutely stunning!

Riding the efficient metro, they visited incredible temples, museums and palaces; enjoyed the old Olympics area and vastness of Lotto World; historical buildings and alleyways of Bukchon old town.

Electronic displays in line of sight at all times, reminded them of the exceptional technology companies, like Samsung, that emanated from these shores.

Spending time in the Gangnam shopping district, they mixed in well with the fashionistas of Seoul and could not help singing to themselves over and over, that one hit wonder or wonders – Gangnam Style. Incredible how quickly its viral uptake took the world by storm. A silly dance being done tongue-in-cheek by a large group of young Koreans.

Wanda recalled seeing coverage on the local Dutch TV news, then switching to BBC moments later and seeing it there too - great to see such fun hit the main news!

Sweet red chilli cake, from a street vendor, proved interesting. Way too hot for Wanda but a delight to Sen's spicier pallet. Fascinating how the simple wagon cooking facility, housed one small chef and her flamed wok-style pan – all under cover. Students in the queue were quick to practice their English and explain eating protocol.

Too soon it was their last night.

They had tickets to celebrate in style, at the traditional Jeongdong Theatre.

This colourful display, of Korean music and dance, was so moving, with its deeply emotive sounds and imagery, simple hand holding acted as a conduit for Wanda and Sen to share every ounce of passion being expressed.

A short walk back to the hotel and they were soon playing out their own passionate encounters and Hug & Fug even seemed to have slight Korean accents!

Very much in love and both excited and nervous about how things might go in Australia, Wanda and Sen considered themselves to be the luckiest couple on earth.

An easy bus ride back to Incheon Airport, not too early the next morning.

'Here we go again. Lady Luck just can't get enough of us!'

Wanda was trying not to look uncool, at the flight check-in counter.

She'd flown business class before.

'Are you kidding?'

Sen had not and was having difficult taking in what was happening. Having simply asked the staff member for extra legroom seats, they were stunned at the response. Economy was overbooked so they would need to put them up top!

It was the business class area but their inflight service would be the same as economy. Was that OK?

Definitely OK!

They were both grinning at each other, like over-excited children, once clear of check-in. What a great way to be making the final leg into Sydney. Big business class seats and hearts bursting with joy!

On boarding, Sen immediately began to discover everything his seat was capable of and Wanda followed suit. Dropped their seats fully down to beds and tested the many options for adjustments. Even had an exit row in front, making it seem as though they had their own separate living space. A brilliant entertainment unit with great sound, there was not one comfort lacking.

Fabulous!

'We can even cuddle up under our blankets and not a soul will know what we're up to!'

Fug was as happy as any revved-up little inner voice could be!

It was only when crew began service that they realised all sixteen passengers on the upper deck, were supposed to be travelling economy. Business class main deck area, had plenty of room to accommodate those paying guests so the airline staff had allocated the entire top level, to free upgrades.

How amazing was that!

Made absolute good sense of course.

Why waste the seats?

What a great pity every airline didn't think that way. Enormous good will to be gained but some seem only intent on how not to serve these days.

As they came in to land the next morning, Sydney was alight with a bright and sunny dawn. Sen had the window seat and a brilliantly clear view across the most beautiful harbour in the world.

'Already even more spectacular than I imagined.'

Tenderly reaching over to kiss Wanda, he thanked her for bringing him there. She thanked him for coming, as they hugged and took on smiles as wide as the sky.

Straight through customs, Wanda ran eagerly into the waiting arms of her special niece Elle. They were extra close and had spent earlier years out bopping and exploring life. Travelled to the US and Europe together. Were always well connected, even after Elle's marriage and having three children - great mates. She insisted on being there for this early morning arrival and couldn't wait to meet Sen.

Wanda was as keen for her to meet him and ecstatic about showing Sen her amazing home town. Sen and Elle hit it off straight away, as she knew they would.

First stop …. Bondi Beach!

'A quick dip for me I think!'

And there was Sen, looking gorgeous as he stripped down to the Australian flag boxers he'd been sent by Elle, soon plunging into the ocean. Quickly realising the ferocity of crashing waves and strong tides, and happy to move on to a nearby café. He had been anointed into Sydney life, in an instant.

'I guess you'll get your car back from Lou will you?'

Elle understood what good thinking it was for Lou to drive Wanda's silver convertible, while she was away.

'That was such a great little find. Worked out so well, Lou being able to get rid of her old hatchback and cover the running costs on your car. She's a good girl. I know she's looked after it well.'

'Not sure actually. We're thinking of living near the city for this short stay so I might leave the car with Lou for now and just get it when we need it.'

Taking the long way around, before crossing the harbour bridge, several stops were made at vantage points in the Eastern Suburbs, to take in the spectacular views of the harbour.

Finally on the bridge, Sen was in awe of its majesty and sheer size.

For their first few nights in Sydney, they'd be staying with Wanda's good mate Cath and her boyfriend Rio, on the north side. Just a few weeks until Cath's daughter Rose got married and she was thrilled to have Wanda arrive and ease tensions around arrangements for that. Lou was chief bridesmaid and she too was about to burst with wedding stress.

Rose could be difficult at times and was clearly on edge about absolutely everything.

Cath hosted a welcome dinner for Wanda and Sen that night. Lou and the new boyfriend Alex would come straight from work. There'd be just the six of them. Nice and early so everyone could get a good sleep and be up early the next morning for the big Australia Day beach breakfast and full day of celebrations.

Alex was perfect! He could not have been nicer and easier to get along with. The look he had for Lou, made Wanda's heart swoon with delight. She observed how they laughed and broke into song, when key words took their thoughts to different melodies. So many things in common and seeming very much the family guy, his head was in the same space as Lou's and she had just as positive an energy, shining out towards him. Wanda knew there and then, this was going to be something serious.

'Sorry I can't join you all tomorrow but I have cricket to win and a barbeque that I really have to be at.'

Alex was a good friend to many and Lou had fitted straight in, with their zany crew. She admired him for maintaining so many life-long friendships, female and male, and they'd already agreed he should carry on with planned Australia Day activities, while she spent some quality time with her mum and got to know Sen.

'Cath's coming down for the beach breakfast so we'll meet you by the bacon and egg rolls bub. Jay's catching up with us later, in the city.'

Wanda concluded arrangements, as they bid Lou and Alex farewell.

'Good luck with the cricket Alex. So lovely to meet you and I'm sure we'll be seeing you again soon.'

She was already thinking what a lovely couple they made and Sen also agreed.

One giant leaping kangaroo suddenly pounced on Sen, as he stepped away from the breakfast tent that Australia Day morning. Loaded with everyone's rolls, it was all he could do, not to drop everything.

The moment was happily caught on film.

Sen staring up into the eyes of this costumed person's kangaroo face, riding high on top of a tall pogo stick - definitely a pic to send back to Holland.

The thong throwing competition, on the sand, did not require people to take off small items of underwear. These rubber foot coverings were already familiar to Sen and he soon entered himself for the big chuck. Quite an art to catching the wind just right but he didn't do too badly at all.

Live music and a great 'country fair' atmosphere.

Sen felt totally comfortable.

As the afternoon approached, it became just the three of them and Lou drove Wanda and Sen to Neutral Bay ferry, to make their way across the harbour for the rendezvous with Jay.

Clear blue sunny skies and a fairly high temperature, had them all taking cover from the sun and realising they needed to apply more sun cream. None of which, diminished their enthusiasm for the spectacle of Sydney harbour, as they sailed into Circular Quay – Opera House to the left; Harbour Bridge on the right; a plethora of different water craft surrounding.

'Can you believe how perfect they are together Lou?'

Jay was thrilled to see how happy his mum was with Sen. The stars had told him this was going to be the one and he'd clearly been right.

What a happy little family they all made. Sen fitted in without hesitation and it was as if they had known each other, a very long time. Wanda looked on with a great sense of satisfaction and again thanked her lucky stars, for leading her to Sen.

It was an amazing day that became an amazing week, busy catching up with so many people and trying to spend as much time as possible with everyone. They moved house twice and were soon in residence with a great mate in Elizabeth Bay.

'Stay as long as you like. I just rattle around in here on my own anyway.'

It was a stunning terraced home, re-worked inside by an acclaimed architect and featured in a leading design magazine.

They were made to feel very welcome but Wanda needed to get back to writing her novel and Sen had loads of people to see about work possibilities. They wanted their own base as soon as possible.

Three weeks had passed by before they knew it.

Sen was now immersed in Wanda's world and loving it. He was sure he wanted to make their home in Australia and working out how best to do that, was his priority.

'It looks pretty small but the back garden area seems to be for the sole use of this granny flat. Nice to have an outside area. Great park and yacht club across the street too. You should easily get a sail there. Apparently people just rock up and put their name down. Boat owners short on crew soon grab you. Wonder if they would accept our six week stay?'

Wanda still had the mansion but it was rented out for lots of money and there was no point disturbing that, for their short stay. She also thought it might be nice for Sen to experience living near the harbour, with easy access to sailing. Most properties wanted you to sign up for at least six months but finally, they came across a possibility.

'The ad says OK for short lets.'

Rushcutters Bay soon became home for the rest of their Sydney stay and Sen had no problem at all just showing up for Twilight Sailing and getting on a yacht. They started their day with a cycle around the park and doing their little stretch routine. Wanda then got straight on with writing or researching for visa insights, while Sen went off to network with job possibilities and literary agent leads.

Still no word from Wanda's big brother Joe and she had left several messages.

'Mum. I've tried so many times, to get Uncle Joe over for dinner or to just catch up wherever. He doesn't even call me back. The last time I did manage to speak to him, he was too busy with all the horses he'd bought and obsessed with how they were going to finally win him big money.'

Lou had been reluctant to say this to Wanda but she had already known this to be the case. The first day they arrived, she called him and it broke her heart to think how he had sold his soul back to gambling yet again. He hadn't had much time to talk but was happy Wanda was back to help him out. Promising to come over to see her and meet Sen, then not calling back to fix a time.

When she rented out the mansion, Joe moved in with a mate that trained trotting horses. He gave him a share in a young filly, in return for Joe's work around the property. The horse developed potential and had even won a race. That was enough to make Joe think his time had come. Now he had three horses. Only his pension and occasional earnings from working as a taxi driver, yet he was happy to max out his credit card and take on costs he couldn't afford.

Months back Wanda had called him from Europe and tried to talk sense into him. He laughed and told her she would see. This time he was going to be a winner!

With no regard for the total debt that surrounded owning horses, he soon owed tens of thousands of dollars, for vet fees, food, training stables, race entry and a host of other costs.

'The first thing he told me on that quick call when we got back here, was how clever he had been to declare himself bankrupt. Where is his sense of honour to meet all those financial commitments he made? It's so upsetting.'

Lou was shocked. She had always been so close to her Uncle Joe and missed him but he just didn't seem to care about them anymore or even about his behaviour.

'I know. Unbelievable really but I don't want to have that conversation with him. Really no point. You know he will turn eighty soon? I don't want to be angry at him. He has to live his own life. Let's just hope we can get a nice birthday happening for him.'

'He doesn't deserve such a nice caring sister as you mum. I still love him too but there's only so much you can do to keep someone in your life, when they don't seem to give a damn.'

Lou was right of course but Wanda wouldn't give up on him just yet. As it happened, the car needed some work doing and Sen had found a place out west, not far from where Joe was living. Wanda caught him at the right time and arranged to meet for a birthday lunch. He wasn't interested in doing anything else for his big birthday, other than trying to pretend it wasn't happening.

The person he was closest to was his son. He lived in Queensland so Wanda would suggest Joe went up there for a celebration with him. They were horse racing buddies too so that could be something nice for them to share for the big 80th.

As it happened, the car fix and lunch date, went brilliantly.

'He is a real character my darling. I'm so glad we were able to see him finally.'

Sen and Joe were quickly best buddies.

'I love where he took us. Was it called Windsor? So much history and Joe had quite some knowledge to share about everything. A charming man! Hopefully we will get to see more of him soon.'

Wanda loved that they hit it off so well. Joe may have disappointed her but he was still the lovable big brother she always cared so much for and she would never forget how he had never shied from filling their mother's hand with cash, when she was little and they had been in need.

Good meetings for Sen all around that week.

'That ABC guy could not have been more helpful. He's introducing me to loads of people and has offered to give me every assistance with finding work. Nothing specific at present but he's going to be a great contact to have.'

Introductions were building up thick and fast. Old Dutch colleagues linked him with several key contacts in television and he met with loads of industry people and media education facilities.

Everything was going very nicely indeed!

Sen was quickly calling the ABC chap for help, with something he had never anticipated, then relaying to Wanda how over-enthusiastic his response had been.

'My old radio show boss in Holland wants me to cover an upcoming visit, from a hugely controversial Dutch politician. I would be the Correspondent from Down Under. I spoke to the ABC guy and he offered me studio time and all sorts of assistance but I think I might just rent a small recording unit to do the interviews. Maybe Jay can help out with the edit and getting it finally down the wire to Holland. The money's not bad.'

Controversial indeed - this Dutch politician was causing all sorts of trouble with his visit. Nasty scenes with protestors in Melbourne, led Sydney police to kick into overdrive with security, for the event Sen was scheduled to attend. All one-on-one interviews were cancelled. Sen had intended for Jay to go along with him as Audio Guy but media passes got cut back and Jay had to stay outside. Riot police and special holding trailers, surrounded the venue but there was no trouble at all in the end. Sen did an excellent report and Jay even let him into his personal studio, to assist on edit. A first! He never let anyone into that space before. They worked until the wee hours getting it done and shared a great bonding experience.

Visa tips had been coming in left right and centre.

'What do you think about this my love? If we register our relationship here in Sydney, it looks like the paperwork for the partner visa, magically cuts itself in half. I'm thinking the sponsored work visa is going to be way more of a challenge. Might also end up restricting what you do. We could not be more committed to each other so this looks like the best way to go. Also easier and cheaper, if we then lodge our application from outside of Australia. Pointing everything to the London address, seems the way to go. We can take it in ourselves, once we get back to Europe.'

They talked for ages about what it meant to 'register your relationship'.

Sen hit google and researched and translated, until he felt perfectly clear on it all.

'From everything I see it looks the same as getting married.'

The grin on Sen's face said it all. He was very happy for this to be the case.

'I guess it sort of is basically the same legal procedure.'

Wanda was being a little coy and trying to keep focus on the efficiency of it all.

'Very OK by me,' responded Sen – and Wanda was quick with her 'me too.'

No appointment necessary.

As they approached the Registry Office, both gave a little chuckle at the girl out front, with her entourage. No doubt that she considered it getting married. She was all decked out in the big white dress and even had bridesmaids. Witness to Wanda and Sen's declaration, would only be the staff member taking the application.

Returning quickly with their receipt, he matter-of-factly informed them that they had 28days as a cooling off period.

Each day thereafter, was count down for Sen.

'Only 20 days to go.'

He would say with a sense of hope and perhaps questioning.

With all his heart, he hoped that Wanda would not change her mind. As much as she had been her often annoying flippant self, trying to convince herself it was only done to expedite the visa more easily, she felt totally committed to her life with Sen and was very happy to have declared that publicly.

There were several moments of concern during those 28 days.

Both of them had times when they felt they could just not say the right thing. So similar in their strength of character, they managed to irritate each other way too often.

Doing the 24/7 thing of course didn't help and yet, they really hated being apart.

When things got heated, Sen locked himself away emotionally and stayed there for hours. Being deeply sensitive and feeling misunderstood, cut him to the core.

Life wasn't meant to be easy heh!

On completion of the 28 days, they celebrated and reconfirmed their never ending love for one another, with a special dinner at the yacht club and swapping of gifts.

A beautiful couple reminding themselves of what an amazing life they had. It might take them time to make the behavioural adjustments they needed to but they had total confidence in their ability to do so.

Rose had pulled herself together by her wedding day. The sun shone and all was well for the beach ceremony. Lou looked stunning, in the tightly fitting apricot bridesmaid dress, and was the first one to appear over the sand dunes. Two musicians sang the bride and her father, down the sandy path to her waiting love. Kite surfers added striking colours, to the deep blue sea and sky background. A short walk to the smart beach restaurant afterwards and they could all feast and party, well into the night. Being close on the tail of Wanda and Sen's public relationship commitment, they considered it a celebration of their own love too.

Partner Visa was definitely the best way to go for Sen but it was incredible what needed to be put together for the application. Certain supporting documents, were best done whilst in Sydney. Two people required to make Statutory Declarations, as to the validity of their relationship and to staying together long term. Elle's husband was an ex-policeman so he was chosen for one and Lou for the other. The words that they both wrote brought tears to both Wanda and Sen's eyes.

So beautiful!

Considering them to be the best possible role models for the family and feeling their love was, without any doubt, complete and enduring. Upstanding examples of how good citizens should behave, they were also extremely talented people that so many others aspired to be like. The declarations went on and on.

Wanda and Sen also had to make Statutory Declarations, as to the nature of their partnership. Words were sincere and grateful, reflecting on how lucky they were and demonstrating their conviction, to sharing their lives for always.

Challenges with demons, and behaviours that upset the proverbial apple cart, would be overcome – not that they had any plan to talk about these in their declaration ….. or indeed to anyone else.

'That's pretty much everything for the visa, right now. Loads of paperwork to get together in Holland once we get back but otherwise, we're in good shape.'

Wanda was happy to put that file to one side for the time being and crack on with the book. She was making excellent progress.

Pity Sen wasn't having the same luck with literary agents and publishing houses.

'These people really make it hard!'

Sen couldn't believe how downright rude some were. How they ever found new talent, was something they would both never understand.

'Maybe our person is in Europe. Think I'll give it a miss for now and concentrate on that TV show format I've been trying to write. Only a couple of weeks before we leave for Melbourne anyway.'

Lou dropped the car over to them, the night before they headed out of Sydney. Alex came along for the farewell to the granny flat dinner, in the back garden. A balmy summer night, with the smell of mangoes streaming down from the giant tree, at the rear of the laneway.

Aromas coming from the kitchen were soon to override that.

Sen had cooked up a treat, yet again!

More than happy with what they had achieved during the Sydney stay, they would be off to explore a little of Australia and to attend nephew Pete's wedding.

After losing his wife Mary in the car accident in Canada, several years earlier, Pete was marrying for the second time, to the mother of his two children.

Things had been touch and go, as to whether this marriage would ever actually take place. The relationship was fraught with trials and tribulations.

She had been the first real girlfriend, as he recovered from the loss of Mary. They got along famously and quickly decided to live together. No plan to get pregnant but they were nevertheless happy when they did.

A perfectly normal pregnancy, with a super healthy young woman.

Why oh why had their baby died at full term?

She had gone along for the routine check-up, with just a couple of days to go to due date. No heart beat! The only thing that could be done, was to force her into labour and deliver their perfectly formed little boy.

They were heartbroken and so was anyone close to them!

Pete was one of the nicest guys on the planet.

How could he be hit so severely yet again?

Everyone had been in mourning for a very long time, still not clear of the wounds from losing Mary so tragically.

Some months later, they happily announced a new pregnancy. A beautiful daughter was born with no problems whatsoever. A further child, under two years later, again with no problems. Both very healthy and alert.

No answers were ever forthcoming, as to why the first child died. They stayed with him for some days, to try to come to terms with it. A funeral service had been held and a memorial created in their garden. That loss clearly impacted their relationship and caused ongoing challenges for them personally, despite moving on to have two beautiful children.

She wanted more than anything, to be his bride and not just the mother of his children. He had been reluctant, having done that once and had his major loss. They purchased a new home together and he could not have been more committed to them as a family but the wedding thing, proved to be a barrier for him. Eventually he relented and did the honourable thing, which seemed to turn things around happily for them. A weekend away to propose properly. The fabulous engagement ring. And now an amazing wedding, that would leave nothing out.

Wanda and Sen visited country towns and vineyards, as they drove the nine hundred or so kilometres to Melbourne. The landscape continued to thrill Sen and he snapped away with full camera gear in use. Giant stick trees, sitting in the middle of sunburnt paddocks, were of particular interest. Old colonial pub stays, got Hug & Fug pumped for some excited love making. The entire journey was a total delight and soon they were at the wedding venue accommodation.

'What a great location. Look at those woods out back and that pool over there. Our bath has power jets too. Should we give them a whirl?'

Wanda was on the balcony and Sen was bringing her a glass of wine, to toast their arrival. Fug jumped straight into his head, at the mere mention of power jets.

'Let's do it! We have two hours before we need to be at the dinner.'

Hot bubbles made for a long, smooth and sexy orgasmic bathing session.

Many of the guests seemed more excited about meeting Sen for the first time, than they did about the wedding. Wanda could not have been more proud of her beautiful man. He looked gorgeous in his immaculate suit and was smiling that huge brilliant smile – his usual charming self to all.

Buses collected everyone for the wedding the next day. Bit of a wild ride but they were soon at the most stunning country farm. The wedding would take place under flowering vines, in an idyllic setting. Close to one hundred guests and the weather was perfect. No expense had been spared and everyone was ready for some fun to be had.

'Aunty Wanda, can I please speak to you in private?'

Tash had tears running down her face and was shaking, as she beckoned to Wanda to follow her to a secluded spot.

• CHAPTER TWELVE •

WANDA'S SURROGATE ENGLISH MUM was Grandmother to Ed. If only she was still alive! She would soon get Ed back on track.

What an incredible lady!

So strong willed and opinionated, Joy had something deep and meaningful to say about every topic you could ever imagine. When Wanda had first gone to England, aged 21, Joy had taken her into her home and made her one of the family. Even when Wanda split with her son Mel years later, they remained incredibly close and she later came to love Larry as well. He would never have established himself as a carpenter, if not for Joy. She had the most remarkable set of books on everything DIY. He studied them hard, bought the appropriate tools and was soon able to compliment his irregular earnings as a musician. When Larry and Wanda married, it was Joy who was there fussing and sorting, getting everything as it should be. Wanda's own mother hadn't made the trip from Sydney. In fact, none of her actual family had. Such a long journey and way too expensive. In any case, they were already planning a trip back to Australia, a few months after the wedding.

Ed was Joy's first grandchild and the apple of her eye. They were alike in so many ways and would talk for hours on end, as he grew up and became a strong-willed young man.

He had emigrated to Australia, with his wife Tash and their three beautiful children, a few years back and become close with Wanda's family in Melbourne. Of course they were all invited to Pete's wedding.

Shocking tales of Ed's deceit were now being relayed to Wanda.

She would never have thought this possible!

He had two brothers and either one of them might be capable of this – but surely not Ed?

'He says he's been having affairs the entire time we've been married and has never really loved me. Now he's fallen in love with someone in Indonesia. I thought the business trips were becoming longer and he was more and more aloof when he returned. We have really good sex so I just don't get it. Can you please talk to him?'

Tash went on to say how she felt Wanda, was one of the very few people he might listen to. He thought the world of her. She had known him most of his life and was the next best thing to his beloved grandma. He already said he was too afraid to speak with his mum and dad. They would be disgusted with him.

'I'm at a loss to know what to do!'

Tears were gushing out now and Wanda had Hug in full support, as she comforted Tash without speaking, all the time thinking to herself.

'They have to work this out. It sounds like he has a real problem. Needing to have loads of different partners and being insatiable with meeting his sexual needs. Nymphomania is a disease and he has to get the right help. All I can do is remind him what he has at risk, with the possibility of losing his family.'

Her focus at that very moment was on Tash. This was not the place to be airing all of this and she needed to snap herself back to the moment and put all her energies into enjoying the occasion. If only for the sake of their children!

Wanda had to bring herself back too. She was devastated by this horrible news but didn't want it spoiling such a happy day.

'OK. Positivity on all counts now please.'

They composed themselves in the bathroom and moved back to mix with the crowd, promising to talk only of the wonderful ceremony and how happy the bride and groom looked.

Wanda had been chatting with Sen for a while, when she saw her chance. Ed and Tash were laughing with another couple, who were just walking off. They were left on their own so she hurried over.

'I don't want all the details of why, where, when.'

Scowling at Ed very clearly, she could also see their three children laughing and playing, on the other side of the lawn so directed her comment towards them.

'They are what matters here.'

Continuing on to tell Ed he needed professional help.

'Get it and get it quickly. This beautiful wife of yours is heartbroken but I think you are both strong enough to pull this back together, with some real effort.'

Wanda grabbed both their heads and gently knocked them together.

'Now please try to enjoy this special day, as the fabulous family that you are. I have complete confidence you guys can rise to this difficult challenge. Please be kind to one another.'

Helping them into a hugging embrace, she was happy to leave them smiling and didn't relay anything to Sen, until they hit bed later that evening.

'I'm so glad you didn't tell me earlier. They are such a fabulous family. Wasn't it nice dancing with them all and being seated together? Such a shock to hear this! Ed does not look the part and Tash is quite gorgeous - and their beautiful children. They seem to have it all!'

Finally Wanda could let go. Sen held her tightly, as she sobbed her way to sleep.

Breakfast the next morning, was held at Pete's house. Then it was off to the airport for a short flight to Tasmania. Just a couple of nights in Hobart and then a rental car, would get Wanda and Sen down to Port Arthur.

She had sent Ed and Tash a message, to say that she was there for them at any time. Only down the line but if there was any way at all that they thought she could help, they should contact her. For now she would keep everything crossed for them to find the right professional help straight away.

Sen was a gem at clearing Wanda's head so they could enjoy the rest of the trip.

Having heard a great deal about MONA – Museum of Old and New Art – that would be their priority for the next day. A short ride along the Derwent River, on one giant black Bond-like ferry, and they were at one of the most eclectic places ever.

The building itself, was an amazing work of art. A labyrinth built into sandstone cliffs, using different metal fabrications to create a magical maze, across three floors. Each corner turned, leading to a freshly inspired display, with light and sound choreographing the uptake of the many incredible works being presented. A soft waterfall wall, dropping different text messages, was a favourite for Wanda.

Totally mesmerising!

Views from Mount Wellington enthralled but the massive boulders, scattered around the highest point of 1200 metres, interested them even more. Wanda and Sen took the last free shuttle bus, back down to Hobart Port and were surprised to see others, choosing to walk the steep 15km return through darkened bushland.

Sad remnants of bushfire disasters, lined their drive to Port Arthur. Stark blackness, being softened slightly, by small green areas of re-growth. The fires of 2013 had been unprecedented in Tasmania's history. Thousands of people ferried off the peninsula to safety, as roads were completely cut.

Port Arthur's history was also bleak, having started as a convict settlement in 1883. A significant World Heritage site, infamous for one crazy man going on a killing spree in 1996 and leaving thirty five dead and twenty five wounded. Simple tourists just like them. What an unimaginable horror!

On their last day, talented crew of a tall ship cruise, demonstrated how to sail such magnificent beasts and highlighted the brilliance of Hobart's harbour. Weather again perfect and lunch taken afterwards, at a cosy harbourside café, before the short flight back to Melbourne.

Their quick visit to Tasmania, definitely left them wanting more!

Lovely to stay with family for one night in Melbourne and do a little city sightseeing too. Being located on a river, it always seemed akin to Europe.

The drive back to Sydney, would take in some of the spa countryside towns but first stop was Sovereign Hill near Bendigo. Recreating the gold rush era of the late 1800s, this open air museum made you feel like you were actually there.

All had seemed well, for the short drive that day but on entry, something suddenly triggered in Sen.

Sarcasm, anger and nasty retorts!

Wanda's behaviour or comments had done it again.

So long without his demon beast but now it was back, in full regalia.

It made her angry to think this special moment was going to be ruined.

What on earth had she said, that was so bad?

She had no idea.

Life, to Wanda, was only about each and every moment that stacked up to give you that day and then hopefully the next and she didn't want to waste any of them!

Maybe it was all just too much and she was overwhelming Sen again.

So many interesting things to see and do around the property but all she wanted to do now, was to get away from him. She really did not like that nasty person she saw, when the demon took over.

They had tickets for the evening show, re-enacting the Eureka Stockade bloody battle, when goldminers revolted against ill treatment by government troops. Wanda had seen it before and knew Sen would love this incredible sound and light spectacular but now what?

'Do your own thing and I'll do mine. If you don't want to stay for the show this evening, just text me!'

Wanda stomped off angrily and was glad to get away.

The feeling was mutual!

Park activities stretched across 25 acres so it was easy to avoid each other. One of the music hall concerts would calm Wanda down. She was soon relaxing with a coffee and muffin, reading literature and checking out the schedule of activities, deciding what she would like to join. Within a couple of hours, she was fully recovered and missing Sen but she knew it would take him longer.

No matter how much he tried, negative episodes like this were really hard for him to shake. She reminded herself how much she loved, that he was a warm and sensitive human being.

Maybe a bit less of the sensitive, would be good though!

Everyone has arguments but he found it so difficult to let them go.

Almost time for the day's proceedings to end and Wanda spotted Sen.

He was coming out of the Chocolateria so she hoped he had a good hit of cocoa, to lift him back to a positive state but she approached with caution.

'I guess we have to leave now and re-enter later for the show.'

Sen nodded and looked into Wanda's eyes, like a scolded puppy.

He grabbed her hand and they walked away, a warm sensation of regret, being sent directly through their palms and making them feel comforted and close again. It always amazed them both, how deeply connected they became, with just simple hand holding.

It was the next best thing, to that skin-to-skin feeling, when hug pulled them close to each other in bed. Going to sleep and waking each morning to their warm body hugs, was high up on their list of life's greatest pleasures.

The night event was very much enjoyed but the shadow of that angry moment earlier, seemed to linger. Not just for the close to that day but also for most of the next. Wanda did the only thing she knew how, which was to try to behave as though nothing had happened. Singing, laughing and talking happy thoughts.

Spa townships of Hepburn and Daylesford, included a visit to the thermal baths early evening. Relaxing into the hot waters, added the required final ingredient, for coming back to their positive and energised selves.

Aroused and longing to please one another sexually and in any way possible, their deep love was again rising above all.

Gentle massaging with favourite oils, once back in their room, calmed and soothed as they eased themselves into slowly peaking sensations and restated feelings.

'I love you so much my darling. It's just horrible when there's distance between us. Whatever it was that I said to annoy you so badly, I'm so very sorry. My heart knows I can be the person you need me to be but sometimes my head is just too quick with going in the wrong direction.'

Wanda was at a loss to understand what it was that happened but she did truly regret it and sincerely wanted for a path to be created, that didn't lead to earthquakes, when things got annoying.

Knowing he wanted to delve deeply into the whys and wherefores, she tried to listen to him explaining how he had felt dismissed but to her, it was all just too negative.

What was the point?

How could she help him understand that it didn't matter if they got annoyed every now and then? The big thing was to not stay in an angry negative mood.

'You can't spend all the time together that we do and not have times of fall out. Let's just accept that it's going to happen and work on how best to let it pass more quickly.'

For Wanda, a change of subject was often the only way to move on.

'I was thinking we might take a bit of a detour from here, to cross one of the biggest mountain ranges and visit the ski resort of Falls Creek. What do you think?'

Sen didn't take too well to subject changes but could see he needed to.

'Sounds fine to me.'

Best if he didn't say anything further at that point and tried to sound positive.

They knew there had been disastrous fires in Victoria, as well as Tasmania, but no way did they realise just how bad!

Suddenly they could see up ahead, that the narrow mountain road, had completely given way!

Sheer drops to both the left and right of this disappearing road and, as they looked out to total blackness, across thousands of hectares of land, it wasn't clear they could make it through.

Turning wasn't an option they even wanted to consider.

So narrow and so incredibly high!

'There's a guy coming the other way in a four wheel drive. See him?'

Merely a dot in the distance but if he made it through, maybe they could too.

'He did it! And he's left a nice dirt track for us to sit in. Yay. I'll take it very easy but won't move an inch, until he gets past us.'

Easy does it. Just as well Wanda loved a bit of a driving adventure.

Finally they came to the resort town. It was summer and clearly not the normal ambiance for hikers but they thought there would be something open. Nothing!

Getting over the top of this ski range and down the other side was seriously frightening. The destruction seemed never to end and, added to that, they weren't sure their petrol would last much longer.

A little too much adventure now - bring on civilisation!

Finally they reached Omeo.

Phew! Huge sighs of relief.

'That was exciting. Not!'

Wanda's head was about to burst from the strain of it all.

'Let's get horizontal and chill somewhere. How about that massive old pub darling?'

Sen was soon inside, making arrangements for their night's accommodation and there they were, in yet another emotionally charged historical moment.

They had made it across the burnt out High Country and were in one of Australia's most intact pioneering villages, with heritage listed buildings second to none – and petrol.

Omeo to Lakes Entrance took them across rolling green hills, to the Pacific Coast, and the clear blue waters of Narooma became their last overnight stop, before returning to Sydney.

Climbing the rocky outcrop, at Narooma's small harbour entrance, they were entertained by one very large sunbathing seal. It was almost as if he was serenading them, as his back arched up high and he made his call to the wild.

Lou's apartment became home, for their last couple of days in Sydney.

Coming to the end of Sen's three month Australian trial, they reflected on what an amazing time it had been. Sen was totally wrapped and had no doubts at all, about coming back permanently. Fingers crossed they could make it all happen.

Not much longer and Wanda should be able to finish writing her novel too!

Talking about it with friends, at a farewell lunch, a quick decision had been made to look at self-publishing and call their venture Hug & Fug Books. Relaying that, to one of their creative friends, an offer was even made to design a logo.

'We are so incredibly fortunate my love. Fancy Bo jumping in over lunch, to say how much she would like to design a logo for us. It was as if she could see actual characters too, when we talked about our little Hug & Fug inner voices. Maybe she can design our special animated people for us too. She clicked into our thinking straight away. Can't wait to see what she comes up with. We are so blessed, to have all these wonderful talents supporting our efforts. Lucky us!'

Lou had spent much of the day before, working up a website for Sen to promote his island home. Marketing was Wanda's game. Surely they could get things moving with his Schier house. Wanda wrote some text and Sen added to it, then translated to Dutch. Lou soon knocked it into a simple web format, with both languages as options. Clever girl! They would take some photos when they got back and she would complete it.

He was glad Wanda hadn't suggested asking any of The Agency team to help out. Not that he had any problem with them but this was his thing together with Wanda and he really would rather keep it separate.

Lou stayed with Alex so Wanda and Sen could have her bed.

Any excuse!

The last evening was a quiet one, getting packed and working out what to leave in Lou's garage or to throw away or give to charity. Farewells had been said and it would be a very early flight so Lou opted for her own sofa that last night. No doubt Spike would be making himself comfortable right alongside her. His dog bed was on the floor but he knew what a pushover she was.

Turned out Alex was just as bad and the three of them, did a lot of cuddling up together so Spike was becoming one very spoiled little Chihuahua cross.

Lou had flatmates, who loved Spike too. How could they not? He was way too cute. They were ready to jump in and look after him, whenever Lou had to be away for work and their rent covered most of her mortgage so that was all working out brilliantly.

It filled Wanda's heart, to see Lou's life in such good shape.

Sen had taken to Lou as well and was also happy to see her enjoying everything to the full. Alex was a lucky guy and it was good that he seemed to know it. Not that Sen had ever seen Lou with anyone else but she and Alex were great together.

'Nothing is ever too much trouble for Lou is it? Can you believe what a great job she did creating that website for my house darling? She's so clever and such a delight to work with. It will make a big difference for holiday lets I'm sure, as well as giving us somewhere professional looking, to point potential buyers at.'

He had been going back and forth, with the couple who were supposed to buy his house. The two ladies had still not sold their place in Belgium but it seemed they had an apartment in Groningen now and were doing very well with their legal business there. Renting a very flash apartment and more than cashed up enough, to go through with the purchase of Sen's house. They could easily have rented out their house in Belgium until it sold. Not so easy to do that on the island. All sorts of rules and regulations impacted that. It was two years ago, they said they'd buy.

 Could they truly believe Sen should just wait for them indefinitely?

The very small amount they had given him, to hold his house for them, did not even go close to covering running costs, all this time. No contract was in place and the entire arrangement was totally open-ended in their favour. Before Wanda and Sen left for the three months in Australia, they met with the ladies to conclude matters. A contract of sale needed to be issued immediately, with a firm date for the normal 10% deposit to be paid – no later than when they would return in April. This had not happened and they were now not responding to any of Sen's communications so that was that. He would assign an agent to sell and forget all about these time wasters. Once they had Lou's website in place, they could promote heavily.

A bright sunny dawn lit their way to the airport, on that last morning in Sydney.

'No upgrade this time bubs.'

Wanda gave Lou a quick call, once they were all checked in for the flight to Seoul.

She was already at work by then.

The quick curb side drop-off, without long goodbyes, was how they liked it.

Lou was happy in the knowledge that they would soon have Sen's application in, for the long term visa, and be back in Sydney to make it their home.

'Great that they're giving us a free night's stopover though.'

Connection for the onward flight to Amsterdam, had a long layover in Seoul so the airline included a free transfer, hotel and dinner for one night. How great was that? Always liked to break the journey to Europe and this would do just nicely.

As it happened, the hotel was near a fascinating port and interesting park so they even managed to do some fun exploring.

'Interesting. I do believe they have an erotic cable television channel!'

They were back at the hotel, chilling out on their bed and surfing TV options.

'Umm. Can't quite make out who is doing what to whom.'

Laughter took over, as they both started to mimic some of the actions and it didn't take long at all, for the groans of pleasure coming from the TV, to be drowned out by the real thing!

It was the middle of April and a wonderful spring day, greeted them on arrival at Schiphol. Early colours, from endless fields of tulips about to bloom, were a sight to behold, as they looked down from their plane, coming in to land.

'Excited to be home darling?'

Wanda always felt like she was arriving home in Holland. Surely Sen must too.

'Ja. Mostly about getting everything finally in place, for making our new life in Sydney. Wouldn't it be great if we could sell both our houses here!? We can but try heh! Really excited to be picking up our enchanted red cabrio now my love!'

The young couple, looking after the much loved car, lived near Amstel Station. An easy train ride from the airport and in twenty minutes they would be there. With them having a new baby and all, Sen had emailed that he and Wanda could make their way to the house for cabrio collection. Wanda hadn't quite understood why one of them couldn't just as easily bring the car to the airport but never mind.

The walk to their house from Amstel Station was a short one but, with all the luggage, and not one taxi in sight, Sen decided to go alone and leave Wanda with the bags.

Again, Wanda didn't quite understand why someone couldn't at least come with the car to the station but whatever!

It made her think back to that evening at Ty's apartment and the feeling she got that the 'kids' acted a little like they were owed the kindnesses, that were bestowed upon them by Ty and Veet. Years earlier, Sen had apparently been caught up in it as well and he and Ty had covered the cost of an annual holiday retreat for everyone. As they all became adults and earned good livings, Sen had backed away somewhat.

It was nice that he wanted to loan the car to the new parents and certainly Wanda had no objection at all …. but…. she did think they might have made arrangements to pick them up, after such a long haul from Sydney. They had bought a gift from Australia for the new baby and she was looking forward to seeing their little offspring.

Sen ended up being much longer than anticipated.

Amstel is one of the largest transport hubs in Amsterdam. Buses starting their many and varied journeys around Europe, from this terminal too – not just the trains.

This was the very spot where Jay had been robbed years earlier; his backpack stolen from right under his legs, as he bought a bus ticket for London.

Not the nicest of places, to be left looking after so many bags.

Strange people wandered around in great numbers and Wanda soon started to feel uneasy. She couldn't help but think how quickly someone could bolt up and take off with their precious belongings.

Not much she'd be able to do to stop them.

Then she noticed one truly suspicious guy, who kept driving in and out, where the buses went. Totally prohibited of course but he didn't care. Another man kept going over to that same car, once it was out of the concourse area. A few words shared and then they'd go back to what they'd been doing earlier, driving around in the continuing circle.

This went on for most of the time Wanda was waiting.

What could they be up to?

She felt as though she'd been standing there all day and was beginning to get annoyed, never mind scared of what might happen.

It was as if this crazy pair, doing their circling routine, had read her mind and it became very apparent, their conversation part, began to focus on Wanda and her bags.

She must surely have some valuables in there, to be looking so concerned!

• CHAPTER THIRTEEN •

WANDA WAS CERTAIN one of the crazy men was headed her way and started conceiving her plan of action.

Would she scream for help? Should she lay herself across the luggage?

'There they are! Finally! My beautiful man and our incredible cabrio!'

Relief swooped over her and the nervous energy began to stabilise, as she told herself Sen would soon be whisking her away from this dreadful scene.

He had quite some navigating to do, to wind his way around and pick her up.

Waving furiously at him and shouting at the top of her voice, to ask if he wanted her move across, seemed to do the trick.

She was sure the crazy guy was headed towards her but, on seeing her gestures and observing Sen waving back, he quickly changed direction.

'So sorry darling. They thought you were coming too and had tea ready for us.'

Tea! Wanda was really in need of a cuppa now but Sen continued.

'I drank it quickly and did the required cooing over the baby. Very sweet of course. They loved the gift and sent a big thank you. Baby was going down for a nap so I said we would come another time. They wanted me to bring you back.'

Thinking about her possibly not behaving as friendly as she would normally like, she was happy with his decision. They would have tea once home.

'Good move darling. I really just want to get settled. Been super weird here.'

No point telling him how scared she was. All good now!

'Tomorrow I have a meeting at the radio station early, then we can drive up to Schier, if that works for you? I think my old show might have some story assignments for me.'

How lucky were they? Two homes for them to live in again and even work.

Hillywood had a couple of paying guests, which would help with running costs there. Holiday makers were starting to fill up the guest apartment at the island house too. Things could definitely be worse. The new website should help loads.

'Great. We can take the shots of the house and get them to Lou. The sooner we go live on the wide world of the web, the better.'

A close friend of Wanda's was having a big birthday party in London early June so they would be making every effort, to get all the final supporting paperwork for the Partner Visa application together before then. Having the Waterside address, allowed them to lodge via the UK and the plan was, to drop it all in to the Strand office themselves, when they drove across for the party.

Sen thought some of the certificates required, would be in his files on the island. Police clearance might take some time to get so that would be applied for straight away. He wasn't sure about his divorce papers and college diplomas.

Wanda loved being back in her Hillywood home and was delighted that she might soon be in the swing of her routine cycle to the bibliotheek (library) to write.

But first, a few days on Schier to get things moving with her first most important role – supporting the many things they had to accomplish together, if they were ever to hope of settling in Sydney.

It was as if their enchanted red cabrio was operating on remote control. Very happy to have its loving owners back and even more happy, to be driving through the stunning Dutch countryside again.

City life was not for it!

The young couple were also not that fussy so a wash was definitely called for. Sen made a quick call at the carwash centre, after his meeting at the radio station and their cabrio was soon gleaming from head to toe.

Motorway driving for Wanda's capable hands and, as soon as they hit the smaller roads, Sen would take over. A fabulously sunny day and down came the roof.

Cabrio cruising again. They loved it!

'Really very cool to be working as a journalist again. They were all raving about my coverage on that Dutch politician's visit to Australia. Now for two more very interesting assignments. One will take me to Zwolle initially, to interview a lady who came from China a great many years ago, with her very large family.'

It wasn't until they stopped for a break that Sen opened up for a chat. Wanda was fine with that and quite happily listened to music and enjoyed the drive. Such amazing scenery. One of her favourite spots was where fields of giant dancing windmills, met the wide open waters of the IJsselmeer.

How could people complain that these statuesque towers were a blight on the landscape? Gracefully spinning in sequence, as their arms stretched out to touch the sky, Wanda saw them as spectacularly choreographed ballet dancers. She would often stop the car, just to watch them slowly turn.

She was keen to ask Sen how his meeting had gone but was slowly learning that her questioning often irritated him and knew it was best to wait until he was ready to share.

'I'm looking at how the Chinese have settled in Holland and she apparently has a fascinating story to tell. So many great leads for interviews. Should be fun!'

As they relaxed and chatted over their prized extra-hot skim latte and applegebak, at a small village café not far from the ferry terminal, Sen was excited to relay everything that had been discussed earlier.

'The second assignment is in Rotterdam. This one is about a small theatre group and how their activities are making a big difference, to the youth of Rotterdam. Not sure about the best people to speak to yet so it's still in the formative stage.'

'Back to the land of the commune and his great many years there, as a young man,' thought Wanda. She was very aware that he still had a soft spot for that town.

'Fantastic! Sounds like you are going to be a very busy man!'

They went on to talk about progress so far with publishing things. Frustrated by unresponsive literary agents and publishing houses, Sen's efforts had re-focussed on self-publishing to get Wanda's first novel live.

'Online tools are amazing and look like even a computer illiterate like me, could get the book onto the big A. That said, I think we should use a graphic designer, at the very least, and make sure it all presents professionally. There are some people out there that specialise in this field so I'm researching all of those right now.'

Bo had nailed it with their Hug & Fug logo. It was exactly what they had in mind. Her enthusiasm for everything they were doing, was adding great impetus – as was Lou's. She had been acting in an editorial capacity for the book and was quick to give constructive feedback before it was handed across for professional editing.

Only four more chapters to write and Wanda was confident that wouldn't take too much longer, once she got her creative groove back.

What incredible weather!

They might even be able to take a swim in the ocean, on this visit to the island. A first for Wanda and she didn't recall Sen ever talking about swimming in that sea either.

A pity the cabrio had to stay on the mainland.

They hated leaving it in the garage, after such a short time since being reunited.

Seagulls gave a welcoming cry, as they stood on the ferry's top deck.

'This really is not my island anymore Wanda.'

Gazing out across the blue still sea, he hugged her tightly and smiled.

'Thank you for introducing me to our new island home of Australia darling. It's quite some island heh? Just a little bit bigger than this one!'

Quiet thoughts drifted back to the three month visit and how well everything had gone. They were both incredibly happy. Perhaps a little strained, when thinking about all the things they needed to do but, for now, just taking in the fresh sea air and hoping everything would soon fall into place.

As the island transfer bus approached Sen's house, a strange feeling came over them. His neighbour had been in to make sure all was well and freshen things up so everything should be fine. Maybe it was the daunting 'to-do' list.

'Wanda look! Tod is on our doorstep.'

It must have been their sixth sense, warning them something was up.

As Tod told his story, it was indeed an odd welcome home.

'Oh my goodness! We have our very own Noah's Ark!'

Wanda hadn't been listening to Tod, as his spoke to Sen in high speed Dutch, but they were quickly inside the kitchen and could immediately see to the end of the very long back garden.

Sen reeled!

He knew this boat was Tod's. What the hell was it doing in his garden?

Years back, Tod had recovered this once sunken treasure - a unique flat-bottomed vessel, especially created for shallow waters and very suitable for sailing the Waddenzee. Tod had made it his mission, to restore it to its former glory.

Farmer friends kept it on their different properties, until they became fed up.

Not a sign of any restoration work being undertaken and the boat just sat deteriorating.

Sen hadn't seen it for years.

Tod went on to tell him that the boat was at risk of the council removing it from the street in front of his government housing and scrapping it, then charging him a fortune for having done so. When his farmer friends had run out of patience, Tod had tried to hide the boat at the back of a trailer parking place. Hadn't taken that manager long to ask him to move it and front of house had been his only option.

She didn't say anything at the time but Wanda actually didn't mind the look of it, way down the back - sort of a very large object d'art. Much better than the old view to piles of used wood, now being blocked by the boat. Also a prettier sight than the orange container, that Tod already had in the garden, full of his and Sen's tools.

Sen was, however, not amused!

How dare Tod think he could just stick this eyesore on his land, without one word!

Tod knew Sen's neighbour was in regular contact and could have posed the question in an email. What a cheek!

No point getting angry with Tod though - little to be achieved with that. Instead Sen went to great lengths, to make him understand that the house had to be prepared for a new agent so they could get selling activated.

The boat had to go and had to go soon! So did the orange container.

Where on earth could he possibly stash these huge monstrosities?

The island was only 16kms long and 4kms wide and most of that was protected.

At least an hour of chats over tea, before Tod finally agreed to find them a new home, as quickly as possible. He'd also be happy to help get the house in order.

Wanda had her doubts but tried to reassure Sen that all would be well.

Meanwhile, the day was becoming even hotter.

Most unusual weather for April.

'Did you hear the forecast on the radio coming here? Temperature is set to drop dramatically tomorrow. Why don't we get into our swimmers and take a brave plunge into the ocean!'

Tod was all about making amends and suggested he leave his bike for Wanda to ride, while they were on the island, then he was on his way for the short walk home.

'I kept swim things in the small bag, in case the hotel in Seoul had a pool.'

And that had been the bag they packed for this island visit.

Excellent!

They were soon in appropriate attire and cycling through the village, to the beach.

Famed for being one of the longest in Europe, it stretched as far as the eye could see. Quite some distance to walk out, crossing small channels that the changing tides had carved into the sand. Wading through knee-high, the colder than cold waters were a good lead up to the real thing.

The plunge was indeed incredibly brave .... and exceptionally brief!

'It reminded me of the ice pool we had to jump into after the sauna in Switzerland. Years since I did that here Wanda. Do you suppose people think we're a little crazy?'

Sen enjoyed that thought, as they relaxed at the beach café and had lunch. Everyone that came over to say hello, took the opportunity to say something about Australia and his house. No secrets on this small island. They even knew about Tod's boat, now residing in the back garden.

The weather didn't wait until the next day to turn cold. By early evening, they were glad they still had loads of wood, to burn in the fire. Wanda had the knack of getting it lighted and loved that she had a task she could be useful with in the house. Sen was always frantically busy with absolutely everything and she often felt a little outside of things.

'I thought those certificates would be in that box but no luck I'm afraid.'

More to add to the list of forms to be completed, to get the visa paperwork they needed. First thing next morning, they began that long process and, as if that wasn't enough red tape, Sen also had to attend to urgent requests that were in the post for his Dutch tax returns to be completed. Not just one but two years and this was going to be some undertaking!

The very important task, of taking good photos and getting them to Lou, was set aside for Wanda. That would keep her amused for a while. First she would dress each area and try to get the lighting as good as possible.

'Great shots darling. You have a gift for photography!'

Sen chose his preferred images and they were soon being sent down line. Lou would be asleep when they arrived but had promised to get straight onto it. It wouldn't take her long to finalise the website. They could rely on her.

Being reliable was as important a trait to Lou, as it was to Wanda.

'That's it Lou. Fantastic!'

A skype call between Sen and Lou tightened up any loose ends in no time. He went on and on about how much he appreciated her work and, after the call, talked about sending her a thank you gift. She was always trying to find her jewellery so he decided he would find a special stand that she could display it all on.

'What a great idea. She'll absolutely love that.'

'When we are next in The Hague, I know just the store for us to find it in.'

They would be going to visit Sen's mother, before they went back to Hillywood so that would only be a few days away.

Their time on the island, moved into top gear and even included more wonderful discoveries. Lots of things Wanda's antiques dealer neighbour might be able to sell, plus loads of trips to the various rubbish points on the island. Only a couple of days but they were in full swing for the final sort out.

'Well, what do you know? I did a big email despatch to everyone I know, with the link to the website Lou's done for your house. My mate Bea, who lives between England and the beautiful French countryside, has fallen in love with your Seascape painting on the living room wall. She spotted it in one of the photos I took and wants to know if it's for sale.'

Sen's eyes lit up. He really could do with some decent money coming in and this painting should be worth quite a bit.

'Am I correct in saying it was painted by Bert?'

She was making notes, as she continued with the history she understood.

'Didn't he train with the famous Minerva Academy? Since he passed away, most of his works have been going up in price haven't they and aren't they quite the collector's item for serious art lovers now? He was actually from Schier wasn't he? Painted so many incredible works from around the island. Really had a sense of the nature and used soft colour tones that are simply striking.'

Quick to relay this to Bea, with an agreed price, she was soon responding in the positive and delighted to make her purchase. But first, what were the sizes please? She had a particular spot on a particular wall, that she wanted it placed. Sizes were immediately sent through but alas, the painting was too big!

'Bummer! Oh well, it got us prepared with information to support a sale. There must be loads of customer possibilities out there. Why don't we hang it in one of the restaurants that already have some of Bert's work?'

A great idea! Sen knew just the spot.

'Not only will he be happy to have the painting on show but he also thinks he knows someone who might be interested in renting my house.'

Sen's chat with the restaurant owner had come up trumps big time and another brainwave had even occurred. Why not promote the house as rent to buy? So many people had property to sell but wanted to move. He could rent his house to them until such time as they sold their place and were able complete the purchase of his. Rents paid, to be deducted from the agreed purchase price. And the restaurant owner had just the lady in mind! How incredible was that?!

Riding the ferry back to the mainland, they felt a great sense of satisfaction, for the things they had accomplished on their first short visit back to the island. Sunny weather had returned and they were excited to drive the lanes in their enchanted red cabrio again. Roof down of course!

New roads to explore this time and the route to mama's house would be quite different. For this two and a half hour journey, their cabrio would set off from Lauwersoog in the direction of Leeuwarden. They would wind their way through the province of Friesland and connect to North Holland, via the unbelievable 32km long Afsluitdijk.

'You are going to love this crossing. I believe it is one of the longest dike bridges ever constructed. Building started in 1927, for a dam to stop the North Sea where it met the Zuiderzee (South Sea), to create the fresh water lake of the Ijsselmeer and allow greater control over the waterways of Holland – much of which sits below sea level.

Another famous work from the architect Dudok, who designed many of Hillywood's historical properties. Besides the dike itself, there are also two complexes of massive shipping locks and a multitude of discharge sluices. A magnificent engineering feat. They took five years to complete it all. The views are stunning.'

Arriving at mama's apartment, they could see her sitting in the window, looking out for them. The broadest of smile, as usual, and she was over the moon to be seeing them, after their great adventure to the Land of Oz Hugs were intense but they were both mindful not too get her too excited, becoming ninety that September.

Age was not on her side, with a mind as sharp as ever but a body that struggled. Not that she ever liked to complain. Her life had been full and happy, with six beautiful children, ten grandchildren and even a few great grandchildren. The sad loss of Sen's dad, several years earlier, meant she lived alone. Still cooking and caring for herself but with help coming in twice daily. Very self-sufficient but also very well supported by family, she was a delight to be around and always happy to chat. Photos and stories were shared. Tales of their adventures, being soaked up with a passionate interest, in the finest of details. They had stopped to buy her favourite cake, at the bakers around the corner, and delighted in sharing that with tea and coffee. Other family called by during the afternoon and it seemed as though they ate and drank non-stop. Mama was tiring and so were they. It was agreed they should go so she could take an afternoon nap, leaving her happy in the knowledge that they would soon be back for another visit.

Once they returned to Hillywood, Wanda and Sen got busy with their separate challenges. It was good to have some space from each other.

Just four chapters to go and Wanda would finish her first romance novel. Getting back into her routine cycle to the library, was an enormous pleasure.

Sen had two radio assignments to get on with, just for starters. He set himself up at the desk in the living room and made sure coffee was always brewing.

Most days had been pure delight but there were also a couple of moments, when Wanda felt it was all becoming too much for Sen. Stress did not sit well with him and the snappy moods took over.

Any couple would feel the strain, with all that was going on in their world.

Wanda loved being on the island but short bursts were enough. She didn't have one friend there and always felt like people were staring and judging. Being back on her familiar turf, she knew she could always keep herself amused. Plenty of friends to catch up with and always something interesting happening in Hillywood.

Having space to themselves, made coming back together so much more fun, as was evident by the first night after a long day apart.

Sen had more than a delicious feast awaiting Wanda's return home.

'I thought we should try some new massage oils!'

Eyebrows were raised and his head tilted ever so slightly, as if to demonstrate one very big secret about to be unveiled.

Lifting her onto the kitchen bench, they kissed with a deeply sexual intent. Wanda's heart pulsed against Sen's and their longing moved to frantic desire.

The massage could wait!

They needed to fulfil the passion that was overtaking them. Wanda's legs wrapped around Sen, as he released the zipper on his jeans. Moving her underwear to one side, he was soon entering her wet and warm centre with his pounding erection. Heads moved backwards ever so slightly, giving them eye contact and a profound view into the depth of their emotions. Pulsing was slow and deep. Connected as one, they reached their peak of orgasm at the very same time. Heaven!

An amorous entrée indeed!

The days that followed were almost as fulfilling.

Amongst the huge list of things that were ticked off Sen's 'to-do' list, he put together an initial proposal for the TV series, that would tie in with the planned series of books Wanda was writing. Meetings had even been scheduled with old colleagues, at a big Dutch production house, to talk through the ideas.

Sen was on fire!

Real progress was being made with the Wanda's writing too and she had decided on an Estate Agent (Makelaar) to take on the sale of her Hillywood home. Now was the time to get things moving. Maybe this agent could even help with the sale of Sen's house.

'How great would it be to have buyers in place, by the time the Partner Visa was granted? Then we could move to Sydney, without having to worry about what was going on with houses in Holland. This agent lady sounds pretty sharp. Fingers crossed!'

Everything they'd read about how long the visa might take, was pointing to six months at the very least and that was from the date they lodged the application. The invitation to the birthday party in the UK for early June, gave them a target date for lodgement. So much easier if they could do it at the same time. They were making every effort but there were still so many bits and pieces to come in. Never mind. They would get there. At least it would be one big thing sorted, if this agent proved to be successful.

'She's coming over tomorrow with her photographer and a guy that does floor plans. Sounds organised.'

April 2013 was also when Queen Beatrix of the Netherlands, would fulfil one of her great desires. She would step down and give way to the heir to her throne, abdicating and handing the treasured crown, to her eldest son Prince Willem-Alexander of the House of Orange.

Wanda and Sen had made plans to join the festivities with Denise and her group of friends, thinking they would be in Hillywood. The entire country was preparing to come out on mass, bigger and better than any Queens Day ever.

Guests then booked into the island apartment and not one person could be found, to prepare it for them so Wanda and Sen decided to drive up and organise things themselves. Maybe they could get everything done quickly and return to Hillywood for the main event.

A sudden change in weather began to take its toll on Sen. Perhaps the ride across on the ferry hadn't helped. They so much wanted to be up on deck, enjoying the fresh sea air, and hadn't realised just how cold they were. Clothing may have been a little inadequate perhaps.

Next morning, signs of a cold appeared with Sen.

'Let's not go anywhere my love, until you're feeling better.'

Hot lemon drinks with honey and staying in bed with the paper. That would do the trick. Wanda could do some cooking for a change and look after her man.

'If you feel better, there is a sing-a-long at the hotel to celebrate the crowning. Maybe we can go to that. Sounds like fun. Or we can just watch it all on television.'

This would be no ordinary affair.

So much to see and maybe TV would be best.

The usual three-day party for Queens Day was always huge and stretched across all corners of Holland but this year, it would become an extraordinary pageant.

A new King to be crowned!

Such a unique occasion and no doubt it would have been great to join the throng and feel the atmosphere but, alas, it wasn't meant to be.

An estimated two thousand monarchs and dignitaries were scheduled to attend, from all over the world, and the party began with an incredible gala dinner event, the night before the crowning. Held at the treasured and recently reopened Rijksmuseum, guests were seated amongst famous artworks, with the outgoing Queen strategically placed in front of one of Holland's most precious works – Rembrandt's Night Watch.

Thousands of people crowded Dam Square for the momentous occasion that following morning. Hearing their much loved Beatrix declare …

'Today I make way for a new generation!'

Her people shed tears and burst into emotional applause, shouting …

'Thank you Queen Bea!'

As the sea of orange stilled, the new King was introduced by his mother. In years to follow, the Netherlands would celebrate Kings Day and that would be on his birthday 27th April. After three successive Queens, celebrations marking Queens Day would no longer take place.

'Thank you for giving the Kingdom thirty three moving and inspired years.'

Willem's own emotions were clearly strained, as he listened to his mother.

'We are intensely grateful.'

Turning to his people to also thank them, a loud cry came from the thousands …

'Long live the King!'

Television was, by far, the best place to be viewing all of these incredible proceedings that day. Cameras were moving from one part of Amsterdam to the next, across the countryside and across the world. Seeing and hearing what was taking place, could really only be done via this remarkable media.

Amsterdam's population was swelled, with eight hundred thousand visitors and the streets were brimming with partygoers. Trying to move around was clearly proving to be a nightmare for all.

Stars for the day, were the very cute young daughters of the new King and their beautiful Argentinian mother, the new Queen Maxima. Eldest daughter Catharina-Amalia, Princess of Orange, would become heiress apparent to the Dutch throne. A weighty undertaking, for this young nine year old.

Relaxing in the comfort of their soft sofa, with snacks and drinks, Wanda and Sen were happy this had accidentally been exactly the right way to take it all in. From early that morning until late that night, they stayed glued to the incredible events as they unfolded.

Two hundred and twenty five members of parliament took the oath, in support of the constitutional role of the Dutch monarch, at an incredibly historic swearing in ceremony.

Entertainers of the highest calibre, performed all over the country, with television taking Wanda and Sen from one fantastic show to the next.

They were enthralled to hear what the media had to say about it all. In particular, when talking about Prince Charles being in attendance with Camilla.

'People will perhaps recall Charles being at the coronation of Queen Beatrix, all those years earlier. Still no signs of his mother moving aside! The people of Britain are not looking at all keen on that!'

In her final speech to the nation, the Queen thanked the Dutch people again, for their support throughout her three decades of reign.

'Without your heart warming and encouraging signs of affection, the burden would have weighed very heavily.'

Coverage talked about the high security alert for that day. Not just against terrorists, who knew they could get decent mileage from impacting an event such as this.

Television viewers were reminded of the horrific happenings of 2009, when a would-be attacker of the Dutch Royal Family, drove his car into crowds watching them in a national holiday parade. Eight people were killed.

Months earlier, there had also been the senseless slaughter of innocents, with the Boston marathon bombings.

Over ten thousand police were on duty in the Dutch capital for this historic event but would that really be enough?

• CHAPTER FOURTEEN •

KING WILLEM-ALEXANDER of The Netherlands was crowned and the party went off without major incident. A great sigh of relief was breathed, by all concerned with its organisation.

Speaking of organisation …. Wanda and Sen were making great progress with certificates coming in and everything was looking good for an early June application.

Where did the time go? Just a few weeks of May left, until they drove to London.

Formats for television shows, were also coming thick and fast for Sen.

His creative juices were in flood mode!

The personal challenges he had experienced with selling his own house, sent him down one road for a TV show that would get to the core of a countrywide problem. Mixing reality television with a type of quiz show element.

'It's about changing blocked patterns of buying and selling property in Holland.'

Reminding Wanda how he had his own buyer, who was unable to move forward until they sold their property, they talked about the chain of actions and reactions that were the root cause of all things stalling the property market and, in fact, the Dutch economy.

'Looks like we might even get government money involved for this one!'

He was excited that his TV show would not only be attractive to viewers but also had the potential to make a big difference to a great many struggling people.

'So exciting darling! They were really quick to say they're keen to move forward. Clever you!'

Sen found it a little difficult to believe, as Wanda congratulated him on his success.

'I have to tweak things a little and speak to a few more people but they are going to pay me an upfront amount to get on with it. Let's celebrate!'

No need to ask Wanda twice. She was always ready for some fun.

'How about that restaurant in town I was talking about, where they do the 'surprise' feast?'

Great idea!

He would book for the following Friday night. Sunday was already locked in for a visit to his mum. How exciting to be able to share this great news with her too.

'Ty and Veet want us to come to their country house for lunch on Saturday to celebrate as well.'

'That was nice of them.' Wanda hadn't seen this second home yet and it sounded lovely. Out in the middle of the countryside and with some quaint villages nearby.

It was their escape from living in the centre of Amsterdam and a renovation project.

Mother's Day in Holland, took place the same day as it did in Australia. Lou had organised Jay and made sure a package arrived for Wanda in time. She loved to make a fuss of her mum and got all gushy, with soppy cards that spoke of Wanda being the best mum in the world. Very sweet!

'Oh lucky me again! Look what I got. Stevie Wonder CDs and a framed photo of the four of us on Australia Day. So thoughtful! We'll be on skype tonight but I'll send a quick note of thanks now, before we go.'

Sen organised gifts to take for his mum. To most of the family, she was Mama An and that was how Wanda referred to her as well. He had great taste and had bought special things for her diary writing, plus the most spectacular floral arrangement.

Didn't stay too long with Mama An. Always mindful of her tiring quickly, a couple of hours were more than enough. Two cups of tea and way too much to eat. She was particularly delighted to hear of Sen's positive experience with his television show formats. She knew how hard he had worked over the years, to get his great ideas out there. Now the first one was being taken up. It had been a very special visit indeed. Hadn't quite worked, to catch up with any of his brothers and sisters though but they would see them again soon no doubt.

'Mama An was thrilled with your gifts darling. It's so lovely how her face lights up and she purses her lips, to pause before expressing what she wants to say.'

They were in the car now and heading into the central area of The Hague, to find the store that Sen had in mind, for buying a gift for Lou.

'Yes. I really think she did. That cake you bought was perfect too. Telling her about our 'surprise' dinner on Friday was precious. The way she wanted to understand how every morsel was presented and what each taste did to our pallets. How fantastic was that meal! Umm...so Lekker! Didn't you just love being able to choose fish or meat and wait and see what came out? Four courses of pure imagination on a platter. I loved those black slates they served everything on.'

Wanda confirmed her equal pleasure at all the taste experiences shared, as they pulled up in front of one amazing shop of treasures.

'And look! Lucky us yet again. A parking spot!'

Mission to purchase one jewellery stand was accomplished but not before eyeing up absolutely everything in this stunning store.

'That is so perfect you clever man. Lou is going to love that. What an incredible shop! Pity we didn't find something for Bo but I'm thinking it might be a good idea to get her an eReader maybe.'

Bo was not only designing them a logo for their Hug & Fug publishing activities, she was also going right into the branding possibilities and looking at illustrations for the two characters. It looked highly likely that she might even help with book cover design and internal layout too. Quite some challenges with differing eBook formats and then for print, it would all be different again. None of it seemed to faze Bo but they had agreed to just take things a step at a time.

First to finish writing the book!

Wanda was convinced she could crack that, before the month of May was out!

Up bright and early each day, she would cycle to the library and get focussed on her authoring skills.

Sen was busy with so many things, including chasing down different angles, for his story on the Chinese settling in Holland. The Zwolle connection had not turned out as fruitful as hoped but a couple of other avenues presented themselves, which looked interesting.

It was becoming a bit of a struggle though and, at times, it seemed to Wanda that she was not helping.

'There I go again. Too many questions and I've managed to annoy him. Back off big mouth!' she would scold herself.

When would she learn?

His whole face would change, as the angry man took over. Jumping on the smallest detail and making Wanda feel like an idiot for saying what she had. The more she tried to explain that maybe he had taken it the wrong way, the more of an argument they seemed to get into.

An acupuncturist, Wanda and Sen had been to, suddenly added a new twist to his story. Her grandparents emigrated from China, almost one hundred years earlier, and they were happy to share information about that and give an overall general view.

Many of the Chinese, arriving in the Netherlands early 1900s, worked for low wages on steamships, often as stokers. They resided in boarding houses in Rotterdam and Amsterdam, in between sailings, and the manager of the house, usually acted as shipping master. First stoker would be main contact person for the group. Simply called 'number one', he was often the only one in the team who spoke a bit of English or, more rarely, a bit of Dutch. House managers contracted with number one. Chinese stokers were paid 70% of a Dutch sailor's earnings and 90% of that went to the shipping master for mediation, board and lodgings.

As steamships died out in the 1930s, men began to be laid off. Some sold peanut biscuits on the streets and a few started Chinese Restaurants. With no legal status or support, the Dutch government also sent many people back to China. Those who remained active in the Netherlands, after the difficult years of World War II, were almost exclusively involved in the restaurant business. During the period of post-war reconstruction, the great rise of the 'Chinese' began in earnest. According to a norm established by the Ministry of Economic Affairs in 1980, it was deemed that every Dutch town or district with more than 10,000 inhabitants should have its own Chinese restaurant.

'That's so interesting and the people you have lined up, to talk through all of this in the interviews, are going to make this story truly special. Good one!'

Sen was pleased with how it was all coming together too.

'Thanks darling. Sorry I've been a bit grumpy with it all. Happy about it now though. Love you!'

A pleasant few days were planned for the island, with Sen being ever so excited to be introducing Wanda to the magical Kallemooi Festival.

'You have never experienced anything like this my love. A little weird to some but I think you will get it. This is only happening on Schiermonnikoog and it's a huge part of island folklore.'

Seven Sundays after Easter, Christians celebrate the coming down of the Holy Spirit - Whitsun to the English, Pinkster to the Dutch. Kallemooi is a part of that and tradition calls for an eighteen metre high mast, to be erected in the village green.

A green branch is tied to the very top and the Dutch flag hung below, with a banner proclaiming 'Kallemooi'. Directly under that, sits a large basket containing one stolen rooster with its bread and water rations, to last it the next couple of days. One special island child, having been selected to steal said rooster and place it in the basket in the darkest hour of night. As midnight struck, several strong villagers, wearing top hats, raise the heavy basket high up onto the mast.

It is said that the 'steal' gives the ceremony magical powers and that the rooster itself, is a symbol of fertility.

Then the three day party begins. Special songs and adults enjoying a little too much drinking, at the island watering holes. Children taken for rides around the island, in horse-drawn painted farm wagons reflecting earlier times, when this spring event heralded fertility of the crops. Traditional games and competitions held for the children over two days, on the village green.

On the third day, the entire island community gathers at the base of the mast, for the ceremony to retrieve the stolen rooster - a procession of children, then return it to the rightful owner. A large group of strong men then lay down the tall mast and carefully remove it to safe keeping, for the following year.

Sen also busied himself with more sorting out of newly discovered boxes. Finding old photos, would take him off to thoughts of times gone by. Occasionally he would share a story with Wanda but she generally felt better, leaving him to it.

Cycling around the island kept her busy. Not such a big land area perhaps but she always managed to find a new discovery.

'When you finish that box, why don't you come for a little cycle with me? I guess you will have seen this already but I would really love to share it with you.'

Once they were on the wooden path, he knew exactly what she had found.

'Quietly now!'

It was a hidden viewpoint that stretched out over the pond. All manner of water birds made their nests around it and you had to silently observe or they would be quickly frightened off.

Wanda and Sen sat in total silence, enjoying every second of this special ambience. Hug was in both their ears and very happy indeed. Such peaceful sights and yet so much was taking place in the reeds. Families of wildlife, all busy with nesting and recreation. They explored nature's tranquil power for over an hour, before deciding to head for their coffee and applegebak.

'How about a cycle to the other side of the island after this?'

Sen could see how much Wanda was enjoying him being out and about with her and there was still a great many things he could excite her with, around the island.

That was a great day. Laughing and holding hands, as they cycled side-by-side. Quickly changing to single file, when cyclists coming from the opposite direction, needed to pass. They must have covered at least twenty kilometres.

As the afternoon warmed, they found a cosy spot at a beach café and cuddled up with a glass of wine and some tasty bitterballen with mustard.

'Let's stay here forever my love. Just holding one another and feeling the sun on our backs, as we enjoy an excellent glass of red.'

Wanda was in heaven and felt absolute gratitude for having her amazing man.

'One slight problem with that. I have this little devil Fug getting in my ear.'

Sen gestured in a way Wanda immediately understood, that he needed to step beyond the realms of hugging. He was hot to trot!

'Maybe we can find a nice spot in the dunes my darling and become horizontal.'

And so they did!

Kissing and cuddling in a tiny nook, out of view from passers-by. Amazed at how they could manage to fully connect their bodies, without having to fully remove even one piece of clothing! Expediting orgasms silently and falling to rest, feeling complete and contented.

The week that lay ahead would be challenging, as they hoped the last certificates would arrive, but they had Wanda's birthday to look forward to at the end of it.

'Great to be seeing these people but I'm not sure I'm ready.'

Back in their enchanted red cabrio, they were en route to Hillywood again.

Sen had done his part of the driving and Wanda was now in the fast lane, for the motorway section. Time was a bit short, if they were to make the meeting Sen had at 5pm.

'Your ideas are clearly explained and I think they're more than enough to demonstrate where you're headed. Nice for them to be able to contribute with strategy too don't you think? Plenty there for feeding a discussion.'

He was not pleased. She didn't know these people and had not one clue as to what their expectations were. How could she even consider that she might?

Whoops! She had gone too far again. But was that attitude really necessary?

Wanda found Sen's persona a bit rude and immediately decided to just not say anything. She felt as though he was treating her like some dumb blonde, who was speaking out of turn.

The silence was deafening!

Dropping her at the house and unpacking things from the car abruptly, he was soon on his way - a quick and fleeting farewell, dotted by an even quicker kiss to the cheek.

'Wow! That was unpleasant!' she told herself.

Returning from the meeting, Sen found Wanda watching a silly program on TV and decided he would just go and sit in the garden. Brief hellos having been exchanged but not another word said.

'Shall I cook some dinner?' Wanda tried to appease and not ask how it all went.

'I prefer to cook,' he replied sharply.

An hour later, they sat eating in front of the television, not saying a word.

The next morning Wanda was up early and off to the library. This would be her day to finish writing the last chapter of the book, if she could overcome feeling distracted by Sen's unhappy mood. It cut her deeply to the core and made her question how he could suddenly become so angry. When these times hit, she even questioned how he could actually even love her, to behave in such a way.

Library brunch consisted of her favourite freshly squeezed orange juice and a toastie, while she read over the last couple of chapters.

Eventually, she managed to close all negative thoughts out and get down to business. She amazed even herself, how strong the positive energy was within. Right throughout her life, it had lifted her up and beyond so many bad moments that might have dragged her down. Reminding herself of all the great times she spent with her perfect man, she was acutely aware of that word 'perfect'.

Maybe that was it? Sen was just so right for Wanda in so many ways but of course no-one was ever perfect. They had so much going for them and no relationship ever existed without ups and downs. It was maybe because the ups were so unbelievably incredible, that she felt so bad with the downs. They stood out too much. Her expectations were way too high and she needed to get real.

Checking her email, she was delighted to find that her good friend Bea had made contact. Wanda had written to friends in London, about catching up when they visited in a couple of weeks. Bea was responding well, with what was sounding like an even better plan!

'We won't be in London then but why don't you pop on down to the French country house for a few days. Nile and I would love to see you and finally meet that handsome man of yours.'

They had the most stunning property near Cahors. Wanda had visited a couple of times before. The last time, being with her brother Joe and Lou, on their big drive around Europe in that green Italian wagon. What an incredibly beautiful part of the world. Being able to cruise those French lanes in their enchanted red cabrio, would be very special indeed. She would forward the email to Sen and ask what he thought.

It was the night before her birthday and still Sen was locked into a sulk. No sooner had Wanda walked in the front door, than he was off finding something else to do around the house.

Apart from forwarding Bea's suggestion, she had emailed him the last chapter of her book and put an excited note with it.

Maybe he hadn't seen them yet?

Surely they would make him happy and help bring him back from the mood.

Wanda went to bed alone and drifted off into a tearful sleep.

How to fathom all of this?

Normally, they made a point of always going to bed together. It was something Mama An had even been clear about. One very important thing to keeping a couple connected.

Not much sleep that night. Sen keeping to his side of the bed and she to hers.

With the new dawning came a whole new world!

Lang zal je leven in de glorius was being sung out loud, as Sen made his way up the stairs to their top floor bedroom.

It seemed as though Wanda had only just fallen to sleep.

She hadn't even been aware of him leaving the room and here he was, singing happy birthday in Dutch and laden down with gifts and a cake sparkling with candles ablaze.

Wanda's head span. That's what he had been organising when she went to bed!

He did love her!

Now she was being very spoiled and Sen was happy and smiling, with an array of different packages all beautifully wrapped. Three of them contained packets of seeds, to plant in the garden. One for tomatoes, to replenish the old plant that had fed them so well and then deceased. Then Lavender, to help out another, that was not doing so well. On entering the house, they often pinched the Lavender, to enjoy its relaxing aroma. Lastly Morning Glory, which gave forth a pretty little blue flower.

Unwrapping continued and she discovered the next gift had stickers to go on the car headlights, for driving in the UK, on the wrong side of the road. She had never bothered with those before but it was good to do the right thing. Sen thought of everything.

Heart shaped cookies were in the next package. So beautiful!

Then finally, the most perfect dress. It fit so well and looked great!

Quite clingy, in a soft black fabric with an assortment of coloured flowers. How brave to choose such a gift and how lovely was his choice.

A very special card accompanied the gifts and on the envelope he had written 'to my diamond wife' and finished off with four pink hearts.

'I love it all! Most of all, I love you! So so much!'

Those last couple of horrible days drifted into oblivion and they were once again, the happy and romantic couple that they could be. Sen had a plan for the day, that he felt confident Wanda would enjoy. It started with breakfast in bed, followed by a fun train ride to Amsterdam. A delicious lunch at the Opera House, then to sit in the sun, looking onto a main canal, for afternoon tea and some great people watching!

Sen's mother had called during the morning and sung to Wanda in English. His brothers and sisters all sent lovely messages. Emailed good wishes were plentiful.

Lou had booked theatre tickets for them to see 'Wicked' in London and sent the voucher by email. Jay emailed a beautiful message, having arranged a dinner, to take place before the theatre.

The love could not have been more plentiful.

She felt overwhelmingly blessed!

Sen was thrilled that Wanda had finished writing her first romance novel and was sorry he hadn't responded to her message with enthusiasm yet. He only saw it late the night before. Also quickly saw Bea's note. How fantastic to drive down to France, after they got everything done in London and enjoyed the birthday party.

Now they could really swing into top gear, with everything to do with the book. Wanda had an editor lined up to cut into it, as soon as the first runs had been finished by Sen and Lou. Work on chapter and character summaries was also under way. The next big thing for her, was to target a large automobile sponsor. How better to promote to their customers, then through romantic travel and family tales of life well lived with their beautiful cars.

Rotterdam interviews got under way for Sen's radio story, which also gave Wanda an opportunity to explore that exciting port city some more. No point him taking the train. She would happily drive him down the motorway and head off, while he had his meetings. When he finished, he could show her the town he loved. She'd been there a few times for big concerts at the enormous Feijenoord Stadium.

Memories came flooding back, to the spectacle that was Marco Borsato's concert back in 2004. This incredible entertainer sang only in Dutch and yet, managed to sell out the fifty one thousand capacity stadium, four times over. His audience hung off every song and knew all the words, singing louder than any earlier football fans to the venue, ever had. Wanda had known some people in the business and managed to get herself invited into the special VIP area. She too was a big fan and was up singing and dancing the entire night. The concert was made even more special, by his being granted the Order of Orange-Nassau for his services to Dutch music and his acclaimed fund raising efforts, on behalf of the War Child cause.

Sen showed her all his favourite spots and, on one visit, they also went to see his brother at work. He was a chef on the magnificent SS Rotterdam Cruise Ship Hotel.

Unfortunately, his brother wasn't working that day. Bad timing on that one. Never mind. Drinks were ordered on the front deck of this historic restored steamship and they took in stunning views that highlighted the non-stop flow of sea traffic on the wide River Maas. As a main connector to the Rhine, it served Europe's largest port well and helped Rotterdam become famous as the gateway to the continent.

'Why don't we take Bea up on that offer darling? It's looking like I will have both of my radio assignments completed this week and that guy on the phone, assured me he has posted the last of the certificates we need for the visa application. All the things we are doing with the book and TV shows, can be done from anywhere.'

Sen was absolutely right. There they go again. Lucky them!

Once Wanda had made arrangements with Bea, another London friend jumped in.

'When I emailed everyone we're catching up with in London and said we would drive to France after the birthday party, Jan and Cat came straight back to say we should also visit them in Spain. Only another thousand kilometres!'

Why not?

If there master plan came to fruition, they would be living way over on the other side of the world, without such easy access to the wonders of Europe.

Their enchanted red cabrio would relish the journey and all the new adventures that came with it. With Wi-Fi and their computers, they could work from wherever in the world.

As Wanda always said, life was for living – today!

You never know about your tomorrows.

The agent would be happy to have a nice clear Hillywood house to show prospects. Drawing up the contract for sale had been interesting. It needed to be in Dutch and English so Sen helped with translating crucial bits. The weather was on their side and the agent seemed hopeful that she might secure a buyer quickly. How cool would that be? No house guests anymore and the mortgage was crippling.

'When the book is clear of editing, we should have that translated too don't you think?'

Wanda was most impressed with Sen's speedy response to the agent for text.

'At the very least, to have it in Dutch for your mum. How amazing is she, about my writing? All those journals she's kept over her almost ninety years. She told me she had a dream to one day use them to write a book about her memoirs. That day passed a long time ago, with her eyes failing. Wish I had a good command of Dutch and could read them. I know you have at different times and you've shared many of the stories with me. So great to have them for the family to treasure forever. Her excitement for my writing, is such a compliment. I'd love for her to actually be able to read it all printed up and bound someday.'

Sen had already been investigating translators. Not just for Dutch but for Spanish too. Other than Chinese, which presented an entirely different set of challenges, it would be the language that delivered the most potential readers. India had enormous volumes but fifty percent of those readers were happy with English.

Dates were checked out and confirmed, as a grand tour of Europe fell into place.

'Fantastic! It's here! Certificate pains now concluded!'

Passing the envelope to Sen, Wanda had suspected it was the post they had been waiting for. Their office had been adamant, it was sent ten days earlier. Even trying to go there, to get another copy, hadn't been acceptable. It was in the post and that was that.

'Excellent my love! All we need now is to get a few of the documents signed by a Justice of the Peace. We're staying at Netty's in Richmond the first couple of nights. She's sure to know a JP. We should get there early evening so hopefully we can arrange it to be done that night. The following morning, we jump on the tube and head to Australia House. From all the forums I've looked at, they reckon late morning is the best time to rock up. Not that you are guaranteed anyone will see you. Should be posting everything in but the peace of mind factor is huge, if we can see someone has received it all. How big is the file now?'

Months of hard labour had gone into getting everything into that file. Reading it all over and over again, they had several occasions when new discoveries were made. Interpretation was all and many of the guidelines were as foggy as a bleak winter's day in London. Thinking you fully understood the requirement and then realising you missed a key element. Finally each and every piece of the puzzle was in place and they were almost ready for the visa application to be lodged. A few more photocopies, the JP signatures, et voila!

Servicing had been carried out on their cabrio and they were ready for more enchanted adventures, starting with one night in Bruges.

'What a spectacularly beautiful city Bruges is. Let the fairy tale begin!'

Just over two hours drive and they had parked beneath their hotel, bags were in the room and they were on hotel bikes, setting out to see the sights. First stop, waffles with chocolate sauce and strawberries, in the medieval main square.

Romance could not escape any loving couple, on a visit to Bruges.

'The beauty of this city, is only surpassed by the beauty of you my darling.'

Sen gazed into Wanda's eyes with total sincerity and declared his undying love. Discovering Bruges together, had captivated their imaginations on so many levels. Concluding with live music, at a bar next to their hotel, added the final animation. Sen spoke softly into Wanda's ear, mentioning each part of her body that he wanted to touch, lick, kiss. Fug was in play but Hug was mellowing his approach somewhat.

'Shall we sleep with the thoughts and awaken to action?'

Wanda understood.

Talking about making love, could be even more exciting than the moves themselves. It was quite common for Sen to wake with an erection. Filling their minds with pathways to putting that to good use, would be erotic. Words and gentle touches drove them crazy for each other that night. They would sleep on those words and dream about what was to come. And come they did!

What an amazing way to start the day.

Lusting after each other, even before their eyes were open!

'I've never been up in that northern tip of Flanders and we have a few hours.'

The ferry was not far away so why not put the morning to good use. Brilliant sunshine and just the sort of day to cruise along the coast in their cabrio. The N34 road travelled right beside the sea and it was a great day for it. Looked like it might only add an extra hour to their journey. Small roads so Sen would do the driving.

'We should be seeing the sea by now. I don't understand. Maybe we took a wrong turn. I can't see the name of this town anywhere on this map.'

Wanda never lost her way but getting out of Bruges had confused them both.

It was starting to get to Sen and the fuel was running low.

'I'm just going to take this next turn. A sign suggested there might be a petrol station.'

Angrily stopping at the wrong tank, he jumped into the car and roughly manoeuvred over to the unleaded.

Bang and scrunch!

An almighty sound of metal on metal!

• CHAPTER FIFTEEN •

ONE PETROL CAP completely ripped off! Horror of horrors! The beloved enchanted red cabrio was wounded!

'Could've been worse! It sounded like we hit the tank. Not a mark on the body of the car and a totally clean break so I'm sure we can get it replaced OK. Still has the plastic inner cap so the petrol's not about to splash out.'

Gathering up screws and bits, Sen safely stored the remnants.

The good news, was they weren't as lost as they had thought they were.

Petrol kiosk attendant not only gave them an easy and very short set of directions to reach the coast; he also suggested a parts place on the way that might have the replacement petrol cap they needed. It had to be the right colour of course and he suspected that might be our main challenge. Not being the latest model car, it might have to come from a wrecking yard.

That drive along the coast was worth the effort. Neither of them had travelled it before and were enthralled by what they found. Would definitely come back with more time. Ostend was of particular note for a decent explore.

Unfortunately no luck with the petrol cap so they would need to do some research on that. One wrecker near the Dunkirk ferry looked promising but alas, the fit was not quite right.

'Lots of Dutch goodies for you and the girls – and for the remarkable Narley, we have his absolute favourites. I guess he might want a taste

237

of the stroop waffels too.'

Netty was thrilled to have them to stay and excited to share the great news that their gorgeous Cocker Spaniel, Narley, had been given the all clear that very day. His treatment was working and the cancer was now at bay. What a relief!

'He's never actually looked ill at all. Just got slow so I had him checked over.'

A simple blood test, close to a year earlier, had revealed the dreaded disease. Netty spared no expense to have him attended to by a top Vet Oncologist and he'd been saved. Something of a small miracle!

It was June and they were on their way to lodge Sen's application for the Partner Visa that would allow them to set up a permanent home together in Sydney. The stress of getting to that point, was beginning to show. Both of them were snappy that morning. Netty had thought her neighbour could witness as a JP but wasn't aware she had gone away. They needed to find someone in town, before they could go to Australia House. More photocopies had to be done too.

'OK. That's done.'

Wanda could feel every muscle in her body twinge. She just wanted it all to be over and not to have to think about this application for a while. Surely it must all be in order!

'Let's head into the Aldwych and have a coffee, now we have all that done. Somewhere we can sit quietly and do one last review of everything.'

Sen was keeping very quiet that morning.

He was nervous and so was Wanda.

The moment was finally upon them. Where on earth were they supposed to go in? This was nothing like the Australia House Wanda remembered from when she first came to London back in the 70s. That had been huge open and more than welcoming spaces. This was a buzzer with a security guard on the other side!

Times had most definitely changed.

Finally they were spoken to through an intercom. After much questioning, they were in. Only one counter open but there was just one person in front of them.

'You need another copy of this document.'

Their hearts sank!

The counter assistant must have sensed their dismay and quickly offered to copy it there and then. She could even witness it, as she was a JP. If only they had known. A few more minutes of her going through each and every page and they were on their way.

'I can't believe it. It's done! Clever you, working out the best way for us to do this. She said that I should hear from my 'Case Manager' quite soon but some visas are taking nine months to come through. Wow! It's in. We're on our way!'

So many months to get to this, they were both in a state of post-traumatic stress.

'Our mission for the rest of this day is to have fun fun fun and seek out new discoveries in London. We have to be at the theatre by 7pm, to collect the tickets Lou bought on line. Wicked is supposed to be fantastic. What a great way to finish off this special day. Jay didn't end up booking that restaurant so we can go wherever we like. He'll cover the cost. Still enjoying my birthday presents. How fortunate am I?'

Deciding to venture out to the new cable car across the Thames, they made their way to the underground. An unusually sunny and warm day. Near the cable car entrance, was a fun café with deck chairs. They would relax there first and have a celebratory glass of wine with some lunch.

What was it in that conversation, that triggered an angry mood in Sen?

'How could he get like this on such a special day?' thought Wanda to herself.

Even the thought of holding his hand, when they finally got up to take the cable car ride, made her body grip with tension. She wanted to be away from him and could not even look into his face. Why this? Why that? He was relentless. They were both in recovery from visa stress and this was not helping.

Arriving at the theatre, things had not changed one bit and Wanda was at a loss to grab hold of her positive self. Sarcasm turned to silence. They watched the performance but neither one really took much of it in.

The rest of that week had highlights of good moments shared with friends, where conversation was animated and everyone was adoring Sen and remarking on what a great couple they were.

Their behaviour with each other was anything but adoring!

Contemptuous might be a more appropriate word!

Could it be justified by the stress release factor, from all that had gone into getting them to this point? Wanda was missing her children and wondering what she was doing with this man, who seemed only to want to criticize and judge everything she said. No matter what it was about. She hadn't even been into The Agency, for fear it would make him feel uncomfortable. That was fine. It was the choice she made.

Sen was feeling overwhelmed and wasn't sure what he was letting himself in for. He felt that he could not ever say the right thing, at the right time. Nobody really cared what he thought anyway, as far as he could tell.

The birthday party was the last strain, during that visit to the UK. Wanda had played in a band with the birthday boy and thought Sen would brighten up, when he saw the room full of guitars they had. He did for the moments other people were present but, as soon as it was just the two of them, the atmosphere turned to ice.

Birthday boy was Kikki's brother and she was beside herself with excitement, to finally be meeting the man of Wanda's dreams. The fact she missed him on that fateful day Wanda and Sen met, was always something she regretted. Signs she had been making, to sell the car, clearly helped attract Wanda's neighbour and led to him telling Sen. Her part in the magic that brought them together was apparent and noted. They all laughed, when they recounted the events of that day. Was it only nine months ago?

The man of her dreams indeed. Her secret thought at that time, was to wonder if he was becoming the man of her nightmares!

She was at a loss to know how to change things.

Straight from the party to the chunnel train crossing. Nothing pre-arranged for accommodation that night, not knowing if they would make the time booked. The train ticket had flexibility so they would just see how they felt and stop at a motorway accommodation wherever.

'I'm really not happy. Can we find somewhere to park please?'

Wanda was aware of her body vibrating throughout and it wasn't because of the train ride. Sen was also looking really upset and the ten minutes it took to find a place to pull up, once clear of the port, seemed to take a lifetime.

'We can't say a civil word to one another and I just can't go and stay with more friends, pretending we are happy. My head doesn't know if it's coming or going and my stomach feels like it wants to throw up.'

As the volume of Sen's questions got louder and louder, Wanda eventually stopped trying to answer and, instead, put her hands over her ears. The ringing in her ears was unbearable!

If she had been sitting at the wheel, she would have started the drive back to Holland and sent a text to Bea to say they had to change plans.

Instead, she got out of the car and walked off around the large open car parking area. They were high on a hill near Calais and it was a warm summer night. Lights from the town flickered in the distance.

Finding a quiet spot to sit, she tried to focus only on those flickering colours and take her mind to a peaceful place. Meditation was not a forte but she had her own technique for finding a point and gazing, as she thought only about her deepening breath.

Half an hour passed before Wanda felt calm enough to move back to the car. She quietly spoke of wanting to head for Holland but Sen was not having it.

'You don't understand what you do to me but I know you don't want to talk about it now - or maybe even ever. You think it is only negative and can't see the point but I feel we need to learn to understand what happens.'

Moving to hold her hand as he spoke, Wanda could only pull away.

'Please let's continue with this great trip we have planned. I will find the nearest hotel and we can get some rest. Maybe talk about it again in the morning. It's been a huge week,' he concluded.

Half an hour later, they were at a roadside inn. Everything was automated and they were swiftly allocated a room by the machine. Both quite exhausted, they fell to sleep in no time, without one more word being spoken.

Wanda was acutely aware of feeling super sensitive, when she woke that next morning. Sen was critiquing the poor state of things at the lodgings and once again, she felt that whatever she said, he was just waiting to pounce with a negative comment. Not able to raise one ounce of positivity, Wanda was at bursting point again.

'I'm going for a drive! Really need to be away from you!'

Anger was taking her over and she hated herself for it. Her entire life, she had made sure she didn't stay around people who made her feel bad. In the shallowest of terms, she would refer to cutting people off, because it stopped being fun.

This was way beyond anything she had ever allowed herself to be caught up in.

Who was this angry person that she had become?

Driving too fast, around the industrial area near the hotel, she realised she had to stop and park to breathe and let it go. Next thing she knew, a police car was stopping beside her. What was she doing there? All in French of course! Fortunately she understood and could reply simply, that all was well. She was just resting and was about to leave.

'*Tres bien et bon voyage madam!*'

What was wrong with her?

She needed to give herself a good shake and get out of the clouds. Did she or did she not want to spend the rest of her life, with this person she thought was the man of her dreams?

OK. He wasn't perfect. She sure as hell wasn't either.

How could she stop overreacting so badly?

Tolerance had gone out the window but she was better than that.

What was she missing in all of this?

She always believed the reason was you, when things were not going as they should be, so what the hell should she be doing with herself?

Going back and forth to Australia, with the intensity of thought being solely around making a new life with Sen - everything happened at such a fast pace.

It was magical and marvellous but the stress factor was taking its toll.

'Just be!' she told herself. 'Stop the thinking for a while and just be!'

Sen was anxious about her whereabouts and pleased to see her smiling, as she pulled into the hotel reception area. He had been waiting with their bags for a while.

The road, towards Bea's house, was travelled quietly and a country farm was chosen for an overnight stop, to break the journey. Icy conditions between them, had been ever so slightly melted, with hand holding.

'Such a beautiful place and we are surrounded by amazing art and stunning farmlands. I love you so much. Please let's stay on track for sharing our life happily together. We must surely be able to stop the madness that takes us over too often.'

Sen's eyes watered as he said this and grabbed Wanda into a strong embrace. Her face rested on his shoulder and she too was weeping. Hug kept them in that hold for some time, while Sen gently ran his fingers through Wanda's hair and rolled his hand across her shoulder, to ease tensed muscles.

'I love you too. So very much. I'm so quick to lose sight of the magic that is us and let myself be too intense, with all the things going on in our life. I'm so sorry my handsome and beautiful man.'

'No. I am the one who is sorry. I just don't know what happens to me.'

This was the Sen she cared so much for.

'It grabs me and I am lost to it but I know I want nothing more, than to be happy with you.'

The romantic farmhouse had a very large bath, which they soaked in together until every tense spot in their bodies was warm and relaxed. A nice bottle of red and dinner brought to the room. Fluffy white robes to keep them snug as they ate.

Lighting was soft and mellow music completed the scene. All thoughts to the stressful week that had gone before, being drowned in the pool of emotions finally being released, as they made love and rekindled the depths of their desire for each other.

Driving past Cahors and having great difficulty with the mixed instructions from Bea, it took longer than expected for them to arrive.

'*C'est magnifique n'est pas?*'

Indeed. Definitely magnificent!

'Coach House awaits!'

Once the welcome hugs and kisses were shared, Bea pointed towards their wonderful home for the next few days. Stunning! Red roses climbing their way across most of the entrance stone wall, to what was once the dwelling for the landed gentry's coach and horses. Entering the large oak-beamed living space, they were directed to the iron staircase to the rear that took them up to the bedrooms.

'Wow. This is even more beautiful than I remember. I think you were still renovating in here, that time I visited with Joe and Lou.'

'Absolutely! You all stayed in the main house with Nile and myself. It was only one night but we had fun didn't we? Really lovely to be meeting Sen and so nice to have you stay a few days. I have so many places to show you.'

Bea was born in Malta, to English upper class parents. A year or two older than Wanda but incredibly attractive, with her dark skin and hair, and very well looked after. Her accent was terribly high English, which had often been misconstrued as snobbish. A little reserved in some cases perhaps but she and Wanda had been close for years, having met when Bea dated A.B. many moons ago. She had been married to Nile for several years and he was as equally lovely. As tall as Sen, and very much the gentleman, with so many interesting tales to tell, from his past career as a private detective.

'We may never leave here,' Wanda said only half-jokingly.

Wanda and Sen had their own kitchen so a plan was laid, for each couple to take it in turn to prepare a meal. Dining in amongst the flower beds, on those warm summer evenings, was indeed special. They joked and laughed until late into the night, one bottle of wine soon turning to two.

Wi-Fi allowed them to do a little work, when it fitted in. Emails were checked regularly and mixed in with little drives around the lanes to different villages. Bea and Nile had a cabrio too so it was cruising all the way. Coffee excursions to various hamlets or just walking the lanes near the property, it was all incredibly peaceful and took every ounce of stress out of Wanda and Sen. Swims in the pool and just lazing in the sun.

Then came the email they had been waiting for.

'Yes! We have our Case Officer. A couple more things she needs for the visa application. Mon dieu! OK. Let's see how we can meet her needs.'

Not too painful but they had to do a bit of quick thinking to keep it simple.

'Wow. She's good. An email back already. She's gone for our suggestions.'

Bea had a fabulous office, set-up with printer and everything they needed. Files were pulled electronically. Printed out, signed and witnessed by in-house JP Nile. Scanned and returned in no time. One very happy Case Officer and the next step would be for a request to come from the designated medical officer, detailing what health check Sen would need to have done. Moving right along!

'Amazing that we were here when this all had to be done.'

Wanda was so grateful to Bea and Nile, who had enjoyed the excitement of it all and wished the visiting friends would stay longer.

'Jan and Cat are expecting us in a few days and we want to be able to explore places, on the thousand kilometre journey from here. It's going to be difficult for us to drag ourselves away from this incredible place. Absolutely love it and can't thank you guys enough for having us.'

Glasses were raised, as they toasted their good fortune to be there together, sharing excellent food and wine, great company and good health.

Driving off to the south that sunny morning, they were soon passing through a familiar roundabout.

'Oh my goodness! This is where that green Italian wagon fell asleep!'

Sen had heard this story before and was fascinated to be reliving some of the journey Wanda shared with her brother Joe and Lou so many years earlier. Her special car at that time had broken down and ended up having to be towed into Toulouse. Joe and Lou needed to get back to Hillywood so off in the train they went, leaving Wanda to relax for a few days, while she waited for the repair work to be carried out. The time to herself worked well and was all covered by travel insurance. Lou enjoyed looking after her Uncle Joe and getting them through Paris, with her limited French. By the time Wanda returned to Holland, Joe had left for his return to Sydney and Lou had sorted herself out, for returning to high school. Wanda had been totally dispensable.

'This beautifully enchanted red cabrio of ours is not going to sleep. How amazing is this car? Not one hiccup in all the miles we've done. Rides so smoothly and always has that extra bit of energy to pass someone, when we need it. I love this car almost as much as I love you.'

He was smiling and full of the joys of their romantic French adventures.

Wanda could not have been happier. Something about speaking French, added a sparkle to this time with her handsome Dutch man. He was more fluent than her but she did OK. Such a passionate language!

Merely watching Sen speak, lit fires in Wanda, and she would want to grab him there and then. Making love to him was always on her mind.

Fug oozed everything French!

At one point, he even directed them to a little car sex.

Quick but satisfying!

Mischievous by nature, it provided lingering naughty thoughts, long after the deed. The power of the mind was almighty and led to tantalising boosts for the libido, with sensitive pumping of the erogenous zones!

Winding their way south, stopping to explore little villages for coffee breaks and lunch, they were stunned to finally come upon Collioure. Wanda had travelled right along the entire French and Spanish coast several times but had never encountered this idyllic Catalan port, situated where the waters, flowing down from the Pyrenees mountains, meet the Mediterranean.

Ancient stone walls surround the port and tiny picturesque alley ways, boasting a unique mix of medieval and renaissance craftsmanship. Known as the city of painters, Collioure had provided inspiration to many a famous artist, including Picasso, Matisse and Chagall.

That night, they stayed in the centre of the old town and right by a canal. Sounds rang out from the castle, as locals sang along and laughed at a theatrical performance taking place. Smells of delicious food, wafted from every doorway they passed, as they wandered around on their discovery walk. Every sense tingled and they had only to look into each other's eyes, to feel the enchantment deep down to their very souls.

A few minutes drive from Collioure, and you crossed the border into Spain. They would stay one night in Valencia, then carry on down to Javea the following day.

'Hi Jan. Shall we aim to be at your house around noon?'

Cat and Jan had owned their hacienda for several years and Wanda already had the pleasure of visiting before so knew roughly where to go. They were much more excited to be receiving her this time, with her lovely new man in tow.

'Can't wait to see you and of course to finally meet Sen. A pity we missed you in London but it's so incredible you could make it down here. We took the liberty of arranging a lunch in the port, when you arrive. Hope that's OK? Really wanted you to meet our neighbours. You know, the couple I mentioned to you before, that live near Hillywood.'

Such a small world!

Cat and Jan were always a pleasure to be around - artistic and interesting. Wanda had worked in advertising with Cat, way way back, when she first joined A.B. in the agency he had in London. Such a funny guy! Never in a bad mood and Wanda loved his silly nature. Still very much in touch with the agency world, even though he had been retired for years, they would gossip and share stories into the wee hours. Bit different this time though. He and Sen got along like a house on fire and nobody else could get a word in edgeways.

Jan was also a delight and an extremely successful business woman. She and Cat had been married to others before and had their children, meeting each other post retirement and deciding they would partner until death do they part. Financially sound and able to travel the world, to take in life to the full, they had stayed at Wanda's in Sydney and in Holland so always made her more than welcome at their houses in the UK and Spain.

'So lovely of you to offer for us to stay as long as we like but Sen has just received an email, from his visa case officer, and has to be in London on a particular day next week, for his medical examination. We want to spend a few nights in Barcelona on the way back too. Need to look at flights. Must be loads of options for a cheapy from wherever in France.'

Mount Montgo sat directly behind Cat and Jan's beautiful hacienda. They could laze by the pool and take in its splendour, which they did, but they also managed to admire it from different vantage points around Javea and take in loads of changing perspectives. The fishing port activities and blue blue waters of the Mediterranean Sea, were also delightful.

Apart from the Dutch neighbours and the lunched shared with them, Wanda and Sen were introduced to many of the owners of other surrounding properties. Not one of them Spanish! As with much of France, locals had often been priced out of their own areas, by the power of the UK pound. So many British, investing in holiday houses and sometimes creating almost ghost town situations, out of season. As the Euro strengthened, this quickly changed and much of the property was now too expensive for Brits and not able to be sold. Prices plummeted and many of the Northern Europeans had jumped in for the bargains.

'Cat is still standing by the open gate. What a great guy!'

The royal wave was a sight to behold. Quite a long street so Wanda and Sen had a little distance to cover, before they could stop reciprocating. Roof was down and the sun was shining. It had been an amazing few days and now they were on their way.

'Barcelona here we come!'

Wanda was so excited. One of her most favourite cities in the whole wide world! The city of Gaudi; of Mojitos on the sands of Barceloneta Beach; people watching from a million café choices around the old town or along La Rambla. The colours of the markets and its outstanding cultural heritage, it was a University town that thronged with learning, music and art. Perhaps the constant excellent weather had something to do with it too. That surely played a role in so many huge convention facilities being established there. Wanda had been to several major events there and had numerous holiday adventures with girlfriends. Loads of memories from Barcelona!

'I saw on the website, that they had plenty of apartments in Barceloneta and we could just rock up and choose one.'

And so they did. Wanda was familiar with the town so managed to find exactly where they needed to be. Sen went in, while she double-parked. How Spanish!

'Looks perfect my love. Only two streets away and he suggested we leave the car up past the Olympic port and take a tram back, once we unload our things.'

Wow. They even had a tiny balcony and you could see the beach, if you leaned out slightly. Great location! On their way back from parking the car, they made their way to Mojito land. They had arrived!

Relaxing, exploring, constantly hot for each other and playing out Fug's every desire, they would have happily set up home right there.

'We need to be out of the apartment by 10am tomorrow so let's grab the car and then venture up to the top of Montjuic. You know the 17th century fortress and parklands, where they hosted the Olympics? Spectacular views out to sea and across the busy port from there. Tonight we can maybe go to that Flamingo show in the Gothic Quarter. Pity the queue was so long at La Sagrada Familia. Can you believe he said to expect a three hour wait!'

An incredible fifteen euro flight had been found, for Sen to get to his medical appointment in London. It was from the small airport of Dole, in France. Around nine hours drive from Barcelona so they would make a couple of overnight stops, before he had to fly.

Who would have thought? Dole was one amazing and very historic town!

Located on the Doubs River, it lay quietly hidden to the north-eastern side of France, close to the Swiss border. One massive cathedral dead centre, towers high above the medieval township. As you wandered the cobbled lanes and canals, you soon learned that this was the birthplace of Louis Pasteur.

'These doorways and courtyards date back to the middle ages. Stunning!'

Sen was posing in another special shot for their memory register.

'So much to discover in this world my darling! What an incredible journey we've had and will continue to have. Love you so much!'

Could it really be their last night already?

Sen would fly to London in the morning, to go straight for his visa medical, then fly straight back to Holland.

Wanda would drop him at Dole airport and would continue with their enchanted red cabrio, for the seven hour drive home, without him.

'I will miss you my love.'

Sen knew Wanda was fine with finishing the last leg alone. She would blast out all her favourite CDs and be singing her way back to Hillywood, on the autoroutes. He would jump on the train from Schiphol and might even beat her back to the house.

Should all be very simple and straightforward.

'Let's check out exactly where this tiny airport is, before we go to that residence we've booked and live out our finale, we've been fantasizing about for the past couple of days.'

'Good idea. Such beautiful countryside but so many confusing twists and turns on these country lanes. Looks like the airport is in the middle of nowhere.'

Fug had them talking about this last night for some time and getting their imaginations into top gear. He loved to add a little intrigue and this Chateau de Trouhans, they found online, did just the trick. A property that could easily have held court to D'Artagnan and provided the perfect erotic backdrop, for him to seduce his captive beauty. Wanda had no problem in playing the helpless wench and Sen was more handsome and gallant, then any musketeer might ever have been.

'Yes. Nice to know the easiest way to get there tomorrow morning. We were lucky to get that appointment. Normally takes months and there's no chance of changing it for ages, if you were to miss the flight.'

'There's the last of the signs it told us to look for.'

It seemed very clear exactly where the airport was so they could see no point in continuing for that final turn. Why waste any more precious time? Room service could only be taken for another hour so they had better get checked in.

That night turned out to be every bit as erotic as they had hoped.

Hot bubbly bath to start, filled with talk of days gone by and the raunchy adventures of D'Artagnan. Sen and Wanda speaking their best French, teasing each other with cheeky facial expressions and body gesturing.

As they savoured every morsel of the delicious feast and ensured each sip of wine, was given time to fill their nostrils before entering their mouths, irresistible aromas and tastes engulfed them.

Gentle kisses accompanied soft touches, to each tender part of their bodies, until they could no longer hold on to the suspenseful intrigue.

Her dashing musketeer lifted her swiftly to the bed and was soon thrusting himself deep within. Enraptured and complete, they were one again! Finally they fell satisfied, into a hot and sweaty melange of flesh - later moving to a peaceful sleep.

'Oh no! We slept through the alarm!'

It had been the most incredible night but now it was morning and Sen's flight was due to depart in just over an hour!

'Do you really think we even have the slightest chance of making it?

• CHAPTER SIXTEEN •

'FINALLY A PROPER SIGN!' He was doing his best with navigation but the earlier turn Sen thought led to the airport, ended up leading them onto a motorway!

'There's the airport down there!'

Sen had no idea how they might get onto that small lane below.

Deep breathing wasn't helping.

'OK. I can see an exit ahead. Not sure if it will lead us where we need to go but let's get the positive energy in place and hope for the best.'

He was exactly right. It took them the absolute shortest way, to where they needed to be. And….the flight to London had been delayed!

As Wanda pulled up out front, within eyesight of check-in, they could see people starting to go through. Sen was out of the car, with no luggage and straight through in moments.

Always the lucky ones!

Wanda watched, as the cabin door closed, thanked their enchanted red cabrio for adding the magic that obviously got them to the right turn off, then off she headed for Holland.

'You're on the train already?'

Turned out Sen was also right about reaching Hillywood before Wanda did.

'I guess you'll have just enough time to get the kettle going for a nice cuppa.'

Sen was way more confident than that.

'I reckon I might be able to go one step further and even have some dinner.'

He would be buying some take-away from the café near the station. Only a five minute walk to their house. Something he did rarely but that would be much easier than trying to shop for things to cook.

Everything had gone like clockwork for his medical appointment. Trains got him from Luton to Knightsbridge without any trouble and he had enough time to grab a coffee, near the doctor's surgery. No comment was made on his state of health. They had to lodge particular information into the visa computer system about him, which was all completed quickly. Sen need not ever hear anything further, unless something came up negative in any of the tests.

Wanda was pulling up outside the house, just as Sen finished putting everything for the dinner, onto the coffee table. Perfect accidental synchronising of journeys.

'Dutch news is just about to start and dinner is served!'

A skype call to Lou had been scheduled for late that evening. Email exchanges detailed several properties Alex was looking at, with a view to buying his first home.

Big news! They had decided they would live in it together!

Lou's flatmates had a friend who was ready and waiting to rent her room, once she moved out. That would completely cover her mortgage and outgoings. She would contribute towards the mortgage Alex took on and they were making every effort to find an apartment with a garden so that Spike had space to run. The three of them were going to set up home!

Skype shrieking - Wanda and Lou were so animated and totally happy. Sen added a little shriek or two of his own, when he got a look in. They both really liked Alex and saw him as a good match for Lou. Pity the market was so hot in Sydney though.

'Three times now! They accept the offer and then bid other people up. Everyone's paying way over the asking price. So frustrating!'

Wanda convinced Lou that they just hadn't found the right place yet. Fate would get them where they needed to be.

'Yeah. You're right of course. Anyway, the other big news is that we've decided to take a two week holiday in August and go to Hawaii. Having fun with planning that. Both of us will finish with the shows we're working on at the same time so we really thought we should take advantage of that. You know how it is mum. Just a gig at a time, with TV work. We might actually be doing the same show, when we get back from Hawaii. Just waiting to hear on that, before we book. Saving well for the trip. Alex has tons of money he's been putting aside forever, to cover the deposit and everything he needs for the apartment purchase so that's sorted.'

Things could not have been better.

Lou even managed to introduce Jay to some work in television. Not anything that really used his talents or degree studies but he was happy to just be earning enough to pay his mortgage and expenses, while he focussed on his DJing, music making and computer gaming podcast. Busy boy!

As July hit in Holland, temperatures began to exceed records. Regularly in the high thirties, Wanda and Sen made sure they took full advantage and had many an afternoon swim in the cooling lake waters of Loosdrecht. Down came the cabrio roof, as they took the short drive around the picturesque lake area. So many quaint cottages and little cafes for them to compare the applegebak offerings and just how hot they were prepared to serve their coffee.

'If it isn't extra hot, it starts tasting like a milkshake to me.'

In the beginning, Sen had thought Wanda was being a little too fussy but he had also become accustomed, to having his coffee milky and very hot.

It was on the way home from the lake one afternoon, that Wanda heard her song.

'That's it! That's our TV Show theme music!'

She pumped up the volume and sang full throttle.

'I've already started writing lyrics but this is the music they will fit perfectly to.'

Sen was making progress, with getting interest in their television series and Wanda's writing had moved along to the next stage.

'Great darling! I can let them hear it at the meeting next week. I love it!'

Sen also had a great idea for a possible sponsor.

'We live cars' is their tag line! They have to see the value in being attached to romantic novels that tell tales of living life to the full in their cars.'

Creative juices just kept flowing with Wanda and Sen. Never a day passed, when they didn't have a new brilliant idea. Sen had TV show formats coming up in his sleep even.

Then came the incredibly exciting news.

'An email from the Australian visa case manager! She thinks there should be no problem at all. Everything seems to be fine. Might take six to nine months, to finally come through though and I have to be out of the country, when that happens. If we want to be in Australia before that, we can. I go in on a three month visitor visa again and she lets me know, when the Partner Visa is about to be granted. Could take a trip to New Zealand or somewhere, for the short time I need to be out, maybe?'

'Yay! That's one huge thing we don't have to think about now.'

They both knew Sydney was where they wanted to be - if only they could get their houses sold in Holland. They did want to stay for the 90th birthday celebrations of Mama-An though so that still gave them some time.

'Let's just do it darling! We'll make something happen with our properties, even if they haven't sold. Why don't we plan to leave Holland straight after your mum's birthday party?'

'OK. Why not? We can work on all our things from anywhere in the world. You know I just had an email about a new policeman coming to the island. He doesn't have money to buy just yet but was interested in the possibility of renting to buy, like I put on that poster. He saw it in the tourist office and then looked at the great website Lou did. Now we have my place with the same agent you're using, I guess I should ask her what she thinks.'

Wanda was disappointed the agent only had two people to view her house so far but the arrangement for Sen's house, was quite different. She was really just handling formalities.

'Yeah. Maybe it's good to ask her what she thinks. She understands all that overbrugging requirement too. I'm going to give her another four weeks with trying to sell my place and then think about other options. Made all the right noises but then not so much action. Looking at her website, I see other places sold. Wonder if my place is too cheap and it's just not attracting the right buyer?'

Off to the island for a week and no doubt, they would hear more about the possible new policeman and his family. They hadn't expected him to be on the island though.

'He was just here for the day. Some meetings to sort out things with

with his new job. How incredible he came and knocked on the door and found us home. Seems like a nice enough guy. He'll be back in a few days, with his wife and kids, to take a proper look. So cool that he loved the house. Fingers crossed they do too.'

Meanwhile, Wanda had a couple get in contact about renting a room in her house for a few weeks. They would be going off to work and no bother at all. Money was good - being paid for by their employers.

Fantastic!

That would keep the Hillywood mortgage covered. Holiday apartment at Sen's island house was also fully booked for most of the summer so they were well covered on all sides.

Close friends in London invited them to their daughter's wedding in the August and now they were also planning a late September departure for Sydney.

'Umm, where in the world shall we visit on the way to that land down under?'

Wanda got into full swing and put on the travel agent hat, she loved so much.

'If you guys are leaving for Australia at the end of September, what are you doing with your beloved and very enchanted red cabrio?'

Denise had a smile from ear to ear, as it occurred to her that there might be an opportunity, for her to buy their very special car. She and Wanda were having one of their regular coffee catch ups in Hillywood town centre.

'Oh wow. Hadn't even contemplated having to sell the car. Can't really take it with us though heh? You know what, it would be amazing to think it was still in the family and you were loving it every bit as much as we do. I'll have a word with Sen and he can let you know.'

A sad moment of realities, when Wanda and Sen discussed the cabrio going but he was of the same mind and agreed, nice to at least sell it to a close friend. He would chat with Denise, when he saw her at the gig they were all going to that Friday night.

De Vorstin was a brilliant live music venue, just at the end of Wanda's street basically. The council had rebuilt an old facility and done a fantastic job. Arts were well supported in Hillywood. This night, they were to see one of their favourite Dutch artists, supporting a huge talent from the United States. The place was packed. Simple sign language would have to do, for the cabrio chat between Sen and Denise.

A bit like watching an old silent movie or playing charades but they communicated fine. He knew she would continue to give the car all the love it so deserved. They would agree a price later. Her current car was on its last legs so she could borrow the cabrio whenever she needed and take it over fully, after they left end September.

Rocking the night away, until way past their normal bedtime, Wanda and Sen's last thoughts for that day shifted, as soon as they lay in bed. Neither said a word but they were both aware of the big hole that would be left, once they no longer spent those enchanted hours together, in their beloved cabrio.

'It's a couple of months until we go darling. Still loads of fun for us to have in our car. Tomorrow it will be remote control to the island. Soon we have another drive across to the UK. Loads of special aura connecting moments to have yet!'

Hugging tightly, with eyelids weighing as heavy as boulders, they were soon off to sleep and so to dream.

Still the heatwave continued, as they made their way to Schier the next day.

'I'm thinking that second promised swim in the Waddenzee might be on the cards. What do you think?'

'Definitely! Policeman and family don't come to the house until 5pm so we have plenty of time. Coffee and applegebak first or after?'

'Ooohh. That's a difficult call to make. Now that you have mentioned it, I don't think I can wait. Let's hit the main hotel and enjoy the front terrace for a bit.'

What a fortuitous time for them to decide to do that!

'Wow! You know they have new owners here now? Well, they are apparently very keen to take a look at my house. Haven't sold their property down south yet but are staying in a disgusting rental on the island so could well be interested in the rent-to-buy proposition we put forward. Saw the poster in the tourist office, which led them to the website Lou did. Fantastic! Things are really starting to happen.'

The lady owner would go to see the house, at some point over the next couple of days. A busy weekend, with full occupancy in her hotel, so she would have to try to fit it in but had Sen's mobile number and would call.

Cycling to a spot further along the beach, Wanda was surprised to see a new building on the sand. It was a life savers hut with a café, built high up on stilts. So funny to see two lifeguards sitting there, watching the very few people actually in the water. Five to be precise!

Then there were seven.

Welcoming cold waters were much deeper than they had been on the first swim. Being so hot and having to walk so far to get across the wide beach, they jumped straight in. Sen was a strong swimmer and went quite some way out. Wanda could swim OK but had been brought up, on the fierce tidal behaviour of Sydney beaches and was always weary of currents. She was soon aware of Sen drifting.

Making her way into shore, Wanda ran along the beach trying to attract Sen's attention. The water was unusually fresh and clear so he was off in another world and enjoying every minute of it. He hadn't realised the current was dragging him out, further and further. It was a seagull that finally attracted his attention.

'Oh my darling! I was getting really worried there. That was some swim you just did. Did you even see how far out you were?'

That swooping seagull had saved the day. No way had Sen been aware of the danger he was in. Wondering what the hell the gull was doing, diving so close to him, he had been astonished to see the shore so far away and Wanda jumping up and down shouting his name. The lifeguards had just kicked into action and were about to launch their high speed boat, for the rescue.

A little relaxing on the upper deck of the life savers hut, before they cycled back to meet the prospective tenants and/or house purchasers.

Wanda made tea and cookies, while Sen showed them around. Three children and the eldest immediately fell in love with the very big boat, sitting in the back garden. Indeed, Tod had still not removed it. They were all excited to be leaving Rotterdam and coming to live in this island paradise. Sen had told them how much the rent would be and the policeman needed to see if his officer in charge, would go that high. They left happy and it was agreed that everyone would consider things.

Sen was sure that the hotel owner would be a better bet, for actually buying the house. They had sold another hotel to buy this one and must be well cashed up. Even though they still had to sell a place to buy, the rent he needed should be much more affordable. Fingers crossed she would call soon and fall in love with Sen's house. Both possible candidates wanted it furnished, which worked really well for Sen too. Should someone move in and not end up buying, the house would always present much better, if dressed with all of Sen's beautiful furnishings and artworks.

Property was on everyone's minds. Alex and Lou had found the ideal apartment and his offer was signed and sealed. No chance of losing out this time and the place they now had, was so much better than any of the others they almost got.

Fate was on their side!

Move in could take place a few weeks before they went on holiday to Hawaii so they would be all settled in and able to really relax, knowing the search for their new home was finally over.

On her discovery mission into everything self-publishing, Wanda was contacted by a Sydney friend, who had a colleague now running a new venture in Amsterdam. Purely for authors who wanted help to publish and they had created an automated system, that had full design support. Having won a 'bright ideas' competition, this new venture had backing from one of Holland's largest banks and a huge international telecommunications company.

'What a lovely young man.'

Regardless of possibilities for doing business, Wanda and Sen met up with this guy to show him some sights. He had been working non-stop since arriving from Sydney and not seen much of Holland at all.

'Zaanse Schans did just the job. How funny was he, posing in the giant clogs and hanging off the windmill railing for that silly photo?'

Visiting his office that following week, the business pitch initially showed some promise. Delving into how their system structured the author's financial reward, didn't however make any sense at all. This was not a path that Wanda and Sen cared to follow.

As with everything they were doing around publishing, they considered themselves to be at the early stages of their learnings. All new information would support their knowledge base and they still had a long way to go.

Things had been hectic. A break was definitely in order.

Ty and Sen made plans for a 'boys only' weekend so Wanda arranged for Anna to visit Holland, for some fun with her and Denise. They were a formidable trio of laughs and bopping madness.

Being aware of some historical data, where Sen had ended up with a new woman, each time he ventured off alone with Ty, Wanda felt a little apprehensive about this trip away. Ty also had a newer and faster car that he wanted to try out and they were thinking German autobahns could be the place for that.All in all, she knew she needed to distract herself big time and Anna was just the person to help her do just that.

Wanda also had the gut wrenching feeling that Ty might do anything he could, to stop Sen moving to the other side of the world. How fortuitous, if perhaps he should fall in love with a new encounter and decide to stay in Holland - a thought being driven only by Wanda's wild imagination. Or was it?

As it happened, Sen was doing his own worrying. He knew how crazy Anna and Denise could be and had heard many a tale of lusty adventures, when the three of them got together.

'Glad I wasn't home when Ty picked him up. Where would you like to go first deary?'

Anna knew exactly where she wanted to head from the airport.

'How amazing is this weather? You OK with the roof down?'

Having lived in the Hillywood house with Wanda and Lou years earlier, she had her favourite old haunts that were high on the visit priorities list.

'Me in the enchanted red cabrio again! Yeah! You know how much I love it! Let's head to the beach first.'

One of their favourite cafes in the sand, made for a delightful spot to catch up, over that much loved glass of red with lekker bitterballen.

'We meet up with Denise later this evening. A great band on in town. Work for you?'

'Absolutely! Can't wait to see her and for us all to have a good old bop.'

Two hours later, Wanda received her first text from Sen. He was missing her already but hoped Anna had arrived OK and wished them all a fun weekend. Lots of love and kisses. She reciprocated along the same lines and all was well. Three further texts throughout the night, with the last one talking about the quiet night they'd had talking over dinner. Sen was now back in his room and wishing her sweet dreams.

As tired as Wanda was, she had not wanted to let the side down. They were still out dancing and didn't look even close to getting home. Her text back wished him *welterusten* and confirmed how much she was missing him. Loving thoughts shared, about wanting to be with her incredibly sexy man.

Anna and Denise were single and determined to see what was out there. She didn't want to spoil their fun but there was no way she had any intention of straying. Watching the two of them was fun but it did have its limitations.

The following day, Sen was messaging about the high speed testing of Ty's car. That was a little disconcerting. Wanda wasn't sure where they were even headed but had understood they planned to spend the last of their three nights, in Hamburg. A wild city indeed! Sen had told Wanda that Ty and Veet had little or no sexual activity these days so she couldn't help but think, they might be frequenting somewhere he could get his rocks off.

With the first night for Anna, turning into a very early morning, Wanda was happy her guest wanted to sleep late the next day. In fact, she was also happy to just go for a quiet drink in Amsterdam that night and re-discover some of her favourite places. Denise had something on already so it would be just the two of them and a whole lot calmer. The second day had been scheduled for a long cycle through the woods and around the lakes so an earlier night was called for anyway.

Not getting a final sleep well message that second night, gave Wanda some concern. Should she text Sen or would that just be seen as intrusive? There had only been one text during that entire evening. Wanda shared her anxiety with Anna, who was quick to brush it off.

'Oh for goodness sakes! He is so clearly besotted with you. There is absolutely nothing for you to be worried about. OK so Ty might want to get his rocks off. Doesn't mean Sen will. I really don't see it. Just let the boys have their space. Not a good look to be seen as the possessive wifey.'

Wanda laughed and it reminded her that she hadn't told Anna about registering their relationship, when they were in Sydney.

'You what?' she shrieked. 'Surely that's just the same as getting married!'

Wanda explained how much easier it made the application for Partner Visa but Anna insisted that she and Sen had married. And why wasn't she invited?

A more relaxing cycle the next day, was followed by dressing up for a special dinner at the 'surprise' restaurant. Being daylight until so late and still really warm, Wanda and Anna sat outside on the tree lined pedestrian street in the centre of Hillywood, enjoying the ambience and people watching. The last night of Anna's visit but they also had a nice long final last day to follow, which they planned to spend by the lake, at a favourite café. From there it would be directly to the airport, for her early evening flight back to London.

'He hasn't sent a text since early this morning. I guess they arrived in Hamburg and it's all a little crazy. Never mind. Just one more night to go! Can't believe how much I miss him. Sorry to be such a bore with it all.'

Anna didn't mind. She knew how incredible their discovering each other had been and was truly happy for Wanda. If only she could meet her Mr Right too. She dated a couple of guys and had loads of mates but, just as Wanda had been before, that really special person had eluded her, since the marriage break up with Mel. The Dutch fling had turned to dust, once she settled in the UK.

'Isn't that Sen?'

Anna was facing towards the end of the street nearest home and Wanda was looking the opposite way.

Wanda turned but had thought it couldn't possibly be. Then he got closer.

'It is!'

She leapt to her feet and ran to the stunning looking man walking her way smiling.

'It's him. My gorgeous man!'

He was wearing a new jacket and looking even more amazing than she recalled. It was like a scene from a romantic movie, as she jumped into his arms and he held on for dear life.

'Love you so much my darling!'

'Me too but what, how, why ..... I thought you and Ty would be having fun in Hamburg right now?'

Wanda had all the facts confused. They had popped in to Hamburg on their way up to Kiel. Neither of them had been there before and thought the waterways looked worth exploring. Not such an interesting place but they managed to amuse themselves. Ty had an encounter that left Sen with an unwanted friend but it had led to nothing more than conversation. The plan had always been for just the two nights away. He hadn't realised Anna was staying three nights but was pleased he would get to spend some time with her too. The lake activities planned for the next day sounded wonderful but, tonight, he would be asking Anna to permit them to hit the sack early. Rekindling of his fire and lust for Wanda could wait no longer.

That walk home after dinner was swift and Anna excused herself, as soon as they walked in the front door. Straight to her bedroom, bidding them sweet dreams with eyebrows raised and a cheeky grin.

'Hot and passionate love making, is the only thing I have on my mind,' Sen whispered to Wanda, as they moved to their top floor bedroom.

Wanda felt her pulse quicken, as he spoke. Desire took over and all she could think of, was being naked and held tightly in Sen's grip. She needed to feel the warmth of his body and take in every inch of his nakedness, knowing full well that he would be boasting a massive erection. She would hold it. Taste it. Knowing it would be thrust deep inside her very soon. Sucking her nipples, as he undressed her, she was almost at her peak before total nakedness was hers to behold. Taking off his own clothes, was frantic. He was about to burst!

Their bodies were so perfect together, their lips both soft and longing. As they kissed passionately and re-discovered every inch of each other, Sen was soon deep inside Wanda and they were as one again. Moans of intense satisfaction, echoed between them, as they climaxed in unison.

Finally falling into a deeply satisfying sleep, wrapped up in each other's arms, both Hug & Fug were completely content!

Sen had received the much awaited call, from the island hotel owner, whilst away.

More than keen, she wanted to know when he would next be on the island. Not wanting to lose her interest, he made plans to go straight after they dropped Anna at Schiphol airport. Should be just enough time to make the last ferry.

'She's coming at 10am so maybe we can cook up some bacon for breakfast and get the sense of smell on our side too. The garden is looking fabulous.'

Wanda took their things in and put the kettle on, while Sen did a mad dash for the supermarket before it closed.

'What do you think? I just had a call from the policeman. We knew they all loved the house but now his lead officer has approved the rent. They want to move in week after next so they can have the kids in school, for the start of the new year!'

A nice dilemma to have!

Well, not quite a dilemma yet. The hotel owner might not like the house. They decided to wait and see. Maybe she was in a position to even buy now, if she really fell in love with it.

'I told the policeman that we would need to get some things in writing, before proceeding. Of course I was enthusiastic and delighted they would make this their home but it would be so much better, if the house was actually being sold. Fingers crossed for the morning.'

The hotel owner was a charming lady and clearly a good business woman. Not quite sure the house was big enough for her family but she definitely did love it.

'I think we need to go with the policeman my love. She already has something that will do for now and we really can't afford to hang around waiting.'

It was agreed. Documents were drawn up quickly and everything was arranged for the policeman to move in with his family. They needed a furnished house so only clothing and personal effects to pack up.

A good friend from Hillywood had the right size van, for getting all the packed boxes back to Wanda's. Everything they needed would be shipped to Sydney before they left at the end of September and they still had six weeks to finally get all that sorted.

Tod had promised to put some new tiles up in Sen's bathroom but that wasn't happening. Maybe the friend coming with the van could do that work. A call was placed and he was more than happy to oblige. Sen would get a vehicle pass for the next weekend and he could bring the van onto the island.

Still no buyer for the Hillywood house and Wanda wasn't at all happy with the agent's input.

'Why say you have people interested and take them to see it, only for them to say they wanted a garage and a big garden. Clearly my house has neither and the information it is not misleading. She just wants to be able to say she's showing people. Total time wasting, if you ask me! Not impressed!'

Something had to be done about that but first to focus on getting everything clear at Sen's house. They would travel to the island in the van and their mate was happy to be enjoying a nice weekend on the island, in return for taking things back to Hillywood. Sen would pay him for the bathroom tiling and Tod would do whatever he could to help. He might even have the boat moved by that weekend.

Arriving at the ferry terminal, just in time to load, they were shocked to find the clearance for the van to travel to the island, had not reached the ferry master. Sen hadn't thought to make a print out of what the council sent him.

What now?

• CHAPTER SEVENTEEN •

'THERE'S THE COMPANY CEO.' Sen gestured to the ferry guy that was forbidding them to board. He knew the CEO well, from having made their corporate video a year earlier. Coming straight across to say hello, Sen explained that all the correct paperwork had been done with council. The CEO made a quick call to the mayor and the van was allowed to board.

The weekend was a great success, accept for one looming issue. Noah's Ark had still not been moved. Tod was there at the house, front and centre, ready to help with the bathroom as promised. Pity he hadn't stuck to the other big promise, to have his boat removed from Sen's back garden.

'Thought it would be easier to get the boat and the container at the same time,' was all he could say. There were things in the container belonging to Tod but best if he and Sen emptied it together so they were on the same page, with who owned what.

Sen was happy to be right by Tod's side, making sure none of his things inadvertently went astray. Still loads of good material in there, from way back when he renovated the house. Much of it would be of use to their mate and could help compensate for the work he was helping Sen with that weekend.

Wanda was tasked with making endless trips to drop rubbish at designated island collection points but the visit wasn't all work. They also made sure time was taken to show their friend around the island, enjoying the cafes and exceptional nature.

A bit of a squeeze, with three of them travelling in the front of the van but plenty of good music and laughs, made the final island sort out a pleasure all round.

'Great work team!' Sen managed to say between songs, as they approached Hillywood on the return leg. 'We need to go back in three days, to meet the policeman and show him how everything ticks. Would be good to have the full inventory prepared by then too so he's clear on what's in the house.'

Wanda had already started detailing everything over that weekend so it wouldn't take her long to finish that.

'His family arrives the following day. I think he's looking to get to us late afternoon so I figure we can go early that same day and be ready in time. What do you think?'

Wanda agreed. It was a plan!

'I think I might have words with the agent tomorrow about my house too.'

In her usual 'moving right along' style, Wanda was onto the next task at hand.

'Great that we now have your place sorted but absolutely nothing happening here.'

Denise worked at the International School and a colleague of hers, had expressed interest in securing a tenant for Wanda's house. She was working with a relocation agent and he had a list of people, who were eagerly looking for property.

Wanda did the right thing and told her sales agent, who wasn't at all happy.

'If anyone is looking at the house, they need to come through me.'

Now this woman was really irritating. How to deal with that one?

Wanda met with the relocation agent and Denise's colleague. They were certain one of the several people on their list, would want the house. An asking rent was agreed and Wanda instructed them to liaise with her agent to gain access. No point alienating the silly cow. The house would be rented furnished, if possible and Wanda could easily prepare an inventory of everything herself. Her agent had only to provide the key to the relocation guy.

The very next day, he had two people viewing and one was quickly contracted to move in, as soon as Wanda and Sen left for Australia. Perfect!

'Can you believe it darling? This stupid agent is acting as if she found the tenant and wants the usual first month's rent. How do you think I should respond?'

Sen would speak to her and see what he could arrange. She was also working in a very minimal capacity, for his house sale. Surely they could work something out.

The agent was a very tall Dutch lady, who had flirted with Sen whenever she saw him. He knew how to get around her and soon negotiated half what she first asked.

That and a million other things sorted, they were on their way back to the island, to organise things with Mr Policeman and his family.

A little weird driving there this time, for what they hoped would be the grand finale. Enchanted red cabrio on auto pilot as usual - Wanda doing the motorways and Sen taking over, once they hit the country lanes. Such a pretty journey! Must stop for some more windmill ballet shots, on the way home.

Could this actually be it?

Years of Sen believing he had sold the house and all the trouble to then get those unreasonable ladies off his radar.

It would be amazing to think it could all be over and going back and forth, with possible renters or buyers, could now become a thing of the past.

The policeman could not have been keener and was making all the right noises about wanting to buy, hopefully before the initial lease expired. He loved all the things that Sen had left in the house too. Particularly the wall full of books and records!

'My eldest son will go crazy, trying to read them all in the first week no doubt.'

Sen hadn't left anything that he wasn't happy to see go. So much had been sold off already but he figured that leaving the house looking great, was a priority. If this family did eventually buy, he would negotiate a good price for them to buy all of it. If they didn't end up staying, the fact it was all still beautifully presented, would make it easier to find someone new. Precious things were already in Hillywood and would be taken to Australia.

'He was here for almost three hours!'

Wanda couldn't believe the policeman had finally gone. All very well to take so long to check everything out around the house but they had both been stunned, when the policeman then started to tell them about the plot he had, for a television show.

It was part of a bigger scheme to have personal effects tagged, for easier recovery after being stolen.

He stood in front of them, holding centre stage, as they sat bewildered on the sofa, trying to look interested. Tea had been served three times.

When he then started to talk about his martial arts and began acting out his moves, Sen decided it was time to let him know they were tired and needed to go to bed. Even then, it was another half an hour before they finally got him out the door.

'Oh my heavens! You know I think a big part of him wanting this house, is because he knows your background in Dutch media. He thinks you can open some doors for him. Wow. Basically a nice guy but his idea had no legs whatsoever. I can't believe how patient you were with him, asking questions as if you had a genuine interest.'

The next day with the policeman's family, was as equally long but that was fine. This was important. A detailed inventory check, with both husband and wife, was crucial. Making sure they were happy it was all correct, before they all signed. An end time, was at least fixed by the ferry Wanda and Sen planned to take back to the mainland. Bags sat in readiness by the front door and they had made it clear which bus they needed to be on.

Somehow Wanda ended up being allocated the very small child to amuse. The elder child had gone off to play with a new friend, before even reaching the house so it was only the middle child, following the inspection parade.

The kids had made themselves at home already and were grateful for the drinks and cookies provided on arrival. They couldn't believe it, when they saw the very large boat they had to play with, in the back garden.

'That will be going soon I'm afraid.'

Sen had to disappoint them. Father was pleased he had. The boat didn't look at all safe for children to play on.

'Here are the keys! Enjoy your new home!'

Sounds from the bus coming up the back street, signalled it was time to grab their bags and shoot out the door. A quick farewell and they were gone. New inhabitants in situ and mission accomplished. Hopefully forever!

'Any sadness to reach this point my love?'

On the open deck of the ferry, looking back to the island, Sen confirmed that he felt nothing but elation, to finally be clear of his house. As he breathed an intense sigh of relief, they both silently hoped this new tenant would mean that was that, for at least one property.

In two weeks, they would drive across to London again. Lots of fun scheduled for that trip, not least of which being one incredibly amazing wedding, but a host of things to get done in Holland first.

Brilliant that Wanda now had a tenant lined up for her place too.

Knowing both mortgages would be covered, they decided to look at more interesting options for extended adventures, in making their way back to Sydney.

'Look at these super cheap flights to Vancouver darling! How do you fancy seeing a bit of Canada?'

'Very cool! You have a cousin there right? Maybe we could also consider adding Los Angeles? I've been having some interesting email contact with an old colleague, who is now Creative Director on one of the big shows for the American market. Maybe we could see him too.'

Sen was pitching their sitcom drama to several possibilities but they still weren't one hundred percent sure, which country they felt would be best to take the lead. They would keep sounding people out and know that fate would land them where they needed to be and when the timing was right.

'Absolutely! Come to think of it, I had an email last week from Elle and they are planning a trip to the States, ending up in Las Vegas on her hubby's birthday. That might fit in really well too! We could surprise him, if we can get Elle to keep the secret. I have close friends in San Francisco as well. Let's see what I can find with flights and see if we can't make this an adventure to remember!'

'Sounds exciting my love! It will be my first time anywhere in North America. Can't wait!'

Wanda loved exploring the world of travel possibilities. The web had so much information and doing your homework, always paid off. There were always new tricks to learn, no matter how much you had travelled.

She made a great discovery for an overnight stop near Calais, which would get their trip to the UK for the big wedding, off to a good start.

'Look at this one darling! Hotel au bord du Lac! Minutes from the Calais entrance to le chunnel. How lucky were we, with that half price train ticket for the channel crossing? And now a fabulous place to stay the night before. We can take a leisurely drive and see a bit more of Belgium, then stay at this cute place in the woods. Only 47 euros and that even includes a breakfast buffet!'

That night was soon with them.

Apart from all the travel planning, Wanda had been busy getting quotes for shipping all the things they wanted to send to Sydney. Never mind heading off to the library each day, to work on her book edit and character and chapter summaries.

She'd been a busy girl!

Sen had been frantic with appointments and clearing tax and other issues needing attention, before they left the country.

They were both thrilled they could now look forward to switching off, to fun times in London.

'What a fantastic place! How could it be so cheap? The restaurant looked excellent too. Shall we dine now my lovely? Or?'

Wanda went for the 'or?'

Pre-dinner sex in the shower! Lovely! Fug could not be happier! Anything hot and soapy got him turned on and the little devil ran riot with both Wanda and Sen!

Coming down off their high, they were quick to hit the restaurant before it closed.

'The food here is great – and so cheap. Speaking of food …. Kiki is expecting us for lunch at her place tomorrow and she's baked something she thinks you will like. How sweet is she?'

She was reading the text message to Sen. He was just staring at her and giving silent thanks for the amazing world that was theirs, as he gave a simple nod in agreement.

Wanda tingled, to think this beautiful man in front of her, actually loved her as much as she loved him. That enchanted red cabrio, having led her to this incredibly gorgeous person.

Blessed also, with two wonderful children and a multitude of fabulous friends, a thought quickly flashed across her mind – Lou and Alex would be returning from Hawaii that very day. So many beautiful messages from them and what a fantastic holiday they'd had! Seemed he was as romantic as Lou and the last day on the island, had seen them get up at 4am and take off
in a hire car with a picnic breakfast, to watch the sunrise from
the island's highest point. They were so right for each other!

 'Weather forecast did not predict this darling!'

As they woke the following day, rain poured heavily. Finally getting on their way, vision was beyond limited. Thick lanes of traffic, crawled towards their Calais departure point.

'Just as well we're so close. Apparently the main roads heading for the port are solid for miles. Major accidents everywhere so let's take it very slowly.'

Wanda took extreme caution, to make sure they arrived at the train safely. Once they hit the British mainland, the weather magically cleared.

An easy drive to Kikki's and they were soon tasting her spectacular chicken pie. She was right. Sen absolutely loved it and of course, Wanda did too.

'Anna and her new boyfriend will be here around 6pm and then we can all walk into the village for dinner. I booked the table for 7pm so a quick glass of wine with them here first. Then we all drive over to Twickenham, to see my gorgeous son play his drums. You know he's with a few different bands but this one has some of the old boys and they're ever so good. Should be a fun night!'

Kikki was happy with her plan and pleased to be with friends.

Great music, great food and great company! Couldn't have been a better recipe for fun!

What a pity Sen had to go off into one of his 'feeling left out' moods.

When they arrived at the pub, the band was playing and of course Wanda, Anna and Kiki wanted to bop around to the fab music. Sen was outside with Anna's new beau, in deep conversation and didn't seem at all interested in hearing the music. All fine but she had expected he might come inside to meet Kiki's son, once the band had a break. Instead, he seemed to wait until they were about to go back on, before walking in for a quick introduction.

Wanda found this a little rude and was not amused!

As the band started to play again, she bid Kiki and Anna farewell. They had to drive over to Clara and Ken in North London anyway so best be on their way. Nodding to Sen that it was time to leave, he quickly said his goodbyes and they were off.

Seething with anger, Wanda did not move to hold Sen's hand but instead hurriedly walked towards the car.

'What have I done now?'

Sen had no idea why she was so mad and Wanda had no intention of telling him.

He persisted and soon they were in the midst of one very loud argument!

Wanda had to stop the car, for fear she was becoming a danger to all on the road.

Sen jumped out and walked off down the street in a huff. Sitting quietly trying to meditate herself back to calm, Wanda was glad to be clear of him. It took quite some while before both could get back to continuing the journey.

A bit of a drive, to get to Ken and Clara and they weren't sure if they would be home from their dinner engagement so a key was left out, in case. For the next few nights, Wanda and Sen would have the top floor bedroom with ensuite, all to themselves.

As luck would have it, they were still out so no need to expose them to the angry state of Wanda and Sen. To sleep and so to dream, hopefully to wake up in a better state. For Wanda, that was the case. For Sen, it would take more time.

'Everyone has arguments. Just let it go. It's this long lasting mood you can't get yourself out of, that really creates the challenge.'

Wanda woke up saying she was sorry for probably over-reacting the night before. Sen wasn't ready to go down the forgiving and forgetting path yet. Trying to quiz her as to why it happened again, she tried to calmly answer until it became clear, she was never going to say that one thing that might put it to rest. So … instead …. she was learning to just stop talking.

Theatre tickets booked for the Friday night, to see A Chorus Line, they would join in the big birthday celebrations for daughter Lia, with a group of people joining for an early pre-show dinner in the West End. Always so much fun to be had!

It was two days since the outburst and Sen was still having difficulty clearing himself of the bad feelings, although he was excited to be going to the theatre and seemed fine with everyone, except Wanda.

So many fabulously talented West End performers, guaranteed you could never be disappointed by any show you saw, although Wanda had seen this one before and felt it was a stronger cast earlier. Often it was the audience that made all the difference. This night they were on great form and a good time was had by all.

Another evening, during their stay at Clara and Ken's, they all stayed in for dinner and watched several episodes of Top of the Lake. A riveting television serial filmed in New Zealand, from Jane Campion, that was absolutely brilliant! They were all hooked and had fun guessing who had done what to whom.

'How do you feel about some more theatre tomorrow darling?'

Wanda hoped this one might bring her loving Sen back and clear his mood.

'I saw Let it Be last year with Jay and it was incredible. Felt just like seeing the Beatles live in concert. Not sure if they have the same cast but what do you think?'

Sen jumped at the offer. He loved the theatre as much as Wanda did and loved the Beatles even more. It was showing at the Savoy, which was an added treat. Such a stunning property! A great evening and they sang and laughed, like the happy couple they could be.

'Wow. That was fantastic! Can you believe how much like the boys they were?'

Their enchanted red cabrio adored cruising around London in the warm weather topless. Before heading a little further north to stay with Bert, they ventured along the Embankment and took in some favourite sights. Big Ben looking glorious in the sunlight and taking Wanda back to those magical days, when she gave birth to her children, from a hospital room just across the Thames. Ah! London!

Wanda's one and only bridesmaid, when she got married, was her long-time buddy Em. Her eldest daughter Jess, would be walking down the aisle the very next day. Nothing had been spared, in making this an event to remember and the carefully chosen stately home venue, would provide the perfect backdrop for one amazing fairy tale wedding. Bert was also attending and was more than happy to be their designated driver.

'Not sure if I told you about her near death experience a couple of years ago? We weren't positive Jess would even still be here, when they found that thyroid cancer. Twenty six years old and not knowing how many more years she might get. It was horrific!'

Even after all this time, the mere mention of it made Wanda's eyes water.

'Her thyroid was removed fully and all signs so far, point to her being totally clear. Quite a miracle really, with it having been so aggressive. Everyone was totally traumatised but her beautiful fiancée kept her positive and her usual bubbly self. Such a beautiful couple! We couldn't believe it, when her singing voice ended up not being affected but she had already made her choice. No more auditioning for parts she didn't get. She would teach instead. Before too long, she had started her own performing arts school and it's doing brilliantly. Now she's marrying her dream man. And he's Jewish too, just like her. Funny thing is she had fought that, just like her mum did when she was young.'

Wanda drifted back to all those nights out bopping with Em and how she would avoid anyone remotely Jewish looking. Her parents kept introducing nice boys.

Em did everything possible, to ignore them. Then she finally met and fell in love with, the most amazing Jewish man.

'The traditions are so strong and I can see that it really makes a big difference, to have that deeper level of understanding.'

Sen had not heard all of this before so was hanging off Wanda's every word. Meeting everyone for the first time, at the wedding the next day, he could see straight away what Wanda meant. The closeness of this family was immediately evident and the love and positive energy flows, were very special.

Choosing not to go for the full synagogue event, Jess had opted to be married by a Cantor and the moving chuppah ceremony, took place in ornately beautiful gardens. Smiles on everyone's faces were as wide as the ocean, as glasses were broken and fun traditions completed the official side of proceedings. Fabulous food and wine, a live band and one hundred and fifty people, who wanted nothing more than to party hard and celebrate this beautiful couple's future.

'What an incredible occasion to be able to share with you all. Thank you so much for inviting me, inviting us. I'd heard great things about all of you from Wanda and of course, they were all true.'

Sen's words to the father of the bride concluded the exchange of farewell pleasantries. Hugs had been handed out by Wanda and a few excited tears shared, when she finally let go of Em. Those happy kind of tears, that people shed when all seems so right, especially when things had once been in doubt.

Mazel tov said it all!

'Tomorrow afternoon, I have the Waterside owners meeting over in Surbiton. The managing agent's office is in the High Street so it's been arranged for fellow owners to meet beforehand, at the pub near the station. Good to have a chat before we all sit in front of this guy. So many things not being managed as well as they could be. Hope we can shake him up a bit. Before that, I thought we could have lunch with some local mates. They can't wait to meet you so I suggested our old café haunt around noon.'

Sen didn't react too well and was not happy that she had not asked him, before making the arrangements.

'Why was everything such a fait accompli,' he thought to himself.

He was quite vocal at expressing his displeasure and Wanda felt as though she was being unnecessarily attacked.

True, she was an organising person. Could that be such a bad thing?

Someone had to do it!

OK so maybe she should have asked him but there were so many different things to arrange. Did she really need to consult him on every single step?

It was so very clear that she was overwhelming him again. When would she learn?

As Wanda tried to reason with Sen, matters worsened.

Once on a roll, he was bringing up all sorts of things he wasn't happy with. Before they knew it, their voices were getting louder and louder.

They were arguing again!

Sitting in their bedroom at Bert's, with everyone having gone to bed, Wanda felt sure the entire house must be able to hear them. Again, she decided her only course of action was to just stop talking altogether.

This infuriated Sen. He wanted answers!

Lucky they had their own bathroom. Wanda put a pillow over her head and did some deep breathing to calm down, while Sen locked himself in for a shower to cool off.

Feeling the tension, even through the closed bathroom door, Wanda had a sense of dread that this would stay with Sen, well into the following day. Shaking and bewildered, she finally fell into an exhausted sleep.

Amazingly close to having so many things in place, for the great life ahead that they planned to share but did she really want to continue down this path, if they were going to keep finding themselves in such an unhealthy angry state?

• CHAPTER EIGHTEEN •

'IT WASN'T MEANT TO BE EASY!' Wanda kept reminding herself, as the new day dawned. Nothing truly worthwhile ever was.

Even the magic of their enchanted red cabrio hadn't helped, on that tense drive down to Dover, for the channel ferry crossing. Well, perhaps it had been silently weaving its spell a little and allowing them some quiet reflective time. They may well have been in the same space but thought paths went in very different directions.

Wanda considered the turmoil she brought into Sen's life.

There he was, quietly doing his radio show and spending long weekends on his island. Trying to sell his house but not really getting anxious about when that might happen, believing he had his buyers already.

If he hadn't met Wanda, he would probably have been fine with living the life he was, for years to come.

But no! One almighty storm arrives, in the shape of this annoying little vixen from the land down under!

The way she managed to rattle his cage, was unbelievable on so many levels.

On the one hand, the sexual sparks that flew between them, made for enough fodder to keep Fug fully engaged forever more. And yet they could also be so warm and soft with each other, presenting Hug with limitless opportunities to demonstrate caring ways.

The full range of passionate emotions, swelled within them both and the sharing of creativity and excitement for life, was so special.

How about all the people and places?

Sen could not have seen that coming. It made loads of people dizzy, just thinking about what Wanda got up to in her world!

Two grown up children and a dog to take into his heart. He felt the love from them so quickly but had he really felt a part of this new family?

So many countries and way too many seriously close friends!

This was a lot for anyone to take on board.

All Sen could think about, was how sorry he was for having upset Wanda so badly, a day earlier. He knew how much she hated getting angry and losing her cool and it made him feel awful too. He also knew that people, who made Wanda feel like this, tended not to stay in her life for very long. She could be quite ruthless, when it came down to that, and would not have a bar of them, once the proverbial worm had turned.

The life that waited for him with Wanda, was going to be an incredibly full one but it was a life he felt sure he wanted. More than anything in this world, he knew his place was by her side and he was determined to make everything right.

Wanda had only to see her very tall and handsome man, walking back to her from the ferry rest room that day, to recall just how much she craved every inch of him. The way his confident stride and upright body moved; his broad smile and cheeky eyes.

Just listening to his soft accented voice, melted her heart every time!

There was not another man in this entire world, who could make her feel so special and she knew how lucky she was to be loved by him and, in return, to love him so deeply.

How long had she searched for this special man to share her life?

She couldn't fail now!

Keeping him and working out how to stay happy together, was her raison d'etre.

There were so many people out there, all alone and wondering why.

Oh to have been more tolerant! Why was nothing ever enough?

What did it take to make some people realise what they had, before it was too late?

Wanda had seen so many of her own friends and colleagues fall into that trap.

She forbid herself to join them!

Sen had popped in to the on-board shop and bought her a beautiful card to say how sorry he was. His loving inscription was sincere, in reminding her how much he loved her and didn't mean to fire up into an angry state. She was his Diamond Beauty and they would be together always. The sparkle that she added to his life, could not be more precious to him.

As Wanda read the card, holding the single silk red rose that came with it, tears welled in her eyes.

Hug jumped right in and they were quickly wrapped up in a deeply loving embrace, knowing they needed to slow the pace and not let things push them to the edge. It would be difficult but they were smart grown-ups and could rise to the challenge – couldn't they?

The rest of that drive back to Hillywood was peaceful, hand holding when it worked and just enjoying the feeling of enchantment again. Every now and then, moving across to share a gentle kiss.

'This is it darling! The next time we leave this house with packed bags, it will be for our big trip back to Sydney!'

The thought was both exciting and daunting. Still so much to organise, not least of which, being several large boxes of belongings to be shipped. Very large bike cartons were discovered for packing. Initially, looking for the right thing to ship Sen's expensive road bike in but then, on realising these were being discarded by the local shopkeeper, they decided they did just the job for everything else too.

'Loads of book cover design ideas have come in via email from Bo. Maybe we can go through them too, when you have a minute.'

They both adored the logo she had come up with. Absolutely perfect!

She had a go at creating characters but they all decided very quickly, that was not within scope for her skill set. Now it seemed the cover design, was also going to be difficult.

Sen and Wanda had a clear view in their minds and wanted the raunchy nature of the story to come across, perhaps using some of the love making accessories mentioned in the text - the magical white feather top of mind for them both.

'Not happening is it darling? Let's not push the boundaries of success. I think Bo would rather stick with what she is comfortable with too.'

Rewards were put in place for Bo's efforts to date but they would look elsewhere for the rest to be completed. Back to that once they were settled in Sydney.

'All the great things she's doing, really don't leave her with time to commit fully to being our digital person in any case so let's be happy with the logo and leave it at that for now heh.'

Sen couldn't agree more.

'And here's another completely different wow factor for us!'

Wanda read Lou's email to Sen and they both had a good chuckle.

She and Alex went skiing! His first time ever and he did really well. They were in the area, visiting his sister and Lou managed to get him on the hill.

'She says he's a natural!'

Lou had said earlier, it was the one little thing they might need to work on, in their relationship. Alex had not been at all keen on skiing, after doing himself a mischief playing cricket and having one very bad snowboard occasion, eons ago. Lou treasured her time on the slopes and had skied since she could walk. Hearing of Sen's bravery, with hitting the Swiss slopes after fifteen years, Alex had decided he might give it a go – provided Sen was right there alongside him, struggling. Somehow, Lou managed to convince him, it might be good to have a shot sooner so he could feel happier about them all going together, next season. Did the trick!

Working side by side, on the long list of things to be done before exiting Holland, Sen and Wanda managed the pace and made sure they took time to chill.

In a few days, they would have their first anniversary but they decided their big trip to Canada and the US, en route to Sydney, would be their celebration. Everything was booked to leave, just two weeks after that special September 14 date.

They would enjoy the 90th birthday party for Mama An and then be up up and away.

All of that said, the incredible day they met soon arrived and it became very clear that neither of them had any intention of letting it pass by, without commemoration.

Wanda could not have been more overcome, with surprise and emotion!

It wasn't just a delicious breakfast in bed; Sen was walking into their bedroom with that morning. He had arranged for Bo to help him have two stunning silver rings created, engraved with their Hug & Fug logo, all the way round.

Beautifully presented, in two little ring boxes sitting side by side on the breakfast tray, as Wanda opened the one he said was hers, he reached for her left hand and ceremoniously placed the ring on her wedding ring finger. After gasping deeply and telling him how lovely it was …. how lovely he was …. she did the same with his ring. Vowing their never ending love for one another, they kissed a warm and sensuous kiss that made both their heads spin.

As they fell back onto the bed, to look up at both ringed hands being displayed, Wanda directed Sen to one of the packages she had for him. Knowing it was his favourite massage oil, she started teasing him before he had even opened the wrapping.

'Shall I start with your back?' She directed Sen to lie on his stomach.

Kneeling over his stunning naked body, Wanda dripped the smallest amounts of oil at strategic points. His ears were particularly sensitive. Just rubbing the lobes gently, caused Sen to adjust body parts that were pushing against the mattress.

Hard shoulder muscles, fought her heavy kneading and, as she pressed into his aching blades, groans of pleasurable release became louder and louder. Down the spine and into the buttocks she continued, another strategic drop of oil being released into the warm crevice between. One gentle finger slide action, clearly arousing and making Sen's back arch.

He wanted more but she moved on!

Leg muscles relaxed, as she swept swiftly along their full length and moved to strong fists, to impact the soles of his feet. Into the base of each toe with a more gentle pressure, widening each gap to grab them singularly and stretch for individual release.

Finishing the back with cupping slaps along the full torso, Wanda beckoned Sen to turn and one enormously engorged and majestic penis was revealed.

Beginning with soft strokes to Sen's brow, she moved gently around his face and again to those super sensitive ear lobe backs. Into the front of the shoulder blades and tops of the arms, continuing a warm flow of movement right along each arm and finishing those off with slow fisting into palms of his hands. As she pulled each finger and shook the arm to soften, a shiver ran down her own spine, holding the hand wearing the new ring and seeing her own ring in that same view.

They were so completely connected and she knew in moments, they would be even more so. She could not keep herself off that towering erection for much longer. As she turned to rub down the fronts of his legs and stretch out to the tops of his feet, her own body was perfectly positioned to allow his tower to move into her welcoming body.

Massaging Sen was as big a turn on for Wanda, as it was for him. Once he was inside her, deep within, erotic sighs intensified as they thrust their bodies together. Turning so that Sen could tease her breasts, it was only a matter of moments before they could hold out no longer. Fug shouted a very loud 'yes', as they pulsed at high speed and took themselves to a dizzy climax. Eventually sinking down from the peak, they hugged and kissed gently, as they shared words of love and fell back into a satisfied calm.

Disturbed by the sound of the doorbell, Sen raced downstairs.

'A package for you my beautiful diamond!'

Wanda couldn't believe her eyes. The most incredible large white feather, all creatively wrapped and with a silk paper note from Sen. It had come all the way from Denmark!

'Umm. Now it's my turn my darling. Onto your stomach you go!'

The love making and massage fest, continued into the early afternoon.

'We are so blessed my love. What an incredible anniversary.'

They had planned to venture up to Amsterdam but it was such a lovely day, they decided to cycle around the forest and into a café in town instead. That evening, they would join Denise and a couple of friends, for some live music at De Vorstin. A totally perfect way to spend any day, let alone this special day, that fate brought them together on, a year earlier.

Did they really start this amazing life together, just because Sen bought Wanda's enchanted car?

Denise had an anniversary gift for them too. Such a sweetie! She was also one very excited lady, to soon be getting her hands on their red cabrio for always and to make it her very own!

Hence the special gift – one beautifully framed photo of their beloved car.

'OK if I use the cabrio tomorrow please? Just want to show it off!'

Such a whirlwind of emotions, in those final couple of weeks in Holland. Everything seemed to be in place for the Partner Visa and making their new life in Australia but a slight fog, blanketed their relationship.

Their cabrio was going to the best new and very loving home possible but they would miss it terribly.

The most amazing trip was all booked, for some incredible fun in Canada and the US, as they made their way to Oz.

Would it all be too much for Sen?

'This trip to Vegas is looking more and more spectacular every day and I really think Elle is managing to keep it a secret. Such a fantastic surprise! What fun!'

Wanda stayed upbeat and Sen seemed happy with everything.

She had secured a great price for accommodation at Caesar's Palace and even booked the best seats to see Elton John in concert, in their Colosseum. She'd seen him perform a few times but Sen hadn't been to anything like the show he put on. Now they could enjoy it together.

One nagging thought, kept rallying in the back of both their minds. Would this be the last time Sen ever saw his mother? She wasn't ill as such but the body was starting to fail her, in so many ways. Her mind was stronger than ever but age was creeping up with a vengeance.

When Wanda said goodbye to her own mother, leaving Sydney with the kids back in 2001, they knew it was more than likely, the final farewell.

The day of Mama An's 90th birthday celebration, could not have been more perfect. Driving to The Hague in spectacular sunshine, allowed for some topless cabrio cruising, before handing over ownership to Denise.

Having rented out the function room, at her local tennis club, family were able to gather, without any unnecessary fuss for anyone. They had all been very conscious of not causing Mama An any stress and kept numbers within reason. Her six children and their partners, plus grandchildren with no partners or little ones.

Mama An was on top form and it all went brilliantly. Ninety pink roses were handed to her, as everyone sang a specially written song, about her family and the roses.

The smile across her face was priceless! Truly touching!

Memorable moments captured on film, with Wanda feeling very much a part of Sen's loving family. They chatted away in Dutch and English, enjoying the beautiful sunshine and laughter, as they celebrated ninety fabulous years.

'We'll be back next April mama!'

In reality, they had no idea when they'd be back in Holland but it seemed much kinder, to give her an actual month to work to and not leave it open ended. She could not have been happier for her son, to be heading off on such an amazing adventure. All the same, she did seem pleased, to know when she might expect him back.

Motorway driving, from The Hague back to Hillywood, saw Wanda at the wheel.

She could tell Sen was feeling a little sad and guessed it might be about saying goodbye to his mum.

'How gorgeous did your mum look today? Always so well dressed and smiling!'

Sen was visibly exhausted and there was no response.

Wanda found herself in that uncomfortable place again, not knowing whether to speak or to just keep quiet.

Sometimes she wondered if it might be a language thing.

Sen was a deeply emotional man and it must be hugely difficult for him, trying to express what he was feeling, in a language that was not his own.

There had been many a time, when Wanda thought she should take more in depth lessons in the Dutch language so they could converse, in his mother tongue. Then she would think about the fact he wanted to improve his English. He even talked about doing some studies, once they were settled in Sydney.

If they had been staying in Holland long term, it would have made sense for her to speak to him in Dutch and take the lessons she needed, to do that well.

But they were moving to Australia!

Was he actually sad about his mum or did something else happen, that she hadn't noticed? Why did she feel asking was so super difficult?

They could be incredibly close and yet, at times like this, she felt as if she was with a total stranger. Something was ticking over in his head and it gave her a sense of a slow burning fuse, soon to ignite an almighty blast.

'Just leave it Wanda,' she told herself. 'Sure he's exhausted from today. Everyone making comments about the rings we now wear. All the questions about what his new life in Australia would be like. He probably feels like he has no real idea what it will be like, even though he made all the positive noises, everyone wanted to hear.'

The silent ride home, ended with a quick peck goodnight. As Wanda tried to close in for a horizontal hug, Sen reacted like a startled and very nervous puppy. She had felt that sudden pull away before and knew he was in an unreachable place.

Wanda dreaded waking, on their last day in Holland, feeling she might be faced with a grin and bear it mood situation.

Sleep eluded her that night.

Never mind. She would soon be on a plane, headed into different time zones. Tiredness was the least of her challenges.

'I think we might have time for a quick cycle this morning darling!'

Wow! This was nothing like the greeting that Wanda had anticipated from Sen.

'My sister is meeting us at the airport for a farewell coffee. I know it's not something you normally like to do but she insisted. Ty was also thinking of coming to see us off but I haven't heard anything final on that. Denise will drop us to the train in two hours. Plenty of time for a quick visit to the woods and a pre-travel stretch, if you like?'

Sen grabbed Wanda in the tightest of hugs and gently kissed her forehead, as he squeezed hard. Relishing, every second of that positive awakening, Wanda was acutely aware of stress releasing its grip on every inch of her being. This was more like it.

'I love you so much my sparkling diamond!'

'A cycle in the woods, fresh air and a good stretch! Perfect!' she replied, after an immediate 'love you too'.

These were the words Wanda hung off, as she summoned all her energy to take in this new day, in full appreciation of the absurdly wonderful moments that made up her life journey with Sen.

Gratitude filled Wanda's heart, as she considered herself blessed with having more love bestowed upon her, than so many people could even begin to imagine.

The love of this incredible man, was so precious to her.

Sure, the ride was rocky a little too often perhaps but acceptance of the bad times, was crucial. Working at shifting the balance to more of the good times and greater understanding of each other, was the way forward.

Wanda had a long way to go with mastering this art.

Sen was so much better at that.

True ... anger and moody behaviour ruled his emotions way too often but, through it all, he never lost sight of what was important.

He never gave up hope for the perfection he sought, in his relationship with Wanda.

The rollercoaster ride would be passionate.

That was for certain!

www.ingramcontent.com/pod-product-compliance
Lightning Source LLC
Chambersburg PA
CBHW060535180626
46817CB00002B/575